MW01071599

Remember Me?

Remember Me?

Rebecca Lickiss

Five Star • Waterville, Maine

First Edition
First Printing: December 2005

Published in 2005 in conjunction with Tekno Books and Ed Gorman.

Set in 11 pt. Plantin by Minnie B. Raven.

Printed in the United States on permanent paper.

Library of Congress Cataloging-in-Publication Data

Lickiss, Rebecca.
    Remember me? / by Rebecca Lickiss. —1st ed.
      p. cm.
    ISBN 1-59414-313-7 (hc : alk. paper)
     1. Mothers—Death—Fiction.   2. Miami (Fla.)—
Fiction.   3. Brothers—Fiction.   4. Fairies—Fiction.
I. Title.
PS3612.I25R46 2005
813'.6—dc22   2005027043

For S., B., and R.
They aren't elves, but sometimes they're naked.

Prologue

"You are impossible!"

Ageon withstood the harsh hiss of his wife's whisper. He'd withstood her screams and shouts for months now; whispers were peaceful, almost dull. The presence of their newborn son, sleeping peacefully in his frilly, antique Victorian bassinet, had changed their lives. Babies really did change things, Ageon had discovered, but nothing could alter how he felt about the beautiful, exciting, enigmatic, dynamic woman who'd amazingly agreed to marry him.

Seeming to sense Ageon's imperturbability, Amelia stalked back and forth across the expensive but tastefully decorated nursery like a caged tiger waiting to pounce. He should have known better than to marry a human woman. Marry your own kind, his mother had told him, find a nice fairy girl who will understand. But Amelia was beautiful, and he'd always been a sucker for beauty. She was, without a doubt, the most vibrant, stimulating woman he'd ever known. Even childbirth couldn't slow her down; their son was barely three days old, and already she was up and rearranging his life.

She turned back to him, glaring. "You're a father now. You have to give that up."

"That's how I pay for all these nice things," Ageon said, waving at the Cassatts and Hummells hanging on the wall; at the antique Chippendale wardrobe, the Oriental rugs, and the Victorian bassinet. "You were impressed enough by them to marry me." That and the fireworks that seemed to constantly spark between them.

Amelia stopped in front of him, tense. "You'll give it up now, or I'm leaving! I'd rather live in an honest hovel than continue in this dishonest house, with these ill-gotten gains."

Trying to hold onto the remnants of his patience, certain she didn't really mean it, Ageon said, "Go then. If you feel you must."

"I'm taking our son with me," she said between clenched teeth.

"I think not." Ageon felt the anger he'd held in check flare. "I'm certain the judge would see that the boy belongs with the parent best able to provide for him."

"And when this judge hears all about your method of providing for the boy, this fairy syndicate?" Amelia folded her arms, and planted her feet solidly into the cushioning rugs. "I'm certain the judge would give him to his mother. I carried him for nine months. I went through labor for him. You did very little."

Just put up with her for the last five years. Ageon knew Amelia had no intention of being reasonable. She never had. It was part of her charm. Also enchanting was the way she always made threats, but never followed through.

At an impasse, Ageon knew he had to find a compromise. "It is common, when a half-breed is born, to separate the two halves of the child into twins, so that child is no longer a changeling, neither one thing nor another. In this case neither fairy nor human."

"I know that," Amelia sneered. "Your point."

"I have the power to divide the two halves of the child. After that we may go our separate ways—the fairy child with me, the human child with you." Knowing he should hedge his bets, give her an out, Ageon added, "Unless you'd prefer to stay."

"Ha."

Ageon carefully lifted the sleeping boy from the frilly bassinet and removed the infant's fluffy-soft blue sleeper and thankfully dry diaper. He tossed the white sheepskin blanket on the floor and gently set the naked child in the center of the blanket. Amelia watched excitedly, though Ageon could tell she was trying to hide her fascination with disapproval.

"What was the name you wanted for him?" Ageon asked.

"Jared." Amelia touched Ageon's shoulder to stop him momentarily. "It's customary to rhyme the names, correct?" After Ageon nodded, she continued, "Then the other should be Zarrad."

"Very well, they shall be Jared and Zarrad. Fairy and human." Perhaps if the fairy child was Jared, she'd change her mercurial mind and stay. He glanced at her, to get her approval for the assignment of the names.

She nodded. The beginning of another temporary truce before their next fight.

Ageon began the incantation, which consisted of a series of simple nonsense syllables, and concentrated on the infant in front of him. He had to see the child, really see the child, see the fairy and the human mixed in him. In his mind an image of the child formed, wavered, and reformed. Once he had the image in his mind firmly, he began to try to separate his mind's image into its fairy and human components.

Salty sweat poured down his brow, and his limbs shook with the effort of will necessary to maintain the image in his mind and separate the dual natures. Ageon forced this mental image into the mind of his infant son. The boy himself had to be convinced that he was actually two people, before Ageon could form separate bodies.

The boy woke, crying. Ageon was amazed at how strongly such a tiny infant could hold to the idea of its own oneness. Continuing to chant, Ageon mentally wrestled to get the boy to accept this new idea. Even when the boy had mentally and emotionally accepted it, the infant body rebelled at separation. Ageon had to push down to the cellular level to separate the dual nature of his son, to compel physical reality to match his mental image.

In the end, two nearly identical boys lay on the white sheepskin blanket—one with almost imperceptible points on his ears and vestigial wings on his back, the other with rounded ears and no wings.

Ageon sagged against the wall, sweating and completely drained from his exertions. No wonder the separation spell was only used on very young infants. Ageon doubted he ever could have convinced an adult that they were two and not one. It no longer seemed strange that a few such attempts on infants resulted in failure or death, and almost all attempts on adults ended in both failure and death.

Amelia quickly sat on the floor and scooped both boys up into her lap, cooing to them and soothing them. Whatever other faults she might have, Ageon had to admit she was a good mother. The infant boys settled back into sleep. She dressed them, putting the fluffy-soft blue sleeper on the fairy boy, and retrieving a white one from the wardrobe for the human boy.

"Jared, my precious little boy." Amelia leaned over and kissed the sleeping fairy infant. She turned her head to kiss the sleepy-eyed human infant. "And my sweet Zarrad. Sleep well, boys." She stood up, smiling down on the babies.

Back in the bassinet together, the boys held hands and

tangled legs in their sleep. Their cherubic faces showed no sign of their recent distress.

A feeling of fatherly pride swelled though Ageon's exhaustion. "Stay, Amelia. We have a family now. Stay."

"Give up your so-called career."

"I can't."

"Then I can't stay."

Ageon sighed and slumped, exhausted. "Separating them was difficult. I have to rest now. We can talk at dinner. Come, you rest, too. You're still recovering from birth. The new nanny will listen for them, and care for them while we sleep."

"I'll follow in a few minutes. I want to watch them sleep," Amelia said.

He understood. Ageon too enjoyed watching the miracle of his son sleep. Now it was his sons. However, the spell had really taken it out of him. He felt as if he would collapse any moment now. He nodded to Amelia, and staggered out of the room, confident that she would change her mind by dinner, if not sooner.

The rest of the house was as expensively decorated as the nursery. The deep, cushioned pile of the carpet kept his feet from thumping as he walked, but he worried about stumbling into, and breaking, some expensive antique knick-knack table or gilt-framed painting. That would give Amelia a real reason to be angry with him. She had good taste, though she couldn't tell the genuine from the fake like Ageon could.

Before he reached his room, a thought occurred to him, and he trundled through his house, wishing he could drop with exhaustion. Down in the foyer, one of his guards, Merce, sat in a hard, gilded wooden chair by the reinforced bulletproof front window, leaning a bit forward to accommodate the vestigial wings sprouting from the back of his expensive dark suit, keeping an eye on the front of the house. Ageon had put that chair there deliberately, with its high back and uncomfortable seat, in an attempt to force Merce to stay awake at his post.

"Merce," Ageon called from the top of the stairs, where he leaned heavily on the thick walnut banister railing.

"Yo, Boss." Merce turned and looked away from the window, up at Ageon.

"Mrs. Silvan can come and go as she pleases, and do what she likes, except for one thing. She can only take one child from this house. Understood?"

"Sure, Boss." Merce looked like he thought Ageon was crazy, but appeared prepared to humor whatever insanity occurred. "Your wife can do anything she wants, except she can only take one child out of the house."

"Good." Ageon left before Merce had a chance to turn back to the window. Now for a much needed rest.

Though still weary from the effort of the spell, Ageon had dressed for dinner, hating the way the coat hampered his wings, though at least with slits his wings weren't uncomfortably smashed beneath his clothes. He flexed his wings, wondering again why fairies weren't born with larger, useful wings, so they could fly. Other than marking who could and who couldn't perform magic, the wings seemed to serve no purpose.

He hadn't seen Amelia, so he made his way to the nursery. Amelia was nowhere in sight.

In the bassinet an infant boy, with rounded ears and no wings, in a fluffy-soft white sleeper, napped.

"She wouldn't!" Ageon stalked out of the nursery and down to the foyer, his anger giving him a temporary vigor. "Merce!"

Merce jumped from his post, standing nearly to attention. "Yo, Boss."

"Where is Mrs. Silvan?"

"I . . . I did what you said, Boss," Merce stammered in the way of someone who knows he's in trouble, but isn't quite sure why. "I let her take as much stuff as she wanted from the house, but I made her put one of the babies back."

"Stuff! Stuff?" Ageon thought his head would explode with anger. "What stuff?"

"Baby clothes and stuff, I thought. I don't know what all was in those bags, Boss. You didn't say to check. But when she brought down two babies, I made her go put one back."

"She took the wrong baby," Ageon bellowed. "Where did she go?"

"I don't know, Boss. Maybe she told Stig before she threw him out of the car to drive herself."

Fearing the worst, Ageon stalked away shouting, "Stig. Axel. Hjell. We've got a job to do."

They found the car at the airport, abandoned, although she had left one suitcase with baby clothes in the trunk and a jewelry case packed with both expensive necklaces and pure junk. There was no record of her taking a flight out, but none of the cabbies remembered her either. Ageon filed a missing persons' report with the police.

She didn't come home. She wasn't in the city. She wasn't in the state. Through his connections, Ageon was able to find jewelry she had pawned, but tracing it proved difficult, and after a while she wasn't pawning anything any more. Amelia had been gone six months, and he thought he'd lose his mind.

Ageon couldn't leave for long without losing control, and anyone that he could trust to go find her he couldn't spare. A geas spell was his only obvious choice, but there was the problem of finding a suitable volunteer.

For such a thing he'd need someone willing, or at least not unwilling; someone with a good deal of time to spare; someone who wouldn't be missed or missing out; and, most importantly, someone he could have some control and power over.

In the hastily thrown together, not so tastefully decorated nursery, Ageon looked at the two identical newborn boys, awake and wiggling in their shared crib. Not his sons, these two were poor orphaned boys he'd generously taken in, temporarily. Community service helped to keep the police off his back. Yesterday they'd been a single changeling, and he'd divided them. His small service for the community.

Now all he had to do was cast the other spell, and he'd have his son back. His fairy son, who would grow up to be even more powerful, magically and otherwise, than himself. The son who would take over the family business. Instead of that weak, inferior, non-magical, unwinged human boy who'd infested the nursery for these six months since Amelia had left.

"Boss, I don't want to question your strategy here," Hjell began, his own changeling nature getting the better of his impulses.

"Then don't."

Hjell subsided, slinking as quietly back to the wall as a half-breed fairy-troll could. He leaned against the wall and kept his mouth shut.

Ageon took a deep breath to steel himself. He hadn't allowed himself much time to recover from yesterday's exhausting separation spell. He had to do this now. He had to. He carefully spread the paper with the words to the spell on the crib mattress between the boys. No simple nonsense syllable chants here. He had to have the commands and releases exactly right, or the spell wouldn't work.

The small pot of expensive gold dust sat in a corner of the crib, far from the kicking legs of the infants. The phial with rose oil sat next to the gold. The unicorn horn lay on the other side of the crib.

Concentrating all his longing and desire for his son, all his will, he dipped his fingers in the gold dust.

Sprinkling two pinches of gold dust into the air, Ageon said, "Golden thoughts in you I place, for another of your race." He anointed each boy with rose oil on the forehead, eyes, ears, mouth, and nose. "My own son will you befriend, and to him all your thoughts will bend. Ever restless till he be found, with this spell you thus are bound."

He placed the unicorn horn over each of their hearts in turn. "Forever faithful you will be, until that twain be seen with me."

Feeling the spell slide easily into place, Ageon locked it with a last sprinkling of gold dust over the infant boys. It seemed too easy, compared with yesterday's spell, until Ageon remembered that this spell merely gave direction to an already existing, ingrained desire for friendship and affection. Nature had already won half the battle for him.

Ageon stepped back to watch what happened.

The human boy he'd named Forrest scrunched up his face, making it turn bright red, and a malodorous stench emanated forth. The fairy boy, Boris, closed his eyes peacefully, made some smacking noises with his mouth, and slept.

"What?" Ageon shouted. "I performed the spell correctly."

"Yes," Hjell agreed from where he stood, holding the

wall up. "But, Boss, they can't even walk yet, let alone find and befriend your sons, their counterparts. You may have to wait a few years."

Ageon frowned at the common sense in this logic. He wanted his son now. All his efforts to track down his missing wife had led to nothing. He couldn't think of anything else. If these boys couldn't lead him to his son, he might not ever find the boy. Or Amelia.

Perhaps he had lost his perspective on this. He certainly didn't want to have any levers an enemy could pull. He sighed, slumping. "We'll take them to the family we found, then. What was their name?"

"Ploof."

"Right. We'll deliver them to their new Mommy and Daddy, tomorrow. But somebody is going to visit regularly, to check up on them. If Boris finds my son, I want to know about it."

"Sure, Boss."

In his son's nursery, Ageon looked into the bassinet, where the boy slept. "Well, Zarrad, it seems your mother made good on her threats finally." He pointed a finger and said sternly, "As of now, you are a fairy. You'll act like a fairy, and you'll look like a fairy. We'll fix your ears, and you'll wear wings under your clothes. And no one will know the difference."

"Sorry, Boss," Stig said, scuffing his feet against the rug in Ageon's office, looking like he wished his small fairy wings could fly him far away from here. "But it's been eighteen years. Once kids get to be eighteen you can't stop them from leaving. They're adults. And both the Ploof boys just took off, and left no forwarding address."

"What do you mean you can't find him?" It took all the

16

restraint Ageon had learned in the long years since his wife left to keep from yelling. What he wouldn't give to be yelling at her and enjoying all the fun that followed. He placed his hands flat on the rich, smooth, mahogany wood of his desk. "He's an eighteen-year-old penniless brat, for pity's sake. Where could he go? Do the Ploofs know?"

"Don't know where Boris is, Boss. Or Forrest, for that matter. The Ploofs seem to think it's pretty much good riddance; they don't care where the boys are either. The kids took what little money they had, and they're gone. They're both gone." Hjell shrugged.

A knock at the door interrupted them.

"Come in," Ageon growled.

Zarrad walked in, scared but hopeful. He twitched the lump on his back under his clothes, the fake fairy wings he hated so much. His ears had the barest hint of a point, from the retainers he wore every night. Behind him slunk a young, human man of similar age, looking at everything with wide eyes. Zarrad smiled tentatively at Ageon. "I think I might have found some extra muscle for the Kirkwood job."

"And he is?" Ageon asked.

"Forrest Ploof, Sir," the other boy answered.

Ageon sighed, tiredly.

After the young men left, Hjell said, "Well, Boss. The spell worked."

"So, where is Boris?" Ageon leaned back in his chair. "And where is my son Jared?" *And Amelia. Where is my beautiful Amelia?*

Chapter 1

"I'm dying."

"Mom, you're not dying," Jared said. The hospital had made an attempt to prettify the room. The walls were a pale rose color, and the chairs had rose and blue cushions on them. But nothing can disguise a hospital bed, with its demeaning side rails and attendant IV. The acid, antiseptic smell, beeping machines, and just-in-case clutter gave the room its true ambiance. Jared stood beside his mother's bed, holding her hand. "They've caught it at practically the earliest stage possible. You're going to be fine."

"No. I've never had to face death before." His mother plucked at the rose and blue blanket over the white hospital sheets. "And now I'm looking back over my life, all my mistakes. I want to put my life in order."

Hallelujah. Jared tried not to show his relief. He'd been after his mother for years to balance her checkbook, pay off her creditors, make out a will, do something to take care of the mess her life seemed to be. If a bout of skin cancer could get her to at least take care of her own taxes, so he didn't have to, he'd be forever grateful. Though the task of putting her affairs in order did appear rather daunting. "I'd be glad to help. Where should we start? Your checkbook? Your will?"

"Oh, none of that stuff. That's not important." She waved her hand negligently. "See, when I was younger, much younger, I made some really big mistakes. Did some things I shouldn't have done. I've always regretted . . .

Well, never mind that. The important point is that there are things in my life I'd rather do differently, and while I can't undo what I did, I can try to make some kind of recompense for my mistakes." She looked longingly up at Jared.

Jared tried to remain patient. Why couldn't she understand that not paying rent and bills and the IRS were serious problems? He hoped she wasn't going to get maudlin about some silly youthful indiscretion she'd committed long ago, and torture him with details he'd rather not hear about his mother.

"Mom, we all make mistakes, it's no use dwelling on them. You've gone on with your life. I'm sure whoever else was involved has gone on with theirs. Let it go. Let's concentrate on now."

"No. Sweetheart, you don't understand. I hurt someone. Several someones. People who were, are, very dear to me. I . . ." She turned to face away from Jared.

"Mom. Let's get you better first; then we can deal with whatever it is."

"Jared." She turned back to him, both her hands clutching his arm, digging her manicured nails into his skin.

"Of course, of course. You know I'll help you. I always do." Jared gently eased his arm out of her grip before she could break his skin.

"I don't want to die with this unresolved."

"Don't worry. I'll take care of it."

"You sound so like your father." His mother patted his arm, smiling up at him proudly.

"What's the problem? What needs to be done?"

For a few minutes the only sounds in the stuffy hospital room were the beeps, footsteps, and hushed whispers of conversations that drifted in from the hallway. Jared had never seen his mother look so uncomfortable, embarrassed, and upset. She kept opening her mouth to speak, sighing, and clamming up, tight-lipped.

He waited. She'd been his only family for years, and he'd been hers, until he'd married Mona, which was another problem he'd have to deal with later. However, Jared had no doubt that he knew everything there was to know about his mother, Amelia Silvan.

"Look in my bag. There's a letter, in a blank envelope."

Jared searched through the small suitcase she'd packed before coming to the hospital. At the bottom, under her red satin bathrobe, he found a blank, blue, card-sized envelope. He started to slip his finger under the flap to unglue it, when she shouted, "No. Don't read it."

"Sorry. Who do you want me to send it to?" Jared asked.

Darting wary looks from Jared to the envelope and back, it took his mother a few more minutes to make up her mind. "I want you to take it to someone."

"Who?" Jared felt his patience starting to slip. He'd never cared for his mother's guessing games.

"You'll know him when you see him."

"Mother! Just tell me who he is." He shook the envelope at her.

"I don't know!" She sat up in the bed, tucking the covers under her folded arms. "I don't know. I don't remember. You'll have to find him."

His patience was long gone, and he trembled with the effort of keeping his temper. "I have a wife, and a job. A life. I can't just wander the world in search of one honest man. For pity's sake, Mother, tell me who he is."

"I don't know. I don't know." Tears welled up in her eyes, her lower lip trembled, and she choked a sob down. "I know where he is, but I don't know who he is. I haven't seen him in twenty-four years."

Jared stared in opened-mouthed shock. "About the time I was born?"

"Yes, since just after your father . . . left." She waved her hand.

Jared had learned not to delve into his father's, or brother's, death. Amelia had told him once, long ago, that his father and brother had died in the separation spell. Hard as it was for him, he'd learned to respect her feelings and not ask any more. Jared flopped, weak-kneed, into the cushioned, hard-backed chair provided for visitors. The jolt of pain as his strapped-down wings hit the hard back of the chair bolstered him and reminded him once again of his mother's foolishness. Why couldn't he just be who he was?

"Who . . . ? How old would he be?" Jared asked cautiously.

"You'll know him when you see him."

"I need more than that to go on." His temper was chasing off any residual astonishment remaining from her previous statement. "A clue please."

"Jared, trust me, you'll know him when you see him. He lives in Miami. It shouldn't take you long to find him." She lifted and smoothed the covers in another bout of fidgeting.

He sat up straight. "Miami, as in Miami, Florida?"

"Of course, Miami, Florida. Where else?"

"Mom, there's dozens of Miamis across the States. We ship stuff everywhere, you know. There's Miami, Mi—"

"Business," she scoffed. "Just like your father, too much business. There are other things in life, you know."

"Like trying to track down some unknown, nameless, faceless man out of the millions in Miami, Florida?" Jared knew the sarcasm was a mistake the minute it slipped out.

Amelia started sobbing. "I knew you wouldn't understand. You'll never let me live it down, never. I'm sorry. I just wanted to make things right."

Jared hurried over to put his arm around his mother's shaking shoulders. Grabbing a stiff, abrasive tissue from the box provided by the hospital, Jared dabbed at his mother's tears. "Hush, Mom. Don't worry about it. Of course I'll go to Miami. Everything's going to be all right."

Taking the tissue from him, Amelia smiled around her tears. "Thank you. I can always depend on you, sweetheart. Take my card; charge everything to my account."

Certainly, her messed-up, unbalanced account. He nodded his head at everything she said, knowing full well he wouldn't follow more than a quarter of her instructions.

Actually, the more Jared thought about it, the more he thought he might be able to make something good come out of this. As long as he didn't learn whatever secret his mother had kept all these years. Whatever it was, it was bound to be complicated, awkward, and irritating for all involved. He didn't want to be involved. However, he wanted to be sure his mother would be all right before he left.

He made his escape shortly afterward. Tucking the envelope into his jacket pocket, he stopped at the nurses' station to ask after Dr. Toscano. The nurse looked at him oddly when he identified himself, but he was long since used to people thinking him strange because of his mother's behavior. Jared tracked Dr. Toscano down in the cafeteria.

Slipping through the jammed-together, half-occupied tables in the vast, echoing room, Jared sat in another hard-backed chair, careful of his wings, across the table from Dr. Toscano. He tried to make his empty, forgot-to-get-lunch stomach ignore the savory smells of institutional tuna salad sandwich and cheap coffee, with promises of a good, hearty supper later.

Dr. Toscano, a thin, gray-haired human, nodded as he

took another bite of his sandwich. "Afternoon, Jared."

"About my Mom . . . ?" Jared fingered the scarred, stained, blue-flecked white tabletop.

"Take a deep breath, and remember how hysterical your mother can be. She'll be fine." Dr. Toscano wiped bread crumbs from his mouth with a thin paper napkin. "This is normally outpatient surgery. Most of it is actually done in the office. If it was anyone but Amelia Silvan, she wouldn't even come in until tomorrow morning, and she'd leave shortly after surgery. But you know your mother; everything has to be a production."

Jared sighed and nodded. He knew that. No one knew it better than he, but sometimes it helped to know that he wasn't the only one who thought so. He ran his finger along a deep groove someone had forced into the plastic table.

"It's only a single, small patch that could potentially be skin cancer. If I took bets, my money would be on benign. The odds are in her favor." Dr. Toscano gulped from his steaming coffee cup. "Still, she'll probably be after all of us about sunscreen and the dangers of tanning."

"She says she's dying. There's no chance of that, is there?" Jared asked, not thinking too deeply on exactly what he wanted to be reassured about.

"Well." Dr. Toscano made the word last through at least six syllables. "She's insisting on general anesthesia, which carries more danger than a simple local. And there are risks involved in any procedure. But, her chances are just about as optimal as they can be for someone with her diagnosis."

Bureaucratic weasel-wording. Jared could recognize standard CYA posturing when he saw it. "She wants me to go to Miami. Do you see any problem with that?"

"Go to Miami?" Dr. Toscano looked surprised. "No. Not at all. Might be the best thing for both of you. Are you sure that's what she said?"

"Yes, that's what she said."

Dr. Toscano nodded, still looking surprised. "Definitely, go." He chuckled. "Run fast."

"Thanks. Take good care of her."

"Oh, I will." Picking up his tuna sandwich, Dr. Toscano nodded. "I wouldn't want to lose my best patient."

The drive to his office gave Jared a chance to think things over. His mother had scheduled four days in the hospital: one before, one during, and two after surgery. This being Thursday, he could fly out to Miami tomorrow for the weekend. He even saw a way to possibly interest Mona, his wife, in a weekend reconciliation.

Walking down the hallway to his office, Jared saw the silhouette of a woman on the other side of the translucent glass window behind the silver lettering proclaiming the door to belong to the SilverProof Corporation. When he opened the door, he found Bathsheba Sparrow, the emaciated, blonde, middle-aged fairy—working days as their office assistant and spending her evenings at night school—slinging a heavy tote over her shoulder as she prepared to leave. She walked out from behind the light-pine reception desk. "Hello, Jared. Goodbye, Jared."

"Evening, Bathsheba. Is Boris still here?"

"In the back," she said, pointing at the door to the back office as she walked out the front.

In the cluttered back office, Boris sat splayed in his office chair while rolling from the filing cabinets, past the fax, where his questing hand pulled the sheet out as the machine spewed it, to his computer-strewn desk. "How's your mother?" he asked as he started to scan the paper in front of him.

"Dying," Jared said dryly.

"That's too bad." Boris had already started typing on his keyboard, entering information on the faxed order.

Jared envied Boris his carefree life, having run off from parents he rarely spoke of, with no ties, no responsibilities, free to do anything he wanted. Jared especially envied the way Boris' openly displayed wings protruded through the slits in the back of his rumpled, wrinkled, oversized shirt, proclaiming to all the world that he was a fairy, able to do magic, and proud of it. Jared wished, not for the first time, that he'd learned magic, that he felt comfortable being a fairy, that his mother hadn't spent his whole life making him pretend to be something he wasn't. His own wings were held down firmly by straps, to disguise his nature.

So, why was it that most people figured it out anyway?

"Would you be able to take over everything tomorrow and this weekend?" Jared asked.

Without looking away from his computer or slowing his typing, Boris said, "So you can go hold your mother's hand? Sure thing."

"No. I'm going to Miami."

The clickety-clack of keyboard keys stopped. When Boris turned his chair around to face Jared, his blue eyes were wide and surprised. "Miami? The boss is going to Miami while Mama languishes in the hospital, dying of cancer?" He grinned. "All right, Jared. It's high time. Cut that umbilical cord."

"Unfortunately, that's not the way it is." Jared sighed and sat at his cluttered desk, shifting the papers around without really looking at them. "She thinks she's dying and is trying to make amends for something. She wants me to go to Miami and find someone, give him a letter. Somehow this will make up for something she did twenty-four years ago."

Boris squinted a bit. "Correct me if I'm wrong, but I hear a certain lack of specifics in all this. Do you know what she did, or who she wants you to give the letter to?"

"I don't want to know what she did. I really, really don't want to know what she did. And she won't tell me who this person is."

"Twenty-four years ago," Boris mused. "You're twenty-four. You don't suppose her husband found out you weren't . . ."

"No." Jared glared at Boris. "Apparently she last saw whoever-this-is after my father died. Probably the funeral home that she used to bury my father. She probably still owes them money."

"I doubt it. While I concede that she probably owes money from that far back, that scenario is far too dull for Amelia." Boris turned back to hunch over his keyboard and resume typing. "It's got to be an old lover, an illegitimate child, or something. Something baroque and indecipherable, that's Amelia's style." He paused a second to glance back. "At least you'll have an interesting weekend."

Jared piled the papers back up on his desk resolutely. "I hope not. I was going to ask Mona to go with me. Maybe . . . maybe it'll work this time."

Resuming typing, Boris shook his head. "You'd have to get rid of your mother for more than a weekend. Which, come to think of it, is not that bad an idea."

"I'm the only family Mother's got." Jared opened his desk drawer more for something to do, and to hide his nervousness, than for any real purpose. "She raised me by herself; it wasn't easy. I owe her something."

"She raised you, or you raised her? It couldn't have been easy for you, either." Boris hit the Enter key with a flourish, then spun around in his chair to point at Jared. "And she

26

owes you a life, Bossman."

"Anything else need doing here?" Jared asked, while ignoring Boris' point.

Letting it slide, Boris said, "All finished. Everything is under control, except . . ." Boris flipped a few pages off the top of one of the paper stacks on his desk, uncovering a brightly-colored printed page. He handed it to Jared. "I pulled the latest on Atlas off the web. They say they're going to be up and running in two weeks. 'Carrying the World.' " Boris' expression and tone conveyed his scorn.

Jared carefully searched the printed page in his hands. The new competition claimed better graphics, faster order turnaround, lower shipping costs, and more products. They certainly had a better advertising budget. Jared glanced uneasily at the small, crowded office containing his Internet/mail-order catalog clearance business.

They were doing well, but not stupendously. He'd been thinking of expanding, but, with his mother's illness and Mona's leaving, he'd been too preoccupied to do anything about it. Now it might be too late.

"Forget them." He crumpled the paper into a wadded ball and tossed it at the overflowing trash can. The ball bounced off the other papers crowding the basket, and began to uncurl as it fell to the carpet. "We'll keep going like we have been."

"You're the boss," Boris said. "Have you told Mona about this weekend yet? Are you going to tell her about the letter to the unknown man?"

"I haven't told Mona yet." Jared stood up. "And I have no intention of telling her about Mom's fool's errand. What are the chances that I'll find someone when I don't know their name, what they look like, where to find them?"

"Million to one against."

Jared nodded. "At least. I figure I'll take Mona to Miami for the weekend. Make things up to her. I'm not putting any effort into looking for anyone. And when we get back, I'll give Mom the letter and tell her I couldn't find him. She'll either have changed her mind and will toss the letter aside as unimportant, or she'll go to Miami herself." He grinned. "Either way, it's not my problem. I'm spending the weekend with my wife."

"Somehow I can't see Amelia taking care of her problems herself. She'll just let it fester another twenty-four years." Boris folded his hands over his chest and leaned back, like a wise old man distancing himself from his own advice.

"I don't care," Jared said. "As long as I don't have to know about it."

"Is there anything important enough to interrupt you?" Boris asked.

"If my mother dies . . ."

"It would take an act of God to kill your mother."

"I thought you were an atheist."

"Agnostic," Boris said virtuously. "Except when it comes to your mother, then I'm born again."

Jared waved his hand, as if to brush aside the extraneous parts of the conversation. "Just use your best judgment. I'll see you Monday."

"Hey, Boss, think maybe you'll lose the wing binders in Miami?" Boris grinned and wiggled his eyebrows.

"One step at a time."

" 'Bye, Jared."

He used the short drive to Mona's office to rehearse different methods of presenting this weekend to her. He finally settled on the near-truth. After signing in at the security desk, he started off through the maze of cubicles, trying not to feel like an overgrown, experimental lab rat.

They both worked with computers, but Jared couldn't stand working in cubes with hundreds of others around him, while Mona thought the idea of working in a business with only two other people insane. One of the many differences between them. Mona was forthright, confrontational, and determined, while Jared tended to be cautious and conciliatory. Mona was human, while Jared only pretended to be. Mona hated his mother, while Jared, well . . . loved and hated his mother.

The lab-maze effect of the office building was heightened by the five-foot high cubicle walls and the vaulting, warehouse ceiling. Sounds seemed both magnified and hushed by the surroundings. The clatter of computer keyboards punctuated the gentle murmur of conversations. As he walked, the interminable breeze of the air-conditioning wafted to him the clashing smells of perfumes, colognes, printers, and half-eaten lunches wrapped and jammed into trash cans. He'd be certifiable in less than a week if he had to work here again, yet Mona thrived on it.

From halfway across the enormous room, Jared saw her head above the wall of her cubicle. She was talking with Sharla, who worked in the next cubicle. He had to stop, pause, and catch his breath.

Mona's beauty continued to awe him, and every time he saw her he fell for her again, just like he had three years ago. Everything about her just seemed so perfect. The way she looked. The way she talked. The way she acted. Everything about her drew him to her. He never knew what it was he'd done to convince her to marry him. He didn't know if he could do it again: win her back, and achieve his dream of a happy family of his own with her.

He caught himself trying to smooth his rumpled shirt, as

if erasing the wrinkles would help. If there was one thing Mona didn't care about it was clothes. Her own tended to be cheap, functional, and durable. Jared straightened himself and continued toward Mona's cubicle.

Sharla noticed him as he approached and made some remark to Mona. Jared could tell it was about him by the sneer on Sharla's face. Mona glanced over at him, only mildly annoyed, and said, "Hello, Jared."

"Hello, Mona, Sharla."

"So how's your mother?" Sharla asked.

"Dying."

"What, still? Try a stake through the heart," Sharla advised.

Mona frowned at Sharla, and made a shooing motion. Sharla shrugged and disappeared behind her cubicle wall. Mona assayed a tight smile. "Well, Jared, what brings you here?"

Jared smiled nervously. "You. I came to ask if you'd like to spend the weekend with me in Miami."

"This weekend?" Mona's eyes widened in surprise. "I thought your mother was going in for surgery this weekend."

"She is. Want to go to Miami?"

Blinking in uncomprehending shock, Mona said, "You're going to Miami while your mother's in the hospital?"

"Dr. Toscano assures me that Mom will be fine. She's just making her usual production out of something that should be fairly straightforward and simple." Jared leaned on the side of the cubicle, and grinned. "Come on, it'll be fun. Just the two of us. Like a second honeymoon."

"Have you told your mother of these plans yet?" Mona folded her arms across her chest, oozing skepticism.

"It was her idea."

"Your *mother* suggested we go to Miami for the weekend?" Mona shook her head. "I don't believe it."

"Mother suggested *I* go to Miami," Jared said truthfully. He reached over the cubicle wall to stroke Mona's arm. "But it wouldn't be any fun without you."

"You're serious." Mona took a deep breath, let it out, then sat in her desk chair. "You're really going to Miami?" When Jared nodded, she added, "Why Miami? We could go somewhere nearer, save the money on airfare."

Jared shrugged, shifting more of his weight onto the rickety metal-and-cloth cubicle wall separating him and Mona. "Mom picked Miami. I don't know why." Or only vaguely why, he amended to himself. "But I thought Miami sounded like fun. And doesn't your sister Nona live near Miami? Maybe we could visit her. I could finally meet her."

"You've been threatening to run off to Nona's," Sharla added from the depths of her cubicle. "You'd be closer, if he took you to Miami."

"Don't help, Sharla," Jared growled. The last thing he needed was all the busybodies surrounding Mona's cubicle turning this into some kind of democratic debate, with nonparticipants voting on the outcome. He had no doubt they discussed him: what a fool he was for catering to his mother, what an idiot for trying to pretend he wasn't a fairy when everyone knew he was, and all the other mistakes of his life. He'd worked here for a short, hellish time and knew the kind of gossips that worked here. They wouldn't say much to his face, but he knew they debated the private problems of Mona's life when he wasn't around. This delicate negotiation concerned him and Mona. He wished everyone else would mind their own business.

Mona sat silently for a minute, alternately frowning and

searching Jared's face, though he had no idea what sign or data bit she was looking for. "Have you already made arrangements?"

"No." Jared walked around the corner to the door of her cubicle. He added in a small voice, "I wasn't sure if you'd say yes."

"There has to be more to this than you're telling me." Mona looked piercingly at Jared. "Does she have something planned? Was she sending you off in the hopes you'd meet some other woman? What is she up to?"

"I don't know," Jared said, the truth tinged with more than a little frustration and aggravation. "And I don't care what she wants. What I really want is a weekend alone with you. I want another chance. I want us, again."

"Go with him!" someone shouted from at least two cubicles away.

"Stay out of this," Jared shouted back.

Mona smiled at him, a real, amused smile. "All right. Let's go to Miami. It's high time you met Nona."

Yes! Another chance. Jared couldn't help grinning. "You won't regret it. I promise."

"We'll see," Mona said. She turned to Sharla's cubicle. "Could you watch my apartment for the weekend, Sharla?"

"Not a problem." Sharla popped up out of her chair, so that her head peeped over the top of the cubicle wall. She smirked at Jared. "I suppose Ploof is watching your place."

"Yes, thanks." Jared made a mental note to check with Boris before he left. Not that there was much to his apartment. When he and Mona had separated, he'd given most of their meager possessions to her. His place looked very sparse and almost uninhabited. Most of his time and energy went to either his business or his mother. Though his business did require him to travel occasionally, the biggest problem with their marriage was the latter, not the former. Their tentative reconciliations these last several months had all been derailed because of the effect of Amelia on his life. Not this time. He hoped.

"We'll change things this weekend." Jared grinned at Mona. "It'll be fun."

Chapter 2

Zarrad held his false wings in his hands, frowning at them. He imagined for a moment his fingers pushing through the thin, white gauze, bending the aluminum wire frame, ripping the flat plastic shapers from their moorings. How he hated these fake wings. The imagined sound of wire breaking, plastic popping, and gauze ripping kept him from hearing the knocking at his door until Forrest started shouting.

"Just a minute," Zarrad shouted back. He strapped the wings on, pulled a concealing plain white undershirt over his head, and slipped into a blue silk shirt. "I'm coming. I'm coming!" He stalked over to unlock his bedroom door, flung it open, and stalked back to his mirrored mahogany wardrobe. Buttoning his shirt, he feigned a casual indifference.

Behind him, he heard the bedroom door close and lock. Forrest's reflection appeared in the mirror beside Zarrad's. "Your father knows about Atlas."

Pinching the bridge of his nose, Zarrad sighed. It had been inevitable, but he'd hoped for a little more time. He rubbed his temples and straightened himself. "I don't care."

"He doesn't believe you can run a catalog company by yourself, and he says no good can come of your messing around on computers. He says he wants you to get serious about the business." Forrest had delivered his lecture by rote, but added with real feeling, "He said, 'Atlas is a stupid name!'"

Zarrad coolly looped a burgundy and blue tie around his neck and began knotting it. "He also says I'll never be good at the business. Just in case he's right, I'll have my own business."

Forrest shrugged, and his reflection disappeared from the mirror. Zarrad heard the quiet shoosh of the cushion on the big armchair and knew Forrest had taken a seat. "Your Papa is worried about Auveron, who supposedly can smell weakness clear from Atlanta."

"I'm not about to let Papa down." Zarrad winced inwardly, realizing that he'd already let Papa down by being human and not a fairy. He rallied and added, "But, I'm not letting myself down either." He admired the effect of his dark tie on the shimmery blue silk shirt, before casually tossing his suit coat on. "And, most importantly, I'm not letting Nona down tonight."

"Right, Boss." The cushions murmured gently as Forrest shifted on the comfortable chair. "Uh . . . was the necklace supposed to be ready today?"

"No. That's tomorrow." Zarrad turned to face Forrest. "If she doesn't agree to marry me tonight, tomorrow she gets the necklace."

"I'm not criticizing or anything, but what does this necklace look like?" Forrest scooted to sit on the edge of the cushion. "I mean, you know women, everything has to match and coordinate. I was just thinking . . . if it's too fancy, or if the stones don't go with whatever she's wearing, she might not put it on. Then the spell wouldn't work. Is it gold? What if she's wearing silver? Does she really like jewelry? Do you really think bespelling a fairy woman is a good idea? What if she figures it out and gets mad?"

"Don't worry so much." Zarrad checked his wallet; he didn't want to run out of cash tonight. "It's a plain gold-

and-silver braided chain. She loves jewelry. She could retire on what I've given her so far." He tucked his wallet back in his pocket, reassured. "The spell will work. She'll be madly in love with me, and I'll tell her never to take it off. She'll do exactly what I say and never know."

"Whatever you say, Boss."

"See you tomorrow."

"Right, Boss." Forrest stood up, saluted sloppily, and followed Zarrad through the house to the door of the garage.

Zarrad slipped behind the wheel of the immaculate powder-blue convertible and drove away, wondering only for a moment what Forrest would be doing tonight. The fact that Forrest didn't seem to have a social life disturbed Zarrad. Zarrad appreciated Forrest's slavish devotion, but sometimes the whole boss-minion thing annoyed him. He wished Forrest had some kind of emotional tie to some other being. The thought that Forrest lived only for him was creepy. It didn't feel natural or healthy. It didn't fit with the rest of Forrest's personality.

Warm, humid air rushed through Zarrad's hair. Alone, with no one to impress or deceive, no rain to make him put the top up on the car, and no problems in sight, Zarrad relaxed into the seat. His fake wings pushed against his back, but even that didn't really bother him. He would be wining and dining the most beautiful woman he knew, and perhaps later . . .

Singing with the radio, Zarrad pulled up in front of the exclusive building where he'd rented an apartment for Nona.

"I'll be right back," he told the valet as he pocketed the keys.

"Sure thing, Mr. Silvan." The sound of the valet's delicate fairy wings rustling in the warm, evening breeze irritated Zarrad. It shouldn't matter to him that he was only a human, but it did, because it mattered to his father. And he should be able to think of himself as plain human, not *only* human. As if human were somehow inferior.

The doorman nodded him in deferentially. "Good evening, Mr. Silvan."

At least he was human, and it irritated Zarrad that it should make such a difference. It shouldn't matter. As he walked in the door, he resolved to think about nothing but Nona for the rest of the night.

Zarrad hummed in the elevator and down the hall to Nona's apartment. Nona, beautiful Nona. Sweet, marvelous, artistic, unpredictable Nona. His very own Nona, well, *soon* his very own.

No one answered when he rang the bell.

Was she still in the shower? Zarrad took out his key and let himself in. The apartment was distressingly quiet. The wicker living room furniture sat empty on the white carpet. The spotless kitchen nook gleamed under the glare of the fluorescent light. No lingering cooking smells remained to hint that someone had been eating here. No one was in the powder-scented bathroom, and the perfumed bedroom looked abandoned. Zarrad flung the closet doors open.

The neat rows of expensive dresses, shelves of folded linens and clothes, and delicate drawers all waited in their places. Nona's perfumes and toiletries still resided in the bathroom and food filled the cabinets in the kitchen. So she hadn't left completely, but where was she?

Checking in the study just off the living room proved that it hadn't been used in a long time. All the easels, canvases, paints, filing cabinets, drafting table, and the desk were covered in a fine layer of dust. Probably no one had entered the room since he'd set it up for Nona when he'd moved her in. She was supposed to be an artist. How could she be an artist if she never did any art?

He found a note on the cushion of one wicker chair. "I had to run home for the week to take care of some things. Will be back on Friday. Sorry. Nona."

Crumpling the note, he tossed it in the trash. Friday. Tomorrow. She'd been gone for two days, and he hadn't known. It was all his father's fault for keeping him so busy with the business. Even Auveron gave it a rest sometimes, especially with that stupid son of his, but would Ageon give Zarrad time off? Never. Zarrad growled at the thought of losing Nona because of his father.

What did she have to go back there for? This was her home now. Didn't she realize it? Had she heard from her sister again, the one with the bad marriage?

Zarrad hoped not. Nona had the irritating habit of citing her sister's marriage as a prime example of why not to marry. Even though, apparently, she'd never met her sister's husband. Why couldn't she tell the difference between him and that loser?

"Damn! Damn! Damn!" Zarrad would have to wait until tomorrow.

Nona, his beautiful, marvelous Nona. Didn't she realize how much he missed her? How much he loved her? How much he admired about her? How much he needed her?

Women! Zarrad managed to walk out of the building as if he'd accomplished his business and had known all along that Nona wasn't there. He barely heard the banal pleasantries of the doorman.

Outside, a dappled centaur idling by the curb with shiny black carriage in tow came to attention as Zarrad walked down the steps. "Need a ride, Mr. Silvan? Just dropped

someone off from the airport, and ready to roll again anywhere you want to go."

"Got my own wheels tonight." Zarrad pointed to his
convertible, waiting in front of the centaur.

"Nice. Very nice," the centaur said enviously, as he adjusted the bandoleers hanging across his bare chest.

Pulling away, Zarrad glanced in the rearview mirror.
Sure enough the centaur continued to watch enviously as
Zarrad moved away. Zarrad muttered to himself, "I bet you
wish you could drive off in one of these, poor bastard
changeling."

Severely depressed, Zarrad drove home and closeted
himself in his office. As always, he found the room to be
soothing and comforting. The office was spacious, and he
kept it immaculate, organized, and efficient: no cluttering
stacks of paper, or casually dropped pens or paperclips, or
sloppy sticky-notes pasted on top of each other. Even the
trash cans were neat and tidy and empty. His computer sat
on the short section of his large, L-shaped wooden desk up
against one wall, and he sat in the dark-leather executive
chair, with the discrete opening in the back to accommodate wings, even if faked. Turned to one side, he faced the
computer; to the other, and he faced the door. Another,
smaller desk with a smaller chair and another computer
hugged the back corner, waiting for Forrest. A few filing
cabinets, a small table with a fax machine/scanner/copier
and printer, and two straight-backed chairs finished the
room's furnishings.

It was important to Zarrad that everything around him
was orderly, and that he was in control. He didn't bother to
tell Forrest that he'd returned or that he planned to spend
the night working on Atlas. He didn't need Forrest around
right now, wheeling around the room, spinning in his chair,

too lazy to get his butt up out of the chair. What Zarrad needed now was organized control and the privacy to sulk.

He hadn't planned to get the Atlas Internet catalog up for another two weeks. But with the time he'd already put in this week and most of the night free before him, he might be able to get it up and running by tomorrow. That was the ticket; charge ahead, get something accomplished, and he'd forget his troubles.

If Zarrad did manage to get Atlas up ahead of time, he'd just advertise it as a pre-opening sales event. Sales, as in things for sale, not a price cut, Zarrad assured himself. He didn't want to go overboard with this. He'd set up some splashy effects on the website, dazzling colors and visual displays.

Humans were every bit as good as fairies, and he'd prove it. Prove it to himself, if not his father, by getting Atlas up and running and making money. Money for Zarrad and Forrest, untouched and unaided by Ageon and his fairy magic. Money earned by human hands with human power.

The fake wings dug into Zarrad's back when he twisted wrong in his chair. He thought about taking them off, but there was too great a chance that someone might come in, someone might see him. Probably only Forrest—who knew already, and had always known, seemingly without being told—but still, Zarrad couldn't take that chance. He sat properly and turned his executive chair back to look at his computer.

For a moment he considered using the sights and sounds of fireworks, but he didn't want to take up too much time. He wanted to get Atlas going as soon as possible. Like tomorrow. That'd show them.

Then he'd just have to hope nothing happened to ruin his new launch this weekend. He had nothing scheduled. Hopefully, fate had nothing in store for him.

Chapter 3

Nona took a deep breath of warm air hinting at the ocean she was heading toward and rested her hands in the driver-instruction-approved positions on the steering wheel. She had to admit Zarrad had been right about the car. A convertible was the only way to drive the highway. If only she could figure out what to do about him.

She loved the car, the apartment, the jewelry, all the little things he gave her, but she wasn't sure if she loved him. Though Nona hated to think that she was nothing more than a greedy leech taking from him without giving anything.

No, that wasn't true. Nona did love Zarrad, but she loved the real Zarrad. She loved the human man who cherished her art, supported her dreams, and thoroughly adored her. But, she hated Zarrad's falseness in pretending to be something he wasn't.

Then there was Zarrad's father, who was the cause of Zarrad's pretend life as a fairy. Ageon intimidated both of them. Rather like he intimidated everyone. Nona avoided him as much as she could.

But what was Zarrad getting out of their relationship? A girlfriend who annoyed him, whose tastes were far beneath his own, and who made him feel inadequate.

The sign on the side of the road told Nona she had only five more miles of highway to go before Miami proper. She had to make a decision. Soon. She couldn't keep tormenting him like this.

If only Ageon would just leave them both alone. If only Zarrad would throw off those stupid fake wings and trash the idiot ear-retainers, and act like the strong, sophisticated human man he really was. If only . . .

She knew the moment she walked into her apartment that Zarrad had been there. The wicker chairs were exactly the same distance from the couch, and all were centered precisely around the coffee table. The throw pillows were sitting formally in the corners of the couch, pointed like diamonds. It looked like something out of a decorating spread for the obsessively orderly and compulsively neat.

Tossing one pillow to land rakishly on one of the chairs, Nona offhandedly kicked a chair out of exact alignment and scooted the coffee table farther away from the couch. The note was also missing, so Zarrad must have found it. She flopped onto the couch to stare out the window.

Zarrad hated her furniture. He'd let her pick it out and had regretted it ever since. Their worst argument had been over wicker. What did that say about their relationship?

Did it mean that they only felt comfortable arguing about insignificant things? Or that they had only insignificant things to argue about? Perhaps she was over-rationalizing everything.

Nona closed her eyes and concentrated. She imagined herself in a little farmhouse, acres of land separating her from her nearest neighbor, green-and-brown-dappled lawn, overgrown fields of wildflowers and weeds, surrounded by forest rolling off into the distance. The clean, fresh scent of yesterday's rain and newly-mown grass coming in through the open window. Outside, two dogs chased each other happily across the yard, playing with a rope toy; from far away a horse neighed, a rooster crowed.

The door opened. "Oh, so you did return."

The concrete and glass, dirt and trash, heat and reek of the city crashed down around her. She opened her eyes. "Hello, Zarrad."

There he stood, all handsome and charming, as he closed the door behind himself. His eyes looked at her as if he were starving, and she his last meal. His smile was fleeting, replaced by a worried frown.

"Where were you? What were you doing?"

"I went to the country to paint. I have a commission, remember?"

"Why can't you paint here?" Zarrad asked for what had to be the millionth time. He waved toward the closed door to the study. A door she'd rarely opened, a room she'd rarely used. He'd stocked it just for her. Told her he wanted her to be able to work wherever she was. Told her how much he admired her art, her talent, her genius.

"I just can't." Nona stood up to him. "I can't paint here in the city. I feel squashed with all this," she windmilled her arms to indicate the city around them, "all these buildings, all these people. It's like it's all pressing in on me. And I can't paint. So, I go to the country. There I can paint and sketch. My muse is there."

"Nona." Zarrad sat on the couch next to her and rested his hands gently on her shoulders. "That's all in your head. It's just your attitude."

"And so are my paintings. They're all in my head and my attitude." Nona stared into his blank, handsome, loving, uncomprehending face. "I don't want to fight about it any more."

"I'm glad you're back," he said, allowing her to drop the subject. He pulled her into his arms, for a long, comforting hug, and a quick, but passionate, kiss.

Nona put her arms around him, bumping into the false

wings under his suit. "Must you wear those?"

"Yes."

She could almost hear the unspoken, "Papa said." She sighed, lowered her arms to areas that were all Zarrad, and hugged him close, savoring the way the musky scent of his cologne mixed so well with the scent of Zarrad underneath. "I wish you wouldn't. You should just be you. Quit acting like something you're not. All your father's money, his connections, and his power can't make you into his fairy ideal."

Zarrad shrugged, trying to act as if he didn't care.

"Did you ever ask him what happened to your mother, or your fairy brother?"

"He . . ." Zarrad shook his head, "doesn't talk about it."

It was more than Zarrad had ever told her about his father, though it annoyed her as much as anything else she'd ever heard on the subject. "He must have told you something."

Nona knew Ageon hated her. If she happened to pass him on the street, he ignored her, and she and Zarrad never discussed him. Zarrad just didn't talk about things that bothered him. So, the fact that his father disliked her had to bother him.

Zarrad squeezed her tightly. "No. I guess they died. And he's had to make do with me ever since."

"You deserve more than just to have someone make do with you." Nona girded herself to tell Zarrad that he deserved better than her, that he should go look, that it was over.

She hesitated too long.

"Dinner tonight?" Zarrad smiled at her, and she melted inside. He was so sweet, so handsome, so charming, so cuddly nice. How could she say no?

Smiling back, Nona said, "Of course. We need to talk."

"I've got some errands to run for Papa, but I'll pick you up at seven."

His kiss was every bit as passionate as a woman could hope for, and he started to slip his hand along her thigh up under her skirt. He whispered, "I missed you."

"Naughty!" Nona squealed, and playfully slapped his hand.

"Perhaps tonight." He waggled his eyebrows.

After Zarrad left, Nona sat back in the couch. She now had four or five hours in which to do . . . nothing. She wasn't a doll to be put back up on the shelf when Zarrad was busy with other things, but she had no business to conduct here, no errands to run, no urgent duty. Just hours to wait in a place she didn't much care for.

Well, there was her commission. She could contact the lawyer for her patron, and let him know she wasn't progressing. It wasn't as if that would be news to him. Mostly what she had for him were more sketches on a similar theme. Which wasn't what was wanted the last time they'd talked. Also, Nona felt uncomfortable around him. Sometimes she wondered if he wanted to date her, or something. All he ever did was take her to lunch once or twice a month, chit-chat about whatever came up, glance at her sketches, and give her some more money.

Nona didn't want to think about him. She'd rather think about Zarrad. She'd rather be with Zarrad, but he wasn't going to be available for several hours.

The only way this relationship could ever work between her and Zarrad was if she had something she could do here. She thought this over for a few minutes. A single glance at the door to her unused study, with its neat, orderly canvases, easels, paints, brushes, pencils, desk, and filing cabinets decided her.

Time to go to the beach. At least she could pretend she was on vacation, and spend her time watching people.

The sand was sun-warmed beneath her, its heat baking into her stomach as she lay on her large, fluffy beach towel in the shade of her rented umbrella. Her swimsuit provided her almost no protection from the sun, sand, and salt water, being far too abbreviated, and intended more for showcasing her rather than actual water sports. Her wings fluttered gently in the ocean breeze, helping to keep her cool.

A dark-eyed, incredibly muscled satyr posed and preened not far away, trying to catch her eye. Nona ignored him. She made sure she saw him well enough—as an artist she'd always admired well-formed people—but she had no interest in anyone that hairy, or that closely related to some sort of animal. Snobbish perhaps, but true.

She made sure she kept her face toward the white-capped waves. Her eyes, behind her mirrored half-wrap sunglasses, could look in any direction she wanted, with no one the wiser. Nona felt it gave her a mysterious, sophisticated appearance, and she certainly didn't want anyone knowing she was actually staring at them.

A line of six gnomes trudged past, through her field of view, between her and the ocean. Stair-stepped in height from the serious, stern Papa in the lead, through a chubby Mama and nearly look-alike girls, to the cute, diapered little girl toddling in the rear with her lacy sunhat falling rakishly over her left ear, they marched on the wet, packed sand at the edge of the water's incursion on the land.

Midwestern, Nona guessed, and working just as hard at having fun on their vacation as they would at keeping their farm and home. She tried to memorize the look and feel of the family. They'd make a wonderfully sentimental painting. Perhaps that was what she needed for her commission. Perhaps this wasn't wasted time.

Off to her right, a movement drew her gaze. A human man preened and fussed as he set up his beach umbrella and chair, displaying his tanned skin, rippling muscles, and the very brief scrap of cloth pretending to be swimwear that was supposed to conceal his assets.

Again, she was attracting males of all species. Nona smiled slyly. This was fun.

Tall and thin, he moved confidently but quietly about his business. He flashed her a tentative smile but turned his attention elsewhere when she didn't respond, apparently assuming her focus wasn't on him. He reminded her in some ways of Zarrad. Except for the fact that he was completely, unashamedly human. Zarrad would never come to the beach with her.

Which brought her right back to the subject she wanted to avoid. She stared out at the waves, endlessly, tirelessly, and pointlessly beating on sands.

She should be forthright, and tell him they were through.

She wasn't the flighty, inconsequential gadfly she appeared to be. She was a woman with her own mind and her own life. She was a power in her own right. And she didn't need him.

Even though he was cute. And had lots of money to shower her with all the things she wanted. And really did seem to care about her. And did want to marry her.

Nona shuddered, and adjusted her sunglasses. Marriage. It seemed so permanent, so confining, so . . . laborious. She'd never been good at making the big, important decisions. That was Mona's forte, and look what a mess she'd made of her marriage.

Serious, sturdy Mona trudging away behind her desk in her office, much like those cute little gnomes. Working hard and earning her daily bread, following all the rules, and being the perfect human woman.

Twins should be more alike, especially twins that had once been only one person. It seemed perverse that she and Mona were so different.

Except, now that Nona thought about it, perhaps in the separation, with all the fairy parts going one way and the human parts going the other, different personality traits had gone one way or the other. It would explain a lot. It would certainly explain why she was so interesting and Mona so dull.

Nona wondered what Mona might be up to at that moment.

Whatever it was, it couldn't have been as much fun as lying on the beach ignoring several handsome men of different species frantically vying for your attention.

Chapter 4

The private carpet undulated gently beneath Mona, and she folded her arms defiantly. They said that flying carpets never dumped their passengers, but every time Mona flew she wanted handles or something. At the very least, the carpet manufacturers could put tassels and six-inch looped pile on the carpets. She just didn't feel safe whizzing through the air above rooftops and treetops with nothing securing her to the carpet except someone else's supposedly safe flying spell.

She wished that it had been Jared's spell; she'd trust that more than some unknown safety technician's. But though Jared was a fairy, and in theory able to perform magic, he'd never learned because of his mother's interference. Now if anything went wrong, he couldn't even use his magic talents.

Beside her Jared fidgeted. Not that he minded the carpets—he actually seemed to enjoy breezing around on them—what bothered him was the backup to land at the terminal. They'd been circling for almost a half hour now, and he was impatient to get to the ground and get on with their weekend.

Another carpet circled at their level, the dark-suited businessman sitting on it too intent on his laptop to pay any attention to delays. Beneath them another two carpets circled. One was a first-class carpet with another suited businessman calmly munching on shrimp cocktail while lounging on a pile of soft pillows; the second was another threadbare, economy model with a couple who were too busy kissing to realize their carpet had started its descent.

Jared smiled, an excited happiness oozing all around and making him handsomer than usual, and patted her hand. "Can you smell the ocean? Are you sure you don't want to get a room in a beachfront hotel?"

"I'm sure." Mona didn't want any money wasted on unnecessary extravagances like first-class flying carpets, or beachfront hotels. Though, considering the threadbare nature of the carpet they sat on, maybe an upgrade carpet would have been a good idea. She just didn't want to pay exorbitant rates for the expensive meals and plush padding on the first-class carpets. She wasn't sure how well Jared's business was going and worried that no matter how this weekend turned out, they'd need the money—for Jared's business, or a deposit on an apartment together, or a divorce.

Mona could sense Jared's impatience to get going and wondered again about this trip. It seemed so out-of-character for Jared. Was something strange afoot? Was Jared having some sort of mental breakdown? An early mid-life crisis? Had he finally had enough of his mother?

"Here we go." Jared leaned forward, placing his hands on the carpet as it dived toward the terminal. Mona felt their two suitcases shift behind her and closed her eyes, clenching her hands into fists. It would all be over soon.

The landing went smoothly, just a minor inertial lurch at the end.

Hoping for the best, Mona followed Jared as he carried their bags into the terminal. She caught a whiff of a far-off ocean breeze sneaking around the oily smells rising from the hot tarmac. It was very different from Wisconsin. It'd been a long time since she'd visited Nona and smelled the beach. The odor brought back to her just how annoying and shallow her sister could be. But Nona was family, and family could be counted on to help in a crisis. Mona hoped there wouldn't be any crisis, just a nice, quiet vacation, with some time for her and Jared to catch up with each other, and reconnect.

Inside the terminal, a brawny faun driving a battered, noisy courtesy cart spotted them and hurried over. "Afternoon, Mr. Silvan. I'll take those." He jumped off his cart and, before either Mona or Jared could stop him, tossed their small suitcases onto the back of the cart. He held his hand out to help Mona onto the one of the passenger seats. "Watch your step, Miss." He smiled, and nodded to Jared. "Sir."

"Uh." Jared stepped hesitantly onto the cart. Smiling wanly at Mona, he whispered, "This will save us some walking."

"How did he know your name?" Mona whispered back.

Jared shrugged. "I don't know."

Mona glared at Jared.

"Any additional luggage or packages to pick up?" the faun asked.

"No . . . uh . . . no. We've got everything with us," Jared said.

The faun nodded without looking back at them. At the main entrance, he jumped down to help Mona off the cart. "There you go, Miss." He waved off Jared's tip. "Oh, no, Mr. Silvan. It's a pleasure to help you." He jumped on the cart, and drove off.

"Do you know him?" Mona stared at the receding cart.

"I never met him before in my life." Jared picked up their suitcases. "Well, that was strange. Let's go get a cab."

In the sweltering outdoors, a line of cabs waited. The

driver of the first in line hopped out of his car and smiled at them. "Hello, Mr. Silvan."

While Mona stared at him in surprise, a dappled centaur pulling a shiny, black open carriage interrupted her view. He adjusted the bandoleers crossing his bare chest. "Carriage ride, Mr. Silvan? For the lovely lady?"

"Ah, uhm . . ." Jared stammered.

The centaur smiled. "A romantic carriage ride into the city, give you some time to relax, look around, talk. She'll love it. Make any stop along the way that you want."

This was getting very strange. Mona glared at Jared, who looked from the cabby to the centaur, confused.

The centaur reached down, took their suitcases from Jared's unresisting hands, and tossed them into the carriage. The cabby on the other side said something rude about the centaur's parentage. The centaur turned his upper, human, body to respond in kind, then shrugged apologetically at Mona.

"We can't afford this." Mona grabbed Jared's arm, hoping to snap him out of his trance.

"No problem, Miss. It's on the house." The centaur winked at Jared. "It'd be a pleasure."

Curling his body backward, the centaur managed to open the carriage door, and flip down the step. "Watch your step, Miss." He winked at Jared again.

Jared helped Mona into the carriage. "Come on. It's different. It'll be fun."

The seats were soft and cushiony dark gray leather. Mona reached for the side of the carriage to steady herself as she stepped across to the other side to make room for Jared, and felt the tingle of a spell. The tiny crackle of a rainbow above her clued her that the carriage was enspelled to keep bad weather out. Such caution seemed unnecessary today; the bright sun shone heavily down on them, with virtually no clouds to offer any relief.

In any case, the spell wouldn't protect against the looming feeling of dread Mona brought with her into the open carriage.

She fumed in silence as the carriage gently started moving. Something very strange was going on, and she wanted to know what it was. She looked at Jared. He smiled wanly at her. She whispered fiercely, "What is going on? Who are these people? And how do you know them?"

"I don't know these people. I've never met any of them before in my life. I swear." Jared patted her hand. "Just relax. We came here to have a romantic weekend." He took her hand in his and kissed it. "You have to admit this is romantic."

And Jared was very handsome; it was all very much beside the point.

"How do they know your name?"

He smiled and shrugged. "I don't know. Maybe Economy Express Carpets is trying some kind of promotion. They have my name from when I bought the tickets. Maybe the city declared this week: 'Be Extra Nice to Tourists Week.' Maybe . . ." Jared sighed.

She knew Jared well enough to interpret that sigh. Her heart sank. "Maybe what?"

"Nothing. Nothing."

"I know that sigh. Maybe Amelia what?"

Jared grimaced. "I think my mother may be trying to make amends. She knows we're here."

"I can't believe she'd do anything nice for us. Especially if it might lead to us getting back together." Mona leaned back against the cushioned leather back, closing her eyes and letting her head loll back, to be warmed by the bright sun.

If Amelia knew where they were at, it could only mean disaster. Amelia was their biggest problem. That woman left chaos and disaster in her wake. Everything she touched malfunctioned, even her son . . . especially her son. Mona's wonderful weekend with Jared was crumbling all around her.

He was right; it had to be Amelia. Something this strange in Mona's life could only come from Amelia.

"Dearest." Jared's voice sounded strained and pleading. "Please. This is our weekend. Just for us. You are the most important person in my life." He caressed her hand softly. "My mother is not here. As far as I'm concerned, it's just us. I don't want anything she has done, or might do, to come between us. Please."

Mona looked at Jared. His eyes were wide-open, whipped-puppy eyes. He was biting his lip like he always did when he was nervous. His warm, strong hand moved over hers with a gentle sweetness. The wind blew his hair back, to reveal his barely pointed ears.

Everything about him reminded her of the first time she'd seen him, at a company function. He'd been so handsome, and sweet, and nervous. His smile had lit up his face when she'd spoken to him. She fell for him almost instantly. He was perfect.

Except for the fact that he left the security of the company to run his own tottering business. And no matter how much she tried to convince him to be himself, he tried to hide the fact that he was a fairy. And, of course, there was his mother.

"Please."

Sighing, Mona nodded. She didn't want anything to ruin

this weekend either. She loved him, and she wanted to work things out with him. Here they were far from Amelia; surely nothing she did, or had done, could come between them.

Jared's face lit up as he smiled. "It'll work out. You'll see. We'll tour around. Take in a few sights. But mostly we'll lounge on the beach and relax."

"And talk."

"And talk," he agreed.

Maybe this weekend would work out after all. She smiled back at Jared. Relaxed against him. Maybe they could rekindle their love. Looking up at the clear blue sky, Mona said, "So, if we go to the beach, does that mean you'll be shirtless? So that everyone will know you're a fairy?"

She could feel Jared cringe.

"I . . ." Jared murmured, "wouldn't want to get a sunburn."

"A sunburn." Mona pushed onward, hoping to make some headway. "I'd be willing to put sunscreen on you." She shifted to look up at him. "Slather up your back and your wings." She wiggled her eyebrows. "Anywhere else that might get sunburned. Or even not sunburned."

His cheeks turned pink. "I appreciate that. It's just . . ."

Mona could almost hear his unspoken thoughts. *I've never done that. Mom wouldn't let me. I don't know.* She wrapped her arms tighter around him. "It's all right. Don't do anything you're uncomfortable with."

Jared kissed Mona's forehead. "She's not here. I promise I'll try at least one thing she wouldn't let me do."

"I'll hold you to that." Mona tried, but couldn't relax against the seat. A question nagged at the back of her mind, something she'd never asked Jared before. "Why, though? Why did she want you to hide what you really were?"

Jared shrugged. "Like usual, Mom got it wrong. She thought that if people knew that I was a fairy and she was human, they'd take me away from her. So, from the time I was a baby, she had me hiding my true nature, strapping down my wings, making sure my hair covered my ears. By the time I realized she was wrong, well, it was too late. It was all habit and ingrained fear." He looked away. "I'm sorry."

"Not your fault." Mona reached up to turn his face toward her. "We'll see what we can do about that this weekend."

Jared smiled.

Chapter 5

Steam from his shower had blurred the mirror to the point that Zarrad could only make out his reflection by the fact that it contrasted with the white bathroom tiles. He scrubbed his head with the towel one last time before wiping the mirror. He stared at his reflection.

"Human. I'm human and proud of it!" Zarrad squared his shoulders and flexed his biceps. Water dripped from his hair and ran in glistening rivulets down his chest. Zarrad was proud of the way he looked, spare and muscular but not overly muscled, tall enough to be tall without risking idiot remarks about the weather up there, large eyes, full mouth, dimpled chin. Perfect.

Turning slightly, he glared at the reflection of his bare, smooth, slick back, trying to convince himself that it didn't matter that he didn't have wings. He wasn't a fairy; he wasn't supposed to have wings.

So, why was he still checking like a little kid, hoping wings had sprouted overnight?

Tossing the towel on the floor, Zarrad stalked from the bathroom into his bedroom, leaving soap-and-cologne-scented cloying steam behind.

Laid out neatly on the down coverlet of his bed were his clothes for the evening. And his hated fake wings. He could have sworn the gauze, aluminum, and plastic things were mocking him. Sighing, he strapped them on, wishing to one day defy his father and toss the damn things away.

But that wouldn't be happening tonight. Papa would

continue to rule and run his life. Zarrad sighed and started dressing.

He was on his second attempt to get his black bowtie correct, when someone knocked at his door. "Enter."

Forrest sauntered in, with his hands in the back pockets of his expensive, crisp trousers, his usual demeanor after a hard day's slouching. "Looking good, Boss. You're going to break some hearts tonight."

"Well?" Zarrad asked impatiently. He didn't have time for Forrest's dawdling slowness tonight. He had a fairy woman to romance and win over. He needed the necklace.

"Was there something you wanted me to do tonight?" Forrest looked genuinely perplexed.

"Don't tell me you forgot the necklace!" Abandoning his lopsided tie, Zarrad snatched up the nearest piece of easily moveable furniture, a carved-mahogany, antique side table.

Running behind the large, overstuffed armchair, Forrest held up his hand to shield himself. "I thought you were going to get it. To make certain it was done right."

"Idiot!" Zarrad threw the table. It bounced off the arm-chair's cushions and toppled sideways to land upside-down on the floor. "I can't pick it up. If I pick it up, everyone will know I bought an enspelled necklace. Fairies don't need to buy things already enspelled. They can do it themselves. You were supposed to get it and bring it to me, so I could give it to Nona tonight!"

Peeking out from behind the armchair, Forrest asked, "How am I supposed to know if they've done the spell right?"

"I'm just as human as you, remember? I wouldn't be able to tell either. Just go get it." Zarrad grabbed his tie and completely undid it, nearly ripping it from his neck. "They're a reputable firm. It should be enspelled; if not,

I'm sure I can get Papa to take care of it. No one but us will know the spell is in the necklace; everyone will think I cast a spell on her. As I would have, if I were a fairy." He sighed. "I wanted to give it to her before dinner tonight, but I can see that's not going to happen."

"Are you so sure this is a good idea, Boss?" Forrest stood up straight, but kept the chair between him and Zarrad. "Giving an enspelled necklace to a fairy to get her to fall in love with you . . . I don't know."

"I didn't ask your opinion. Just get me the necklace. I'll deal with Nona." Zarrad turned to face the mirror for another try at the bowtie. "I always get what I want, and I want her."

"But—"

"No buts, just get it."

"Where're you going to be?" Forrest's reflection appeared in the mirror beside Zarrad's.

"I don't know; she hasn't decided yet. Check the usual places. If you can't find us, page me." Zarrad angrily finished tying his bowtie, which didn't dare finish off crooked this time.

"Sure, Boss." Forrest slunk toward the door. "No problem."

"Don't screw up this time!" Zarrad shouted as the door shut. He sighed at his reflection in the mirror. If his reflection could be trusted, he looked perfect, almost fairy-like, but he doubted the rest of the evening would be so easy.

Why couldn't things go right just this once? Would some great cosmic plan be disrupted, if just this once things went smoothly?

Jared tried to soothe Mona. Patting her hand wasn't working, and she'd moved out of his embrace a while ago.

He tried putting his arm across the back of the cushiony leather seat, to ease it around her. She squirmed away, and he only managed to get a twinge from his strapped-down wings. He sighed and said, "Everything will be fine."

"I could have done without the extended tour," Mona said through gritted teeth.

"I think we took the most direct route," Jared said. "That's what I told him earlier."

"I heard you," Mona growled. "But I don't think he was listening."

The centaur pulled the carriage to a stop in front of the hotel, leaving Jared no more time to calm Mona. Jared so wanted this weekend to go well. The weather was cooperating, warm and clear in the twilight, a sweet breeze cooling the city, but all the plans he'd made seemed to be coming apart.

Perhaps this hotel had been a bad choice. Mona had wanted something cheap, but he intended this weekend to be nice, very nice. So, he'd booked them into a nice hotel. Not the most expensive one in town, but a nice one. It was definitely more expensive than one Mona would have picked.

He withered under her glare as the centaur pulled their suitcases from the carriage and set them on the well-swept cement curb in front of the hotel. Jared hadn't meant for her to be so upset. Then again, he hadn't planned for everyone to know his name and run roughshod over his plans either. How did everyone know his name?

Pulling out his worn wallet, Jared motioned to the centaur that he was ready to pay. At least it would delay his next argument with Mona. Though she was right; he could see from the meter on the centaur's hitch that this had been one expensive, yet ruined, romantic impulse.

"Oh, no, Sir!" The centaur moved to block Mona from seeing the exchange. "I wouldn't dream of it. It's on the house." He winked at Jared and extended his hand, palming the money Jared offered. Jared knew the tip was cheap and hoped the centaur might say something to him about it. That way Mona would know he wasn't just tossing money on the street.

However, the centaur and carriage pulled away without saying a word, and Jared could see Mona standing over their suitcases like a snarling tiger, daring the bellhops to try to take them. He could make out the bellhops' tentative expressions in the twilight.

"I'll get the bags." Jared waved to the bellhops.

One nodded back at him. "Yes, Sir, Mr. Silvan."

"Mr. Silvan?" Mona mouthed as she glared at Jared.

What was going on here? How did these people know his name?

"Boss!" someone shouted behind Jared.

Jared glanced back, and almost didn't recognize Boris running across the street in the gathering nightfall. His surprise at seeing his partner quickly gave way to shock and concern for his business. "What are you doing here? Has something happened?"

"Good thinking, being right across from the jewelry store. Even I could find you," Boris whispered to Jared. Then, smiling at Mona, he held out a box with a flourish, and said loudly, "I'm sorry I forgot to get this to you earlier."

"I thought you said he was minding the store," Mona growled. "Why is he here?"

It was so unlike Boris to interfere that for a moment Jared was speechless. Usually Boris was very businesslike, efficient, and effective, if rather casual and rumpled. Everything about Boris was unusual tonight, from his crisp, expensive-looking clothes to an unaccustomed slouch. And what was he doing in Miami?

Boris spotted the suitcases in Jared's hand and seemed confused. "Did you want some help with those?"

"No!" Jared found his voice again. "What are you doing here? Has something happened with the business?"

Waving the box, Boris looked even more confused.

Mona snatched the box. "What have we here?" She opened it, and examined the expensive gold-and-silver plaited necklace. She glared at Jared. "You can't afford this."

"I don't know anything about it!" Jared turned on Boris. "What are you doing here? Who put you up to this? Where did you get that necklace?"

"Ah. Ah." Boris started backing away from them, down the sidewalk, his shoes scraping across the cement as he tried to feel the walk beneath them without looking away from Jared and Mona. He just kept moving away without turning his back to them.

"Just get back to the business. And stop interfering," Jared shouted.

"This goes back. Now." Mona slapped the closed box down hard on Jared's suitcase, causing him to lose his grip and drop the suitcase and the jewelry box.

"Shop's closed," Boris said, just before he turned down a dark, side alley and took off running.

"Jared?" Mona said warningly.

"I'll take care of it." Jared handed the jewelry box back to Mona. "Tomorrow. Right now, let's get checked in."

They walked toward the hotel doors in stony silence, and one of the bellhops opened the door. "Evening Mr. Silvan. Miss."

A stray breeze blew Mona's hair into her face, so Jared could pretend her angry gaze wasn't burning holes into him as he ushered her into the hotel.

"Who are these people?" Mona whispered fiercely.

"People who work at the hotel? I don't know."

"They know you," she accused.

"No they don't." Jared ground his teeth.

"Then how come they call you by name?"

"I don't know. Maybe it's a slow day, and we're the only people checking in tonight." Though that very question was burning through his mind also, and he'd dearly love to have the answer. Assuming it wasn't his mother. Jared dropped the bags on the floor with a thump and smiled at the woman behind the gleaming walnut check-in counter.

"Good evening, Mr. Silvan."

Jared glared at her and demanded the room he'd reserved. The desk clerk kept trying to upgrade their room, but Jared growled and grumbled every time she tried. She finally shrugged, as if giving in to his whimsical ways.

One glance at Mona convinced Jared he was in for it tonight. He signaled for a bellhop to get their bags. Another extravagance, but he'd take any help to delay the moment Mona started reaming him for things he had no control over.

Mona didn't say a word until they were alone in their room. Then she just folded her arms, and sighed. "Is there anything you want to tell me?"

"I wish I could." Jared flopped onto his stomach on the hard bed, the thin pillow muffling his voice. "I wish I had an explanation for this. I wish I knew what was going on."

She leaned against the wall next to the bed. "Amelia?"

He sighed and rolled to face her. "Mother knows I'm here. I neglected to tell her I was bringing you. So I doubt she called ahead to make arrangements for us." Jared looked at Mona pleadingly. "You have to believe me. I don't know these people. I don't know how they know me. I'm sorry I don't have a better explanation."

"When I saw Ploof, I guessed it wasn't Amelia. I can't see Boris having anything to do with one of her schemes. But maybe he's changed. This is much too strange," Mona said. Her lips thinned. Even mad and windblown, she was the most beautiful woman he knew. He had to find some way to make this weekend perfect, to make her see how much he loved her, how wonderful their life together could be.

Reaching for her hand, Jared said, "How about we go out to eat? I thought I saw a steak place down the street. Would you like steak?" When she didn't move, didn't even twitch a flawless eyebrow, he added, "If you'd prefer seafood, I'll check with the concierge, and find a nice spot."

"Steak is fine. We'll walk." Mona headed for the bathroom. "And in the morning the necklace goes back. Right?"

"Promise." Jared looked at the unassuming black jewelry box. Unfortunately it didn't say where it was from. Boris had said he'd picked it up across the street. There were a lot of shops across the street. He'd have to contact Boris. What was Boris doing in Miami?

At least Mona was still talking to him. That was the most important thing this weekend. Keeping Mona happy and talking to him. Convincing her to come back to him.

He unpacked their bags, a quick chore since they'd only packed for the weekend. Mona had always been a light traveler.

Having finished that, Jared had nothing more to do. The room was a standard hotel room, clean and neat, everything in its place. He adjusted the phone slightly to a more aesthetically pleasing angle, then headed for the window, to check out what part of the city they'd have as a view. From their window he could see buildings, streets, cars, all the usual suspects in a city. For a moment, he wished he'd gone ahead and gotten them a room on the beach, but he doubted the view would be worth the aggravation to Mona. As he closed the curtains, there was a soft knock at the door.

Opening the door, he found someone in the navy and gold uniform of the hotel, waiting with an iced bottle of champagne and two glasses on a room service tray. "Your usual, Mr. Silvan."

"What?" Mona shouted from the bathroom doorway. Jared winced; he hadn't noticed her opening the door to the bathroom. The mingled scents of her makeup and perfume wafted out of the bathroom with her.

Jared glared at the waiter. "What is going on? I didn't order anything."

The waiter blinked. "I thought . . . I mean the ticket . . . I was sure this was yours."

"He said, 'Your usual,' " Mona growled as she grabbed Jared's arm and turned him to face her. "You want to explain that. You've been here often enough to have a usual? At least that explains how they all know your name."

"Oh, no, Ma'am." The glasses on the tray tinkled as the waiter shifted it. "I said, 'Your order.' " He made a great show of picking up a piece of paper from the tray. "I see. I'm very sorry, Mr. Silvan. I have the wrong room. Sorry to have disturbed you."

"Mr. Silvan?" Mona screeched. "And how does he know you? Hmmm? Explain that." Her grip on Jared's arm was becoming uncomfortable.

"I don't know. I've never seen him before in my life."

Jared slammed the door in the waiter's face. "Why won't you believe me?"

"Every time I start to believe you, something like this happens." Mona stalked over to the bed and sat. "And you have no explanation. You could at least try to come up with something that explains all this."

Jared sat beside her. "I don't have an explanation, because I don't know what is going on here. I'm sorry. I really am, but there's nothing I can do about it."

The situation had Amelia written all over it, but Jared had vowed not to even speak his mother's name or refer to her at all after the disastrous carriage ride. He wasn't going to let her interfere with his reconciliation with Mona. He wasn't about to let Amelia mess this up, as she had so many other things. Why couldn't she just once stay out of his life?

Then again, if it was Amelia, what was Boris doing in this? He wouldn't have cooperated with Amelia for any reason.

"No." Mona stood up and stepped away from him. "No. I let it slide with the baggage handler, and the centaur with the carriage. I didn't demand an explanation about the expensive jewelry. But enough is enough. What is going on?"

"I don't know." Jared jumped up from the bed. "Why won't you believe me?"

"Would you believe you?" Mona shouted back.

"Yes!" Jared screamed, but in his heart he knew he wouldn't. He grabbed his jacket, and stormed out the door. "I'll be in the bar, if you change your mind."

As he waited in the elevator lobby, Jared's temper cooled. How was he ever going to convince Mona to stay with him now?

★ ★ ★ ★ ★

Zarrad watched Nona pick at the tray of shrimp, lobster, and calamari hors-d'oeuvres. He'd made his reservations for this very exclusive restaurant, this very table overlooking the city and ocean, months ago. He'd planned every second, every aspect of this crucial moment, and it was all falling apart.

The hushed clinking of crystal, silver, and porcelain could barely be heard above the soft strains of Mozart coming from the string quartet in the corner. Strategically placed pots of lush green plants gave diners a semblance of privacy. Elegant waiters quietly fawned over every patron's little gastronomic whim. The crisp, white linens contrasted nicely with Nona's skimpy, glittery, little black dress.

Everything was perfection. Everything but . . .

"You're cute, Zarrad." Nona looked up at him momentarily. An expression flickered across her face that gave him hope; then she looked back at her plate. "Very cute. But I think—"

He grabbed her hand. "My love, you don't have to say a word. I've been thinking about us, too." Where was that idiot Forrest with the necklace? Maybe he should just go ahead and propose. Maybe she'd surprise him and say yes. Maybe Auveron would give up and go move to Hawaii.

"Yes, ah . . ."

"I've been thinking that maybe it's time we . . ." Zarrad searched for the right phrase. "Get serious" was definitely the wrong thing to say. "Better express our feelings, our passion, for each other."

"Oh, Zarrad." Nona shook her head sadly.

This wasn't working.

"One moment." Zarrad reached for his pager, tapping the buttons to page Forrest with his location.

"Is something wrong?" Nona asked, looking relieved to change the subject.

"I had a surprise for you. It's late getting here."

"Oh."

The expression on her face told Zarrad everything he needed to know. She'd planned on breaking up with him, but now wondered if she should stick around for the surprise. He hoped Forrest would get there soon. Otherwise this would be his most complete disaster since . . . well, since he'd survived the separation and his fairy brother hadn't.

Forrest arrived with the first course. His crisp suit was almost as exclusive as the elegant waiter's. Though, of course, the waiter wore only black and white. "You need something, Boss?"

"The surprise," Zarrad said. "For Nona."

"Surprise?" Forrest looked confused.

"The necklace I sent you to get." Zarrad could feel his face heating up and turning red with anger.

"I already gave you the necklace, Boss." Forrest slumped, almost cringing, managing to get one awkward step away.

Chapter 6

"What are you talking about?" Zarrad shouted. "You hadn't gotten it earlier, when I spoke to you at the house."

"Well, no, but then I did, and—"

"Where is it?" Zarrad stood up, hands twitching.

"I gave it to you. Remember?"

"No you didn't. You didn't have it. How could you give it to me, if you didn't have it?"

By now the hushed clinking and murmuring had ceased; everyone in the restaurant stared at them with varying degrees of disdain. The waitstaff stood paused at their tasks, some with steaming, spicy plates of food held high.

With everything slipping away from him, Zarrad couldn't get his temper under control. To make matters worse, Forrest had the usual stupid-minion look on his face. Zarrad drew a deep breath. "Tell me where the necklace is, before I strangle you."

Forrest motioned with his hand to Nona, and Zarrad noticed that she had stood and was grabbing her purse.

Nona stood poised for a moment, glaring at him in disgust, her glittery, clingy little black dress shimmering. One hand resting on her hip, the other waving her matching glittery black purse at him. "When you're done being macho, don't come looking for me. We're through."

Her hips swung in a sultry, mocking way, and her gossamer, vestigial wings fluttered good-bye, as she glided out of the restaurant and Zarrad's life, to the staccato clicking of her stiletto heels. Everything he ever wanted was walking out the door, and he could feel his panic rising.

"You idiot!" Zarrad swung his hand, as if to knock Forrest upside his head. Forrest ducked, and Zarrad stalked out after Nona, shouting, "Nona!"

A quick look proved she wasn't in the elevator lobby outside the restaurant. Or the lobby on the ground floor of the building. She wasn't in the quickly cooling dark outside on the street. She'd disappeared somewhere into the depths of the dark night. Zarrad felt his heart break. He loved her so. Why couldn't things have gone right this once?

Zarrad stalked back in, looking for Forrest. He'd find Nona in the morning and mend this somehow; right now he intended to deal with his sorry lackey. For once, someone was going to pay for everything in Zarrad's life going wrong.

He looked in the lobbies, and the restaurant, and even the stairs, without any luck.

Forrest had managed the same disappearing act Nona had pulled.

It was probably just as well. Zarrad didn't want to add murder to his list of sins.

Jared slumped down in his booth, keeping his back and his strapped-down wings from touching the back of the seat. He wondered where he'd gone wrong. A romantic weekend in Miami with his wife. A few days to spend quality time with each other. What had happened?

He sipped his second "Dog House Special." He wasn't certain what it was, but it had seemed an appropriate name for a drink right now. It tasted sufficiently alcoholic, and slightly fruity, though it didn't have one of those little paper umbrellas in it. Somehow he'd imagined that all drinks in warmer climates had little umbrellas, or at least green sprigs of tropical plants sprouting from them.

The hotel bar was handily situated next to the lobby. He'd had his choice of a small, dark booth by the windows, any of several small, round, dark tables with comfortable chairs on the far side of the bar, or a small, dark booth near the entrance that allowed him to watch as people walked through the lobby. He'd picked the booth nearest the door to the lobby and now kept watch from the bar's twilight recesses, in the hope that Mona would come get him.

Loud pop music blared from speakers farther in the bar, but the noise was muffled this close to the lobby. He could have watched the news on the bar's TV, but he wanted to keep an eye out for Mona. There was the occasional movement in the lobby, as guests came and went. Which proved that they weren't the only guests expected tonight. So, that ruled out that theory.

He carefully thought back over what had happened, but couldn't see where he'd gone wrong. He couldn't see that he'd done anything. Stuff had just happened all around him, and he'd been unable to stop any of it.

There was the problem. He hadn't done what he should have done, and stopped the nonsense when it first started. He had to quit reacting when he was taken by surprise. He had to take charge and make things go right.

Slumping a little more, Jared tried to think of how he could take charge of any more unexpected surprises this weekend. It would have helped if he knew magic. He'd have stopped the nonsense early on, if he'd only known magic.

How was it that Mona, completely human and unable to use magic, never tolerated any nonsense from anyone?

Something was really wrong here. Jared vowed that if he got the chance, he'd make it up to Mona somehow.

71

★ ★ ★ ★ ★

Nona hurried down the dark, deserted alley, the loud thumping of her heels echoing around her. A cool breeze stirred the rotting stench from a dumpster into her path, and she tried to run faster. Fluttering her wings didn't help get rid of the stench.

Zarrad would never think to look for her here. Which would be unfortunate, if she met some thug intent on robbery or rape. Though, since Zarrad had to be furious with her, she'd chosen to take her chances with ordinary thugs. They could have her money, as long as Zarrad didn't kill her.

She couldn't believe she'd told Zarrad they were through. Nona almost wished she could take it all back. Almost. She was several blocks from Zarrad, she hoped—assuming he'd stayed at the restaurant—and she figured she'd gone far enough that she didn't have to hide in alleys any more.

Stepping out onto the sidewalk, Nona headed for the lamppost on the corner. Better to be somewhere with a lot of light and people.

Looking up and down the surrounding streets, Nona saw no sign of a cab. She never could find one when she needed it. Zarrad had always taken care of that. However, she did see a familiar hotel catty-corner across the street. She could get a cab there.

No cabs waited in the hotel's drive, so Nona sauntered in as if she were staying there. She figured she'd just walk up to the concierge's desk and have them call one. She'd stayed here often enough before Zarrad had gotten her the apartment. No doubt they'd be eager to get her a cab, hoping for one of Zarrad's usual later monetary rewards.

"I'm sorry."

Turning, she saw Zarrad standing next to her. Only he'd changed from his black tux and bowtie into a rumpled khaki button-down shirt and blue jeans. She'd never seen him in blue jeans before. Of course, he'd never apologized before, either.

"I'm really sorry. I shouldn't have lost my temper." He reached out and stroked her arm with his fingertips. His eyes glistened with wide, whipped-puppy sorrow. "I just think you're the most beautiful woman in the world. And you deserve everything that life has to offer. And I wish I could make everything perfect."

"Oh, Zarrad." Nona put her arms around his neck.

Why had he never shown her this side of him before? A sincerely remorseful, romantically babbling Zarrad was irresistible. He probably feared what his father would say, if he was found groveling over a woman.

She couldn't stay mad with him like this.

"Forgive me?" His alcohol-scented breath was hot on her throat as his hands squeezed her waist.

"Of course."

"I was in the bar." He touched the thin shoulder straps of her dress. "Did you want me to change for the restaurant?"

"No." Nona smiled up at him. "I don't want you to change a thing."

Zarrad grinned the biggest, sloppiest grin Nona had ever seen on him. Taking her hand, he led her to a small, intimate booth near the entrance of the bar.

"You are the most beautiful woman in the world." Jared smiled down at Mona blearily. He probably shouldn't have downed the rest of his drink in one gulp when he'd spotted her, but she didn't seem to mind that he was buzzed.

He didn't remember that expensive, glittery little black dress either. Had she bought it just for this trip?

His heart soared. There was only one reason a woman wore such a dress: to catch the eye of some man. And she'd come here with him. Maybe this weekend would work out.

Mona giggled and nuzzled his shoulder as they scooted into the booth.

The seat really was too small for both of them; the booth had been built to accommodate two people facing each other, but if Mona didn't mind, he didn't mind either.

Her hand slid up his back until she reached his wings, hidden under his shirt. "You're really cute, but these have to go. You need to be yourself."

Jared tried to think that through. He must have misheard her. Was she telling him she didn't like the fact that he was a fairy, or that he should quit hiding his wings and be proud he was a fairy? He thought she'd been urging him to show his true nature earlier; maybe he'd misinterpreted her.

"You don't like my wings?" Jared asked, hoping he was wrong. He wasn't that much different from a human. He had the wings and ears, but he'd never learned magic.

"No. I don't like your wings. I never have." She twined one lock of his long hair around her finger. "I wish you'd get rid of them."

Shocked, Jared stared at her. His throat threatened to close up and choke him, and his stomach sank. Mona had never said anything before to indicate she didn't like the fact that he was a fairy. Had he really thought she wanted him to be proud to be a fairy, when all along she'd wanted him to become human? He felt crumpled and ugly. He'd hidden his ears and his wings, but the thought of having them removed was more than he could bear. "I'm sorry. I can't. It's who I am."

"But it's not who you could be." She reached up and started to tuck his hair behind his ear.

He stopped her, and pulled his hair back to cover his ear: his repulsive, ugly, pointed fairy ear. "I'm sorry. I'm sorry. I wish I could make things perfect for you, but this is the way things have to be."

Mona growled. "Some parents really need to learn when to let go. You're grown now."

"Yes, but . . ."

"Yes, but . . ."

Jared reached for her hand. He had to change this conversation. Talk about something else, anything else. He had to make things go right. "Let's talk about something else. Are you hungry? Did you want a steak or something?"

"I'm fine. Hors-d'oeuvres were enough for me."

"We could order from the bar here, if you'd like." Jared swallowed to clear his mouth and stall for courage. "Or room service, if you'd prefer."

She giggled, and kissed his chin. "You mean you don't have everything all planned out? Every second of every minute, every move, every little thing?"

"I wish." Jared smiled at her, relieved. This was better, much better. "Things rarely work as I plan them. I just hope that I can make you happy, no matter what."

"Oh, that's so sweet."

"Did you have a plan?"

"Me?" She giggled again, and traced her finger down his nose to his lips, sending a matching tingle down his spine. "Never."

He smiled at her joke. Mona was the least spontaneous person he knew. She planned almost everything. His best bet was to let her have her way on whatever she wanted to do.

"Well, what would you like to do?"

Wiggling her eyebrows and snuggling up against him, she whispered, "How about room service? A little champagne to begin with, and maybe pizza later?"

"Anything you want. Your wish is my command."

"Is that a fact?" Mona snarled from the other side of him.

Jared looked up.

Mona was standing next to the table, in a sensible—but nice—tailored gray suit, arms folded, glaring at him. And Mona was snuggled up next to him, in her almost-nothing little black dress, tickling the opening of his collar.

Things weren't going as well as he'd hoped.

Again.

Chapter 7

Jared knew he was a little buzzed from the fuzzy, out-of-focus feel of the world around him, but he didn't think he was that drunk. He looked from one woman to another. "Mona?"

The woman snuggling into him looked up. She abandoned Jared to hug the standing woman and squeal, "Mona!"

How could there be two of them? Jared wished he hadn't drunk so much. He'd understand things better.

"What is going on here, Nona?" Mona said.

The woman in the glittery black dress jittered, nearly dancing with excitement, reflecting little sparks of light around the bar. "We were out for the evening, we had this fight and ended up here by accident. I can't believe you're here, too. How did you get here?"

"I flew here this morning." Mona angrily pointed at Jared. "With my soon-to-be ex-husband."

"What?" The other Mona glared down at Jared.

Jumping up, Jared desperately grabbed the sensible Mona's hand, knocking the glittery, agitated Mona out of his way and nearly onto the floor. "Mona, wait. I thought she was you. That you were her. That she was Mona."

Mona reached around the other woman, to flutter the other woman's fragile, gossamer wings. "She's a fairy. This is my sister Nona."

Noticing the wings for the first time, Jared felt like an idiot. How could he not have noticed? How could he have made such a simple mistake?

"I'm sorry." Jared motioned to the empty glasses on the table. "I guess I drank more than I thought. I didn't notice that she had wings. I just didn't see them." He extended his hand to Nona. "I'm really glad to meet you. Sorry about the misunderstanding."

"Misunderstanding?" Nona glared at Jared, ignoring his outstretched hand, placing her fists on her hips. "Which misunderstanding would that be? The one where you were dating me? Or the one where you were married to my sister?"

"You're dating her?" Mona shouted. "My sister!"

"No!" Jared clutched her hand desperately, his Mona, the real Mona. His hands were starting to sweat and he feared his ability to hold her was slipping away. "No. I swear it! I never saw her before tonight, and I thought she was you."

"Liar!" Nona shoved Jared's shoulder, before turning to her sister. "We've been dating for over a year now. He even pays for my apartment in the city here. He's even been trying to convince me to marry him."

Shock made Jared gape at Nona. How could she say such things? He couldn't think of anything to say, with the buzzing in his head so exaggerated by the clashing perfumes of the two women. The situation was completely out of control, doomed and hopeless.

"Well, that explains how everyone knows you." Mona pulled her hand from his slippery grasp.

"Of course everyone knows him," Nona snarled. "This hotel used to be 'our place,' before he got me the apartment."

"Is that where all your money goes? An apartment for Nona?" Mona pushed Jared roughly against the booth table, and he fell back onto it.

The empty glasses bounced off Jared's back and fell ringingly to the floor, followed seconds later by the clatter of the menu and holder. The salt and pepper shakers, tilted over and spilling, dug into his back, and his legs flailed for purchase in the air.

Nona put her arm around Mona. "Honey, money is not his problem. With all his connections, he has more than he could possibly spend."

Stunned, bewildered, and buzzed, Jared grabbed the edges of the table in an attempt to right himself. How could this be happening? Why would Nona do this?

Mona burst into tears and leaned on Nona's shoulder. "He said he wanted to take me to Miami for the weekend. Some time for us to be alone and rekindle our love. Something special, just for us."

"Special, huh?" Nona whacked Jared's stomach with her purse, knocking the air out of him. "Planning a threesome?"

"It's over," Mona shouted at Jared, tears streaming down her reddened cheeks. "I'm going to get my things, and I'm leaving."

He had to do something. Find some way to stop this madness. Some way to make Mona understand that Nona was lying. But he couldn't think of one thing he could do.

Nona patted Mona's shoulder. "Come stay with me. You can help me pack up my stuff. We can put this two-timing turkey on the chopping block and relieve him of his little pin-head."

As Mona nodded and turned to go, Jared threw himself off the table, not managing to stand, but at least landing on his knees at Mona's feet. He wrapped his arms around her nearest leg to keep her from leaving. She managed to get to the doorway between the bar and the lobby before he stopped her.

"Mona wait!" He buried his face in her hip, as he clutched her thigh. Her skirt was scratchy against his cheek, but her leg was warm and soft beneath his hand. Being this close to her, holding her, smelling her, afraid to let her go, he sought desperately through his reeling, dazed brain for the magic words to keep her with him. "You have to believe me. I've never met Nona before. I don't have an apartment for her. I've never dated her. I love you. You're everything to me. I can't lose you. I'd go crazy. Please believe me."

"Let go of me." Mona swatted at his head, but Jared only held her tighter.

"I admit I cuddled with her when I thought she was you. But I *thought* she was you. I thought *we* were going to the restaurant. You and I. Believe me, please, Mona. You have to believe me. I love you."

A sharp, stabbing pain hit Jared in the back, in the extremely sensitive spot right between his strapped-down wings. Mona wrenched her leg away from him. Pinned to the ground, literally, he could only watch helplessly as she walked away. His hand reached out toward her, but her disappearing shoes were already beyond his grasp. The pain in his heart was worse than the pain in his back.

Gasping, he turned his head to see what had him pinned. Nona stood over him, one spiked heel digging into his back, her other foot planted solidly near his elbow. He had a perfect view up her dress, but right now he was more concerned about the expression on her face as she watched Mona walk away. She looked rather like a furious tiger to Jared.

"I'll keep him here until you're done, Sis."

Nona looked down at him as she might a cockroach she was grinding underfoot. "Look while you can, scum-bucket. You ain't ever going to have this view, or anything in it, ever again."

"I don't know you! Why are you doing this?" Jared asked despairingly. "Why?"

She growled at him and moved her heel deeper into his back. Jared groaned in pain and frustration.

Mona could barely see through her tears as she raced through the quiet hotel corridors to her room. She tried wiping her face with her hands, but they were already too wet. Her cheeks were slick and hot, and all she wanted was to find someplace to hide. Where no one could see how humiliated and embarrassed she was.

How could she have been so deceived? Had she really never suspected that shy, handsome Jared was really leading a double life, cheating on her with her own sister?

They always said the wife was the last to know.

Arriving at her room, Mona gratefully shut the door behind her. Finally, somewhere soothing and private. She took a few moments in the bathroom to splash bracing, cold water against her face and compose herself.

The suitcases had been emptied, of course. Growing up with his mother had given Jared a compulsive need for order around himself. She hastily threw her clothes into her suitcase, repulsed to think that Jared had touched them. Had touched her.

How could she have believed him when he said he meant to reconcile with her this weekend?

How could he have brought her to the same hotel he'd romanced her sister at?

Why would he?

In fact, now that Mona thought about it, why would he bring her to Miami if he was secretly romancing her sister? Why risk getting caught?

Did he think he was so clever he could get away with it?

That neither sister would notice a thing?

Mona spied the jewelry box, sitting out on the bed.

Had he wanted to be caught? Had he finally been driven crazy enough by his mother that he'd snapped? Or did craziness just run in his family? Either way she had to get away from him. Now.

She threw the box with the necklace into her suitcase and closed it up. The *thrip* of the zipper closing sounded final in the hushed confines of the neat room.

Whatever he was, crazy or sane, she deserved something nice out of this weekend; the necklace would be it. She didn't really want a memento of this weekend, but she could sell it and get something back for her trouble.

Grabbing her suitcase and holding her head high, Mona headed for the lobby.

It was over between her and Jared. She might as well get used to it. She could put the pieces of her heart back together later. At least she'd never have to deal with his mother again.

Flat on the floor, with Nona's heel still in his back, Jared kept his arms over his head protectively. Nona had taken to leaning down to slap him with her purse.

"You are so low, they're going to have to make a whole new category of low, just to fit you in."

He flinched as her purse connected painfully with his knuckles. He just wanted this to be over. He'd given up on getting anything sane out of her. Even with Mona gone, she wouldn't admit she didn't know him. Whatever she had against him, she wasn't going to give it up easily.

"You creep. You jerk. There aren't any words to properly describe someone as . . ." Nona rambled off into a growl, and her heel twisted on his back.

His whole body twitched, and an impulse to respond overcame him. He flailed one hand behind him, found her leg, and tried to knock her off balance and off his back.

A few quick words of magic rolled off her tongue. Jared didn't recognize them with his limited exposure to spells, but their import became clear when he realized she suddenly seemed to weigh several times more than she had before. It felt rather like an elephant was stepping on his back. Except it was an elephant wearing spiked heels. He couldn't dislodge her. He desperately wished his mother had let him learn magic, or that he'd defied her and learned it secretly.

Her purse pounded new torture onto his unprotected head and he let go of her leg, returning to shielding his head as best he could, and waiting until it was over.

"Unmagical loser!" she shouted. "You fake. You fraud. You couldn't cast a spell if your life depended on it. You can't even say the release that would get you free now. Fool!"

Footsteps approached, Jared recognized Mona's shoes from the little peephole between his arms.

"Let's get out of here," Mona said flatly.

"Certainly." Nona wrenched her foot across Jared's back before following after Mona.

Jared barely heard the tearing of his shirt over the pain slashing through his wing. The pain subsided in time for him to see the two women reach the hotel lobby doors.

"Mona!"

She didn't hear him, or didn't care if she did; she just walked on out the door with her suitcase and her sister.

Slowly, careful of his aching back, Jared got to his feet. His legs shook. While he didn't yet trust them to get him safely to his room, he didn't want to stand around in the doorway between the bar and the lobby.

The lobby was ringed with people in the hotel's navy and gold uniform. A sprinkling of people in tourist and business attire completed the lobby's new decor. It appeared that everyone who worked at, or was staying at, the hotel had gathered to stare at him.

He tried to smooth his hair and shirt, but any movement of his arms made his back throb. Dignity was out, so Jared just staggered slowly through the gaping crowd in the lobby toward the elevators.

"Sir?"

Jared turned to find a male fairy in a hotel uniform behind him. The fairy looked more surprised than shocked, and somewhat concerned.

"Your wing." The fairy reached tentatively for Jared's back.

Over his shoulder, Jared could see his left wing sticking out of his shirt. He closed his eyes and ducked his head with a stab of fresh shame. He'd hidden his wings all his life; they'd never been exposed in public before. He'd hoped to change things this weekend, but not this way.

"Just leave it." Jared turned so that his back was away from the fairy.

"But Sir, you're bleeding."

"Leave me alone," Jared pleaded quietly. "Just leave me alone."

"Yes, Sir." The fairy faded away as the elevator arrived.

Staggering into the elevator, Jared sighed as the doors closed behind him, giving him some measure of privacy and dignity. He wasn't certain what hurt worse, his wing or that his life was shattered. The corridor to his room seemed unbearably long.

Alone in his room finally, Jared started to sit in a chair, but his back and wounded wing wouldn't let him lean back.

The bleeding seemed to have stopped, so he didn't have to worry about leaving blood all over everything. After a few moments perched uncomfortably on the edge of his seat, he decided to try the bed. He lay face down on the hard mattress, but that only served to remind him of being pinned helplessly to the floor in front of everyone.

In the bathroom, he tried peeling his shirt from his back, but it had become stuck to his wing with dried blood. Jared didn't much care for the idea of further tearing his wing. So, he stripped off the rest of his clothes, and turned the shower on. With the shower set to as hot as he could take, he stood under the steaming water, letting it pound the back of his shoulders and stream down his back and wings, until the soaked shirt fell off painlessly.

After throwing his sopping shirt into the sink, he stood under the pounding hot water for as long as he could stand. The heat soothed his nerves, and the pounding helped ease his tense muscles, but the streaming water and soap stung the wound on his wing and back.

Gently, he dried himself with one of the fluffy towels, letting his back and wings air-dry. The soap-perfumed steam swirled around him as he thought.

He had to get Mona back. That's what he'd come here for this weekend, and he had no intention of letting her crazed sister ruin everything. Besides, if Nona was as crazy as he feared, Mona might be in danger.

But how to find them?

Nona had said she had an apartment. She had to be listed somewhere. Someone had to know where she lived, and he'd keep looking until he found out.

Examining his wounded wing in a towel-cleared section of the steamed mirror, Jared found a jagged red gash roughly the length of his finger, with blood slowly oozing out. He decided he'd have to wait until morning, to give his wing time to heal up enough to allow him to wear a shirt.

But only until morning. If that wasn't enough, Jared would just get himself a shirt with slits in the back to accommodate his wings.

He'd find Mona, even if it meant deliberately going out in public with his wings exposed for the first time. Well, at least one thing would change this weekend.

Chapter 8

"I don't know, Boss." Forrest stood beside the gilded armchair in Zarrad's bedroom with the morning sunlight streaming in through the window. "None of this makes any sense."

Zarrad discarded another tie, tossing it on the tangled, multi-colored pile on his bed. His anger had run aground against the unbreakable rock of Forrest's patient recital of the exact same story, over and over. It made no sense, but perhaps somewhere, in some forgotten detail, was the key that would open the door to understanding. So, Zarrad stood at the open doors of his mahogany wardrobe and tossed rejected ties onto his bed. Surely he'd eventually find the perfect one for strangling Forrest. "Tell me, one more time, what happened to the necklace."

"I walked out of the store, saw you and Nona across the street, in front of the hotel, took the necklace over to you, and left." Forrest shifted from one foot to the other, while a crafty, bovine look crossed his face. "No, wait."

After patiently leaning on the open wardrobe door for a minute of quiet to assist the gears grinding in Forrest's brain, Zarrad prompted, "What?"

"I didn't give you the necklace," Forrest said.

"Ah ha!"

"Nona took it."

"What?"

"Nona took it, because you had the suitcases."

"What suitcases?"

"I don't know, Boss. You had these two suitcases. I never seen them before."

Pinching the bridge of his nose, hoping to stop the headache growing there, Zarrad said, "I had two unknown suitcases, and Nona took the necklace. What happened then?"

"I left." Forrest's forehead wrinkled; Zarrad assumed he was thinking hard. "No, wait. She was unhappy about the necklace. You said you didn't know anything about it, and you'd see that it was taken back. I got out of there before anything else happened."

Zarrad looked at the pile of ties, wishing he had found one to strangle Forrest with. "She must have recognized the necklace was enspelled."

"And after they guaranteed no one would know." Forrest sighed. "I bet I know what happened after that. She put a spell on you, so you'd forget I'd delivered it."

"That sounds too calm for Nona."

Forrest nodded.

"And it doesn't explain why you thought I had two suitcases."

"Unless I wasn't far enough away, and caught some of the spell's backsplash."

"I thought you were immune to that kind of a spell."

"Have been, up until now. Maybe this spell is different. No one ever did figure out why I was immune. Maybe it wore off."

Glaring at Forrest, Zarrad considered the idea that he possibly shouldn't be listening to such rantings. "But why suitcases?"

"I don't know, Boss."

"Unless there's more to the spell than my forgetting the necklace." Zarrad looked around his bedroom. Everything seemed normal. Being human, he might not be able to cast spells, but he'd been around them enough to understand them and figure out any he didn't already know. Though he didn't like the way his back was starting to itch, as if expecting a knife. His fake wings had saved him from those more than once. They worked pretty well as body armor. "If this is a spell we're dealing with, then the suitcases and everything else must represent something. The hotel was the one she and I used to use, so that's where that comes in. But I don't understand the suitcases. What's connected with suitcases?"

"Travel," Forrest said quickly.

"Baggage, as in personal issues and problems," Zarrad mused. "A change of scenery, a life change. A journey, growth. Travel is supposed to be broadening." He patted his muscular stomach absently, checking to make certain it hadn't blown up and bloated overnight.

"Clothes," Forrest stated.

"Do I look okay? I mean, do you see anything different about me? Anything wrong?" Zarrad smoothed the slightly starchy front of his button-down shirt as he looked down at himself. Everything seemed normal.

"Looks fine to me, Boss."

The light blue shirt and dark blue trousers, dark socks, and black belt were what Zarrad remembered putting on. He didn't see his underwear hanging out, nor did he appear to have put it on outside his clothing. It appeared he had the proper number of heads, limbs, digits, and other parts. Zarrad sighed. "I don't have time for this."

"So what do we do?" Forrest asked.

Pointing at Forrest, Zarrad said, "You are going to watch over Atlas, make sure the system stays up, and if any orders do come through, make sure the system works. I didn't spend all last night and the night before getting things going early, just to have everything blow up on me this weekend."

"Right, Boss."

"I'm going to go talk to Nona and smooth things over."

"Um . . ." Forrest inched behind the armchair. "Your father could tell you if she's put a spell on you."

"No. I don't want Papa finding out about my fight with Nona." Zarrad shook his head, thinking of how angry his father would be if he found out Zarrad and Nona had argued in public. Again. Ageon had never approved of anything Zarrad did, said, or touched, and that included Nona. If his father found out about this fight and the spell, Zarrad would have to listen to a rant on how he couldn't take care of himself without magic, how he wasn't good enough for anything, especially the business. Which reminded Zarrad about his other business. "And I don't want him finding out about Atlas, either."

"Yes, Boss." Forrest slouched out.

Nervously checking himself in the mirror, Zarrad wondered what exactly was the spell Nona had put on him. One of the many problems with being human. If he'd been a fairy, like his father wanted, this wouldn't be a problem. Not only would his father not worry about him taking over the business, Zarrad himself wouldn't have to worry about his ability to withstand a magical fight. Or his ability to recognize spells like the one Nona had put on him. He still hadn't figured it out as he slowed his convertible to a stop in front of Nona's apartment building.

He remembered her telling him they were through, but discounted it completely. She surely hadn't meant it. They had their differences, but Zarrad knew she loved him. Probably that memory was a part of whatever spell it was she'd put on him.

Checking his watch showed it was nearly noon; surely she'd be awake by now. Though, since it was Saturday, there was really no telling. Nona might have decided to get up at a normal time, or she might still be sleeping in after a restless night from their fight.

As far as Zarrad was concerned, things would work whichever way. If she was up, he'd take her to lunch; if not, they'd have lunch in, after he woke her. A sly grin spread across his face. He knew just exactly how to wake her. He'd start by kissing her shoulders . . .

He tossed his keys to the valet, and smiled as the gnome day-doorman held the door for him.

"Good afternoon, Mr. Silvan."

Checking his hair in the elevator's mirrored doors, Zarrad finger-combed some stray, wind-swept locks down. Since the elevator assured him of relative privacy, he adjusted his suit coat across the fake wings on his back, and smoothed his tie.

The nervous adjustments of his clothing hadn't given him any more confidence than what he'd started with, before he left on this errand.

The more he thought about it, the more it made sense for Nona to have put a spell on him. It explained a lot. But—

It didn't explain why she'd then go out to dinner with him. Usually when Nona got mad, she just pitched her fit where she was. Then they'd separate for the night, and the next day she'd be cooled off, so they could talk. But—

Nona hadn't pitched a fit; she'd just walked out.

Zarrad checked his shoes as he stepped out of the elevator. Clean, matching, correct number, and on the right feet.

Perhaps she was ready to get serious about their relationship. Maybe by walking out, she was signaling that she was ready to quit acting childish and consider commitment. That would cover personal issues between them. But if she'd cast a spell on him, he probably shouldn't interpret it as willingness to work on their relationship. And the "we're through" certainly didn't sound like someone who wanted to get serious.

Maybe dinner hadn't happened at all. Maybe those memories were also part of the spell.

Maybe this was her way of setting an ultimatum for him to start acting, and being, the person, the human, he really was. If that was true, then . . . what would he do?

Zarrad paused in front of Nona's door, his mind reeling with possibilities.

But that wouldn't explain why Forrest remembered all this craziness, too.

Sighing, Zarrad knocked on Nona's door, not daring to use his key since she was possibly, probably, still angry. Whatever had happened last night was over now, and it was time to get on with their lives.

Jared carefully strapped down his wings with an elastic bandage, surprised at how much better his injured wing felt afterward. The elastic bandages were nowhere near as good at concealing his wings, but they were ever so much more comfortable. One thing to remember, if he did decide to keep on concealing his true, fairy nature. On his quick jaunt down to a local drug store earlier—with his injured wing brushing painfully against his shirt—he'd picked up pain-killers, elastic wrap bandages, and a hotdog breakfast. After easing his oversized T-shirt back on, he deemed himself much better prepared to face the world.

Mona was somewhere in this city. Unfortunately, she

was with her crazy sister, Nona. And he was going to find them, rescue Mona from her sister, and salvage his marriage.

He spotted the letter his mother had given him as he put the bottle of painkillers into the dresser drawer with his clothes. Amelia, intruding on his life again. That he was also supposed to be looking for some unknown man didn't help his stomach, still queasy from his breakfast of spicy hotdog of dubious origin. He didn't have time for his mother's silliness. Still, he did have an obligation toward her. She was his mother.

Stuffing the letter in the side pocket of his rumpled cargo pants, Jared headed out of his room. If he stumbled across this man while looking for Mona, fine, but he had no intention of spending any effort finding whoever-it-was.

He had a woman to locate and seduce.

Nona wasn't listed in the phone directory, but someone had to know where she lived. He'd start with the hotel employees, and work out from there.

Jared hoped Nona wasn't so crazy she'd hurt her own sister, though she was obviously seriously deranged, and a pathological liar, and given to physical outbursts of temper. He had to find Mona soon.

Nona had been expecting the knock on her door. She knew without checking it was Zarrad. In the past—before she knew what a chrome-plated cad he was—she would pretend on the day after an argument that the argument had never taken place.

Not any more. Nothing was ever going to be the same ever again.

Flinging the door open, Nona snarled, "What do you want, you snake?"

Zarrad smiled tentatively at her. "You."

"If you think you can just waltz over here this morning, like last night never happened, you're even stupider than you are unmagical." Nona started to shut the door, but he put his hand on it, keeping it open partway.

"Nona, I know we've had our differences, but we can work things out." He gave her his best, charming, impish look. How could he be so handsome, and yet so slimy? "If you would just let me in, I'm sure we could talk it over, and everything will be fine."

"Work things out!" Nona screamed. "I'd rather be dropped in a pit of snakes. At least they're honestly creepy."

"Please, open the door." Zarrad leaned against the door.

"You are not coming in here ever again." Nona pushed back, against the door. "Just go away now, because nothing you say is going to help you."

"At least tell me about the spell," he begged.

The door slowly and inexorably started opening, as Zarrad pushed against it, protecting himself from any spells Nona might try by hiding behind the bulk of the solid wood door. Until Mona, hearing the commotion, joined Nona.

"Forget it, jerk," Mona shouted. "We want nothing to do with you. You are out. Out-classed, out-numbered, and outside."

With a final push, they closed the door. Nona switched all the locks on, including the magical spell-lock. "Good riddance."

From the other side of the door, they could hear him yelling for them to open the door, to talk to him, to work things out.

Mona put her arm around Nona and pulled her away from the door. "Come away. We shouldn't even listen to him. Give him half a chance and he'll try sweet talking us into believing anything he says." Nona felt her shudder. "Look how easily he sweet talked me into coming here. Thinking . . ."

It was Nona's turn to comfort her sister. She led Mona into the gleaming kitchen. "Don't think about him. Think about yourself."

"I don't know." Mona scrubbed tears from her eyes as she leaned against the cleared counter. She'd barely stopped crying enough to sleep. "He's acting so crazy. I'm afraid what he might do."

"Him!" Nona snorted. "He'll just go crying home for help." She paused, as she lifted the lid of the cookie jar, thinking of what sort of help Zarrad might be able to muster at home. Maybe Mona was right to be worried.

"A fat lot of good that would do him." Mona reached into the cookie jar, stirring her hand around and coming up empty.

"Oh." Nona looked around the kitchen trying to think of what else she had to offer to comfort her sister. Ice cream? Heading to the freezer, she reflected that Mona was probably right about running home for help. Zarrad's father had never liked her, and even actively discouraged Zarrad's interest in her. She couldn't see Ageon helping his son win her back. Though, maybe Ageon hadn't liked her because he was afraid of what she might do to Zarrad's marriage.

Worse, there was no ice cream in the freezer. In fact, there was very little beyond the ice spilling out of the ice maker.

"What with everything being so messed up, and her twittiness in the hospital," Mona said. "Though that may be what's driven him to act so strangely."

Nona stared at her sister. Was there another woman—

beyond the two of them—in Zarrad's life? The cad! Wishing she'd been able to injure him through his fake wings with her heels last night, Nona motioned for her sister to follow her.

"Come on. There's nothing here for us to drown our sorrows in. So we aren't going to drown them. We're going out on the town and celebrate getting rid of that loser." Nona grabbed Mona's arm and dragged her back to the bedroom. "We're going to dress up, just like when we were younger and on the prowl. We're going to hook ourselves up with a nicer class of men."

Mona sighed as she followed Nona into the bedroom. She hadn't ever cared for dressing up and prowling around. That was Nona's thing. Still, Nona needed cheering, too. Maybe this would help.

She put on the first dress Nona pulled from the crowded closet. A deep-red, swirly, clingy thing, with ruffled sleeves and a sheer overskirt that stopped just above her knees; it reeked of Nona's perfume. She discovered why as Nona applied her perfume liberally while still standing in the closet, before handing the bottle out to Mona.

"Try this. You'll love it."

Already Mona hated it. It was heavily floral, almost sickeningly sweet. Her taste and Nona's had never run to the same things. Strange that they'd both been attracted to Jared.

"Don't you think I should wear something of my own?" Mona asked, without much hope.

"Did you bring anything really nice?" Nona's knowing smirk irritated Mona. Especially since Mona hadn't brought anything except her casual clothes, not expecting to need anything else.

Well, truthfully, with no intention of letting Jared take her anywhere she couldn't wear casual clothes. To keep the prices down as much as possible.

"Did you bring any jewelry?" Nona still smirked knowingly.

"No," Mona forced herself to say. Then she remembered the necklace. "Wait. I didn't bring anything, but . . ." she paused, not wanting to say Jared's name, "he gave me a necklace last night. As a present. It was a surprise to start the weekend off, I guess."

"That sounds promising. Put it on."

Looking at the silver and gold necklace glittering on its bed of dark velvet, Mona had to admit it looked pretty, and to her—admittedly inexpert—eyes expensive. After she'd fastened the cool, plaited loop around her neck she turned for Nona to admire it.

Nona grimaced. "No diamonds, I see. Typical of the man. You'd think he'd learn eventually. But still . . ." She half smiled and shrugged. "It looks good on you."

Undoubtedly leaving unspoken the idea that Nona wouldn't have worn it under any circumstances.

Mona turned away to grimace. She loved Nona. Nona was her sister. But why did Nona have to be so shallow?

Sighing again as they left the apartment, Mona wished she could just go to some cheap all-you-can-eat buffet and stuff herself for a couple of hours. Someplace with lots of rich, fattening entrees, butter-loaded breads, vegetables in cream sauces, and sweet deep-fried desserts.

Nona looked trim and neat in her form-hugging, lacy, violet dress. She nearly floated down the corridor, as if those tiny wings could actually lift her from the ground. Mona felt like an overstuffed sausage in the tiny, expensive, red dress Nona had loaned her. Everyone said they looked exactly alike, so why did Mona feel like a plump, dull human next to a flighty, flirty fairy?

Maybe this wasn't such a good idea.

But then, had coming here this weekend with Jared been all that better?

Squaring her shoulders and holding her head high, Mona was glad to see that Jared had left, not just the building, but apparently the area. He was nowhere in sight. She and Nona could storm the city without him tagging along behind them, begging and whining.

Though Mona did wonder where he was, and what he was up to. This weekend had gone seriously wrong for both of them. She worried what he might be planning to do, or worse that he might do something seriously insane.

Chapter 9

Zarrad leaned back against the driver's seat of his car, his fake wings digging into his back, his hair fluttering in the wind as he drove, thinking. With Mona here, no wonder Nona was acting so strange. Obviously Mona had finally left that loser of a husband she'd picked up. But why had she chosen now to come here? He'd been so close.

Did Mona's presence have anything to do with the spell Nona had cast on him? Life was getting far too weird right now.

A movement on the sidewalk to his right caught his attention, and he realized Forrest was there waving frantically at him. He'd been paying no attention to where he was going, just cruising along slowly in traffic. Barely moving at all. Irritated at himself and Forrest, Zarrad pulled the convertible to the curb and waited for Forrest to catch up.

"Hey, Bossman, you need to check your pages sometimes," Forrest said.

"I check them when I check them. What do you want?" Zarrad glared at Forrest, wondering what had gotten into him. To have Forrest scolding and ranting about pages, that just didn't happen. Forrest never spoke that way to Zarrad. Nor had Zarrad ever seen Forrest dressed in old, faded blue jeans and wrinkled T-shirt. First Nona started acting strange and now Forrest. Maybe it was the spell. It'd have to be one complicated spell. "Aren't you supposed to be at home, minding the business?"

Forrest glared back. "We have a problem. That business

venture we discussed Thursday, well, it's arrived early, today." He pointed at his feet, as if to emphasize the immediate presence of the problem.

Zarrad almost asked what business venture, then he remembered: Auveron, who could smell weakness clear from Atlanta. He growled softly to himself. This time Auveron was mistaken. He and his father merely hadn't had much time to see each other for a while; they weren't arguing. Not really, Zarrad hoped.

"You want to head back?" Forrest asked.

"Yeah. Okay." Zarrad turned the car off and tossed the keys to Forrest. "I'll go see about this 'problem.' You keep an eye on the girls for me."

"Girls? What girls?" Forrest looked completely baffled. Which was an expression Zarrad was accustomed to seeing on his face, not the fierce-eyed defiance that had been there before.

"Nona and Mona."

The bafflement disappeared from Forrest's face, replaced by sympathy. "I take it things didn't go well."

"No." Zarrad didn't want to talk about how the girls had pushed him out and ignored him. "Just find them and keep an eye on them. Maybe you can figure out what is wrong."

"Where'll I find them?" Forrest asked.

"Start with Nona's apartment. If they're not there, ask the doorman. Nona can't help chatting with everyone she passes. She'll probably tell him." Zarrad walked off, muttering to himself, and trying to decide if he should go straight to his father, or try to take care of this himself. He hated going to his father for help, but this time at least half the problem was his father's. First he'd make a few phone calls; at least he knew he'd have someone he could trust watching over Nona.

★ ★ ★ ★ ★

Boris alternated between looking at the keys in his hand and watching Jared's disappearing back, as Jared pulled out a cell phone. When he'd found Atlas up and working the previous night, with their "pre-opening sales event," he'd paged Jared. And paged him again in the morning, with no answer. So he'd hopped a plane, figuring this was definitely a problem worth interrupting Jared's romantic weekend getaway with Mona.

He'd expected Jared to grab Mona and leave immediately for home. Or something.

This he hadn't expected.

At the very least, Boris had expected they would sit and brainstorm some way to counter Atlas' move. Though, maybe Jared had his laptop up in his hotel room, which might perhaps be nearby. Maybe Jared wanted to handle it himself. Though, if things were going badly between Mona and Jared, perhaps Jared just needed a little time to himself.

Not, Boris realized, that spending time trying to salvage his business would help Jared mend things with Mona.

Maybe between Amelia being in the hospital and his marriage to Mona going bad, Jared had finally snapped. Boris hoped not. If that were the case, then Atlas might be the straw that broke the camel's back.

Too late, Boris realized he didn't know where Nona's apartment was. He slid behind the wheel of the convertible, glad that for once Jared hadn't let Mona force him into some ugly, practical, cheap, compact rental. This was a much better setup.

Sticking out of the glove box was a corner of an envelope. Surprised that the preternaturally tidy Jared hadn't closed the glove box neatly, Boris reached over to fix it for him. The letter tumbled out, onto the floor, and Boris noticed it was addressed to Nona.

Well, now he knew where Nona lived. The rest of the glove box was stuffed with papers and junk, more like a normal car than a rental, but on top was a well-worn map of Miami.

In a few minutes, Boris eased the car back into traffic, and headed for the address on the envelope.

He'd find Mona and Nona and see if he could talk to them. Jared obviously needed help. Mona might be mad at Jared, but she'd never seemed the type to hold a grudge. If Jared really needed her, Boris was sure she'd set aside her anger to help.

Jared wasn't just his boss, they were friends.

If Mona wouldn't help, Boris knew someone who would.

His brother, Forrest.

If he remembered correctly, Forrest had said he was heading for Miami when they'd split up, after they'd run away from home. Family was family. You could always count on them for help.

Jared walked down the street, making sure the breeze didn't blow his hair back off his pointed ears, and wondering what to do now. He dodged the crowds on the street, barely paying attention to the passing people. They were little more than obstacles to get past as he walked. Occasionally a thick cloud of perfume or an overloud voice screaming into a cell phone would cause him to actually look at someone, but they were not important to him.

The hotel employees hadn't known where Nona lived and seemed to think him very strange for asking.

Well, after the way she'd treated him last night, it probably did look strange for him to be asking after her. But she was the only way he could find Mona.

He checked his watch; it was nearly noon. Most people would be looking for lunch.

More importantly, Mona would be looking to get lunch. Probably at an all-you-can-eat buffet, with Mona as upset as she had to be. Somewhere she could sit for hours and stuff herself. Come to think of it, he was a little hungry himself.

Grinning to himself, Jared headed for the nearest door. All he needed now was a phone book listing of every all-you-can-eat buffet in Miami. He'd find and check every single one.

As he opened the first shop door he came to, he thought for an instant that he saw Boris drive by in an immaculate, powder-blue convertible. He shook his head. Boris was back home, minding the store.

Probably just coincidence, and a trick of the eye that made whoever the man was look like Boris.

In a city as big as Miami, he could probably find look-alikes for many people. Maybe even himself.

He needed to check his pages. That's what it was. His subconscious made him think he saw Boris to remind him to check his pages. Jared told himself firmly that he didn't have time for that. He had to find Mona. The business would just have to get along without him for one weekend.

Zarrad squared his shoulders as he searched out his father at home. Hjell stood outside the door to Ageon's office; his father would be in there.

The hulking, half-breed's delicate, gossamer fairy wings fluttered as he put one enormous, heavy troll hand on Zarrad's shoulder. "The boss said he needed a few minutes of privacy."

Sighing, Zarrad said, "We've got problems with

Auveron. I need to talk to him."

"Huh," Hjell grunted. The heavy hand lifted off Zarrad's shoulder, and Hjell rapped his knuckles in a pattern on the door behind him.

In seconds the door opened a crack. Ageon whispered, "What?"

"Auveron," Hjell whispered back, and flapped one giant hand at Zarrad.

Ageon slipped out, closing the door behind him. "What about Auveron?"

"Forrest found me a little while ago." Zarrad tried not to twitch his false wings. "He and I had been discussing Auveron last Thursday, and now Forrest says he's here."

"Here?" Ageon roared. Zarrad flinched and nodded. Ageon sighed. "And how does Forrest know?"

"I . . . I forgot to ask." Zarrad withered under his father's glare.

Blowing out a long breath, Ageon studied Zarrad. He folded his arms across his chest. "At least it's good to know you've been doing something other than chasing that flighty flirt and playing at being a dot-com."

Zarrad felt his face flush, and bit his lower lip to keep from saying anything they'd all regret later.

Turning to Hjell, Ageon said, "Get Stig and Axel; tell them to see what they can find out about Auveron."

"I made a few calls on my own." Zarrad shifted his weight from foot to foot nervously. "Little Jimmy was seen in town last night."

Blowing out a breath, Ageon nodded to Hjell. "Go."

Hjell nodded, and headed down the hall.

Trying not to squirm while his father stared at him, Zarrad stammered, "I, uh, I wouldn't want anyone to hurt you. I just thought you should know."

"Hmm," Ageon hummed neutrally. "I can't talk long."
He glanced back at the dark, solid door to his office. "But
about this on-line business of yours . . ."

"Yes?" Zarrad said warily.

"All the financial aspects are handled through the computer, right?"

"Yes."

"Could be," Ageon's head tilted slightly, and one eye
shivered in a wink, "very useful."

"It's my business," Zarrad said, while over and over in
his mind he thought, *No, no, no.* Atlas was the one thing he
had that hadn't come from his father, or been touched by
his father. It was his and his alone, and he wanted it to stay
that way.

Ageon frowned, as if reading Zarrad's mind. "I'm your
father. Your business is my business. We're family."

"It's mine," Zarrad said stubbornly. He tried to stand
straight, as if he weren't afraid.

"This is yours." Ageon waved his arms to indicate the
well-appointed corridor they stood in, and the house beyond. "Everything I've ever done is all for you. Why do you
think I work so hard? Why do you think I care about you
and protect you? You're my son. You have everything. I saw
to that."

"This is yours, all yours, all for you!" Zarrad shouted.
His arms windmilled around in imitation of his father's.
"This overstuffed museum of a mansion is all yours. The
money is yours, the power is yours. And, as far as I can
tell—from the way you treat me—I'm just your most in-
competent, idiot minion." He stalked off down the corridor.

"Zarrad!" his father shouted behind him. "We'll talk
about this later."

★ ★ ★ ★ ★

Ageon watched his son walk away, while surreptitiously casting a spell to see if Zarrad had been enspelled. No aura of ensorcelment appeared around any part of Zarrad, so his behavior couldn't be due to a spell.

Just the usual angry Zarradness. Ageon sighed, wondering why his remaining son had to be so trying. Zarrad sometimes reminded Ageon far too much of Amelia. They were both human.

Why couldn't either of them understand?

And Auveron. Something would have to be done about Auveron. Something permanent.

How had that idiot Forrest ever discovered the wily Auveron here? There was more to this than met the eye.

Ageon slipped back into his office, to finish his business there, before he had to go look into this new problem.

Zarrad stomped through the house, thumping his feet as hard as he could into the plush carpeting. He momentarily considered slamming his fist into the wall every so often, to leave a trail of indents to mark his path, but that would only lead to another confrontation with his father, which would lead to more wall punching, which would lead . . .

He'd done that before, and finally realized he only ended up with swollen, aching knuckles for his effort.

Just once he wanted something of his own. Something his father had never, and would never, touch. Something his father wouldn't hijack for other purposes.

But, Ageon was his father, the only family he really had.

His office was next to his suite on the second floor. Zarrad decided to check up on how Atlas was doing, since Forrest had abandoned it to find him and tell him about Auveron.

Why had Forrest abandoned Atlas? How had he found out about Auveron? Zarrad decided to worry about it later.

The dark, solid door to his office was a near twin to the one for Ageon's office. Behind it, Zarrad hoped to find tranquility, order, and a few moments of happiness.

Opening the door, Zarrad found the office just like he'd left it: immaculate, organized, efficient, and operating. Everything was just as he'd left it, except for Forrest sitting splayed in the executive chair, grinning like a loon at the computer screen on his immaculate desk.

"Hey, Boss! Everything's running like greased lightning."

Chapter 10

"What are you doing here?" Zarrad roared.

Forrest blinked. He sat up properly in the executive chair, causing the dark leather to squeak quietly. "I'm keeping an eye on Atlas, like you said."

"I told you to keep an eye on the girls." Zarrad really did want to punch the wall now.

"What girls?" Forrest asked, looking terribly confused.

This was sounding altogether too familiar, and Zarrad found he had less patience with every repetition. Soon he would have none left. "Nona and Mona."

"Mona's in town? Did you get to meet her?"

Zarrad growled incoherently for a moment. Now that he thought it over, any tie seemed appropriate for strangling Forrest, no matter what color or style. Too bad for him that Forrest never wore one. Though perhaps that was why Forrest never wore one.

"Yes, Mona is in town. I think that may be why Nona is acting so strangely."

"Ah," Forrest said. "So, how'd it go talking to Nona?"

Grabbing Forrest by the collar, Zarrad lifted him out of the chair to his feet. Since Ageon paid Forrest to be Zarrad's bodyguard, Zarrad shouldn't have been able to do such a thing, but his anger and frustration added to his strength.

As Zarrad spoke, he roughly shook Forrest. "I told you she wouldn't talk to me. I told you to follow them, and keep an eye on them, and try to figure out what was wrong with them."

"Uh, Boss . . ." Forrest clung to Zarrad's wrists. "The last thing you told me was to keep an eye on Atlas this morning. That's what I've been doing. And everything is going well."

"Everything is not going well." Zarrad slammed Forrest into the wall. "I found you on the street. You told me about Auveron. I gave you my car and told you to follow the girls, while I took care of our 'little problem.' "

"I've been here all morning, Boss."

"What about Auveron? You told me there was a problem with Auveron. I checked around, and Little Jimmy was seen nightclubbing here last night."

"I don't know nothing about that."

As Zarrad started to slam Forrest's head repeatedly into the wall, Forrest shouted, "I think I have it. I *think* I've been here all morning."

"What are you babbling about?" Zarrad screamed, letting go of Forrest's shirt.

Forrest scooted away. "I was just thinking. Maybe this is more of Nona's spell. Maybe she's following you around and messing up our memories."

"So where's my car?" Zarrad sounded more strangled than patient to his own ears.

"Nona has it?" Forrest offered.

Zarrad growled quietly. It made sense. If Nona and Mona had followed him until his meeting with Forrest on the street, they could easily have taken his car and left him with a memory of giving it to Forrest, and made Forrest think he'd been home all morning. Though Forrest was usually immune to spells of any kind. Life was not fair.

"All right, all right." Zarrad flopped into the dark-leather executive chair, making it creak, while Forrest sat gingerly in a straight-backed chair near the door. "We have to find Nona and get this taken care of."

"Are you sure about that?" Forrest asked cautiously. "Every time we get near her, something strange happens. Maybe we should leave her alone for a while, to cool off. We could just stay here and watch Atlas."

Ah, what a temptation. Zarrad glanced at the soft glow of the computer screen. But its siren call didn't touch him this time. As Forrest had said, everything seemed to be running smoothly on-line, without need of assistance.

Also, if they stayed here, Ageon would be bound to find them and put them to some little job, rather than let Zarrad have time to work on his own project.

And they needed to know what it was that Forrest had found out about Auveron. If this spell had made him forget what had happened this morning, which had clued him in to Little Jimmy, well, that could be a real problem. Nona would have to understand that.

"No." Zarrad sighed. "Father is taking care of Auveron and Little Jimmy, and Atlas is taking care of itself. We need to find Nona and resolve this."

"Sure, Boss, whatever you say." Forrest stood up. "So, where do we start."

"I'm going to check Nona's apartment. You check the hotels in town, see if she's checked in somewhere." Zarrad started for the door, which Forrest deferentially held open. "Oh, and check under her sister's name; they might try registering under her name."

"What is her name?"

"Mona."

"Mona what?"

"I don't know. Try 'Bryce,' like Nona. If Mona's left her husband, she's probably gone back to her old name."

Boris pulled the luscious convertible to the curb at the

address listed on the envelope. Maybe Jared had reasons other than Mona and money for not wanting to rent such a car. The seat squished his wings very uncomfortably. However, Boris had to admit it looked cool.

The building that matched the address looked nice, clean and modern and light, though not to his tastes. He didn't much care for towering luxury apartments. He liked a place with a front yard and a porch, a small slice of suburban paradise. Not everyone's cup of tea, but to each his or her own. He checked the apartment number on the envelope before he got out of the car.

"Park your car, Sir?" a uniformed, human valet asked, as Boris stepped up onto the curb.

"Actually, I was looking for someone in apartment . . ." Boris checked the envelope again, clutching it against a gusting breeze, "one-one-four-seven."

"Oh, Miss Nona Bryce. She and her sister have gone out for the day."

"Did they say where?" Boris looked up and down the crowded street, as if they might still be hanging around. He knew it for a vain hope.

"They didn't tell me, but they did speak to Durward." The valet motioned to the gnome doorman, standing quietly by the door, looking off somewhat to the left and pretending he couldn't hear them.

"Thank you." Boris nodded at the valet and approached the gnome. "Excuse me, Sir. But would you know where I could find Mona Silvan?"

"Mona Silvan?" The little gnome's shaggy eyebrows lifted in surprise.

"Yes. I believe she was staying here with her sister, Nona Bryce."

"Her sister is Mona *Silvan?*" It was a good thing the

gnome's shaggy eyebrows had moved up, because his eyes now goggled nearly out of his head and the eyebrows would only have been in the way.

"Yes." Boris shoved the rumpled envelope into his back pocket to keep the wind from blowing it away. It also kept his hands busy, so he couldn't strangle the cunning gnome.

Gnomes all thought they were so sharp, but if you knew their tricks—every one of which Boris had been exposed to, starting in elementary school—you could save yourself a lot of annoyance.

The greasy little con thought he could get more money out of Boris by acting like he knew something incredible that Boris didn't. Fat chance. Boris had no intention of tipping anyone for a little friendly information.

However, just because it wouldn't look good for Boris to actually strangle a gnome—what with his height advantage and being a fairy and all—didn't mean he wouldn't use what he had to his advantage. He loomed threateningly over the ugly little swindler. "Where is she?"

The gnome turned pale. "Zarrad Silvan's wife?"

Boris grinned evilly. If the lisping little swindler thought using the bossman's name would impress Boris, he was dead wrong. Boris had no intention of believing in psychic powers. Mona had probably mentioned her husband's name.

"Yes. Now where is she?"

"Wherewolf Whillies," the trembling gnome whispered. "Just down the street."

"Thanks." Boris settled for patting the gnome on the head, rather than passing him any cash.

You just had to know how to talk to people, Boris thought, as he slid behind the wheel of the convertible. Nice and polite, but firm.

★ ★ ★ ★ ★

Zarrad had taken one of his father's spare cars, a large lumbering Caddie that, while plush and comfortable, was not what Zarrad preferred. Ageon tended toward vehicles that hinted at muscle power and menacing threats, with shiny, black exteriors and hushed, dark, mysterious interiors. Zarrad preferred something fast, free, and risky. Though he did have to admit the plush seats better and more comfortably cushioned the false wings fastened to his back than his sports cars.

For the second time that day, he pulled up in front of Nona's apartment building.

The valet nodded to him nervously. "Park your car, Sir?"

"No." Zarrad approached the doorman, the same gnome that had been there in the morning.

"Good afternoon, Mr. Silvan." The gnome twitched apprehensively, his hand shaking as he reached for the door.

"I'm not going in." Zarrad tried to smile, but being so harried and frustrated, it felt more like a grimace. "I was wondering if you knew where Nona was?"

"Ah. Yes." The gnome pointed one shaky finger down the street. "She and her *sister* said they were going to Wherewolf Whillies."

"Thanks." Zarrad nodded to the gnome, and hurried back to the car.

Maybe it was the unusual car he was driving, but Zarrad could've sworn both the valet and the doorman watched nervously until he'd driven away.

Jared staggered out of the restaurant, slightly dazed and definitely worried, wishing the smell of grease and potatoes wouldn't follow him everywhere. He had a horrible fear that it would never fade, and he'd end up reeking of greasy dives for the rest of his miserable life.

His stomach roiled, as he walked through the thinning afternoon crowds. Lunchtime had come and gone, and he hadn't found Mona. He'd searched every all-you-can-eat buffet he could find in this part of town.

A few of the restaurants had required him to pay before entering. Between his own inborn obsessions and the ones Mona had impressed on him, he'd been unable to pay without eating something, to get some sort of value for his money. The result being that he was so stuffed, he was sure he'd never need to eat again.

Where was Mona?

Obviously not at an all-you-can-eat buffet. If Mona and her sister weren't following Mona's standard operating procedures, they had to be going with Nona's.

Which in its own way made sense. Nona clearly had a great deal of influence on her sister, far too much influence. Jared could be certain of that.

Now, what had Mona told him about Nona? What would Nona do? From what Jared had seen, it could be anything. The woman was pure insanity. She dressed differently, so if he thought of something the opposite of what Mona would do, he might have a chance. So what would be the impulsive, unexpected, insane thing to do on a Saturday afternoon?

Jared leaned against the side of the building he'd been passing. It was all rough, tan brick, with no windows on the first floor, perhaps a bank, or some such thing. For the most part, the few people walking past ignored him. Occasionally someone would nod at him, by way of saying, "Good afternoon," Jared supposed.

A few stepped warily away from him. He didn't think he

looked like a bum and certainly couldn't smell like a bum. Though, with all the greasy dives he'd been through, perhaps he shouldn't be so certain his morning's shower would hold him through the day. He hadn't asked for any handouts, but maybe Miami had a better class of bum than he was used to. Looking up and down the street, Jared didn't see any other bums. This didn't look like the right part of town for them.

The breeze gusted past, fluttering Jared's shirt, cooling him from the steady, relentless heat of the sun. He considered moving to the other, shaded side of the street. Maybe Mona and Nona had gone back to Nona's apartment.

His hand patted his pocket absently, reminding him of the letter there.

Why had he listened to his mother? Why hadn't he let Mona convince him to take her somewhere closer to home?

The more Jared thought of it, the more a nice, little, isolated cabin in the woods sounded vastly more romantic than a day at a hot, jam-packed beach in crowded, noisy Miami.

Far, far away from Mona's crazy sister, Nona. She was enough to make Jared thankful that he had no siblings.

A large, shiny black limousine pulled up to the curb in front of Jared, and an older man got out. Jared caught the sound of the end of his name. "—ared."

He didn't recognize the man, who turned for a second to say something to the driver of the car. A lump centered on the upper part of the back, under an expensive suit, let Jared know that this was a powerful fairy he was dealing with. A lawyer, perhaps?

Nona's lawyer, on loan to Mona?

Jared groaned quietly. This was all he needed.

The fairy turned around. Jared tried to look calm and

not twitch with nervousness. He thought he recognized something about the man. It wasn't his eyes, or his nose, but something looked familiar.

The fairy was tall and broad-shouldered, with a thickening middle and graying hair. He swaggered over to Jared like he owned the city.

Closing his eyes momentarily, Jared hoped this meeting with Mona's lawyer wouldn't be too painful.

Chapter 11

"Have you been able to find anything out?" the fairy asked without preamble.

"No. I've searched and searched. But I can't find—"

Holding up a hand and making a shushing noise, the tough fairy glared at Jared. "Not here. It's too public. No specifics."

"I understand." Jared nodded. "So what now?"

"Here, take this." The fairy reached into a coat pocket and pulled out a roll of money, which he handed Jared. "Spread it around as you see fit. Something is bound to come up." He turned and started back for the limo.

"What?" Jared asked, stunned. He stared at the fat, green wad resting in his palm. The top bills were fifties and hundreds.

"Use it. You know where," the tough fairy said over his shoulder as he opened the limo door, preparing to get in and leave. "And stay away from that woman. You've got business to take care of."

"Wait a minute!" Jared shouted.

The disappearing fairy just waved his hand, dismissing Jared, and closed the door to the car.

Jared watched as the dark, shiny limousine slowly and smoothly pulled away. He looked at the money in his hand. Then, realizing he was on a public street, promptly stuffed it in his pocket.

Good lord! What was going on?

Rerunning the conversation in his head didn't help Jared

any. Now that he thought it over, it didn't make much sense. Where would Mona get that much money?

Nona.

Anger welled up in Jared's confused mind.

How dare that woman try to buy him off! Did Nona honestly think he'd leave Mona for a wad of cash? The woman he loved? The woman he'd romanced, and married, and adored?

The black car had disappeared from the street, but Jared doubted the tough fairy would tell him where to find Nona. Nor did the fairy seem like the type to simply take the money back and leave Jared alone. His sort usually just escalated the violence until they got their way.

Jared had to get the money to somewhere safe, until he could return it to Nona. And let her know he couldn't be bought. No matter what, he would always love Mona.

As he flagged down a taxi, Jared realized he finally had proof of Nona's intentions. He wouldn't return the money to Nona's hired thugs; he'd make sure Mona knew all about Nona's underhanded dealings.

Assuming Mona didn't already know.

And wasn't already afraid. Or worse, enjoying all the things Jared couldn't get for her.

Slumping in the back of a beat-up taxi, Jared wearily gave the driver the address of the hotel.

He'd have to think this through, before he did anything else.

Everything he did just seemed to make things worse. And make him more confused than ever. All he could be certain of now was that he really, truly, honestly loved Mona, and wanted to be with her the rest of his life. He wanted her to be happy and to have all her dreams come true. He just wanted to be a part of it, that's all.

★ ★ ★ ★ ★

Wherewolf Whillies was every bit as awful as Mona had expected. Exactly the sort of place she usually avoided and the sort that Nona preferred. Of course, Mona had never particularly cared for dating, or clubbing, or any of the other foolishness that went into introducing people in the hopes that they'd pair off in relationships of varying potential. It all seemed so artificial and deceptive. Jared had felt the same way; at least he'd always given Mona that impression. They'd met at a company function, but somehow he and Nona had hooked up. Mona hated to think of her sister and Jared meeting at a place like this. It was Nona's style, though.

As her eyes adjusted to the dark interior, and her ears adjusted to the screeching music, Mona recognized the place as some sort of dance club. The sort that passed itself off as trendy and chic, which overcharged for drinks and snacks, and which pretended to be discrete while feeding tabloids juicy tidbits of gossip. At least it would probably be such tonight, for now the place was catering to a mid-afternoon crowd unwilling to wait until evening to start their fun.

Perhaps the darkness was to simulate night, since Mona could see that some of the lights were off. The place seemed to be lit by floodlighted posters and flashing neon artwork. Behind the bar, a sequence of neon showed a werewolf running from some sort of ghoul. Or perhaps they were dancing. It was difficult to tell.

Nona made some complicated hand signal to a handsome satyr behind the bar. He nodded and smiled. Obviously, Nona was a regular. She turned back to Mona. "He's so sweet, but, uh, not the right sort."

"What sort would that be?" Mona asked, trying not to

feel oppressed and surrounded. Darkened interiors never seemed cozy and mysterious to her; they always made her feel the place was hiding grime, or cockroaches, or watered-down drinks, or something equally horrible.

"You know," Nona whispered, waving her hand over the table. "Not like us."

Ah, unseparated, and worse, half-animal. Mona felt sorry for the poor guy, working here, putting up with snobs like Nona, being cheerful and courteous with stuffed shirts for tips. Not, she had to admit, that putting up with snobs like her would be any better.

The quiet clicking of his hooves on the hardwood floor as he approached caused Nona to look up, smiling at him. "Thanks, Clyde."

Clyde smiled back at her. Mona couldn't tell if he really thought Nona liked him, or if he didn't care as long as the tip was good.

Nona slipped him some money; yes indeed, the tip was good.

"Thank you." Mona carefully didn't smile. She didn't feel like it, and he probably had to put up with enough falseness anyway.

"Sisters?" he asked.

"Yes," Nona purred. "We're on the lookout. If you spot any likely prey, let us know."

"Yes, Ma'am."

"Not me, thanks." Mona glared at her sister. "I've had enough of men for a while."

"Don't be stuffy. Just because he was a jerk doesn't mean they're all jerks."

Clyde beat a hasty retreat. Either because he didn't want to be mistaken as a jerk, or fearing that being male was the same as being a jerk, and his presence would just pull him into the argument.

Nona sipped her drink. "Come on, we're here to have fun. Relax a little."

Picking up her drink, Mona tried to relax. One sip of her drink and she grimaced. It was fruity and sweet and consisted mostly of crushed ice; she hated it. And the stupid little umbrella with pineapple and cherry skewered on it. One of those frowzy, expensive drinks that cost more than a six-pack and delivered less.

Where did Nona get the money for this sort of lifestyle? Expensive apartment, stylish clothing, cool car, frequenting chic and popular hot spots. Nona was a starving artist who worked only when the muse took her, perhaps once or twice a year, without any other visible means of support.

So where did the money come from?

Not Jared. Mona knew his salary, both from before he'd left the company to start his own, to now, when she'd occasionally checked his books. Nona's money hadn't come from Jared.

"Nona, where do you get your money?" Mona asked, fingering the necklace Jared had given her, wondering if she really wanted to know. She hadn't known Jared as well as she thought. Did she really want to know all her sister's secrets?

"Oh no." Nona sighed, looking over Mona's shoulder. "I should've known."

Wondering if there really was something wrong, or if Nona just wanted to change the subject, Mona turned around. A man was walking straight toward them from the restaurant's front door. As he passed by the various dimly-colored lights, Mona could just make out who it was: Boris Ploof, rumpled and wrinkled in his oversize T-shirt and faded blue jeans, with his hands jammed in his pockets, looking disgusted and disheveled.

"What do you want?" Nona demanded sullenly. "Or should I even bother asking?"

"Go away." Mona felt the direct approach would be better. She certainly didn't feel like chatting with Ploof.

"I just want to talk with you about the bossman." Boris stood with his feet planted solidly on the floor, facing both of them. "He's got some real problems, and you can't be so heartless that you won't even help him. Talk to me. What is going on here?"

"That two-timing rat can go gnaw on his cage." Nona flicked her drink-wetted fingertips at Boris. "We're not interested in whatever he, or you, have to say."

"Well, that takes care of you," Boris said dismissively. He looked down at Mona. "Come on, talk to me. I can't help, if I don't know. What is going on?"

"It's over. I'm not talking about it," Mona stated. She picked up her drink, letting the cold exterior cool her temper. "I have nothing more to say." She sipped the icky, sweet concoction.

"This has Amelia written all over it, you know that," Boris muttered. "Don't do this to him."

That hit too near the mark for Mona's conscience not to twinge, but there was no way Amelia had done all this. Jared had done himself in this time.

Nona flicked more of her drink at him. "Go away, or I'll call the bouncer." She grinned evilly up at him. "He's a friend of mine, you know."

Ploof backed away, still looking disgusted.

Nona leaned in toward Mona, giggling. "What an idiot."

As he slouched away toward the bartender, Nona had her back to him. Mona could see his wings twitch under his jacket, but she didn't care if he was irritated. The wing twitch only reminded her of Jared, trying to pretend he was human and not fairy. So why did it suddenly seem so endearing? Jared's problems only made him exasperating, Mona sternly told herself.

She tried to smile at Nona.

"Ooooh," Nona cooed. She pointed surreptitiously toward someone behind Mona. "Here comes someone with potential."

Mona grimaced. She really should have gone to an all-you-can-eat buffet. She wondered if the bartender had any ice cream in the back. Of course, they'd need a bucket of chocolate syrup to go with it. They'd probably go get it for the right tip, too.

Zarrad eased the lumbering, black behemoth of a car into a parking space near his wonderful, beautiful, powder-blue convertible. Things were finally coming together. He stopped to check his car; everything was still there, no scratches or rips. Sighing in relief at his good fortune, Zarrad headed for Wherewolf Whillies.

Forrest had been right again, a banner week for him. Nona had to have taken the convertible out of spite.

Had she also concocted the story about Auveron too? Might Forrest actually have stayed with Atlas all morning? If so, Zarrad was in for a hard time with Ageon later.

Grimacing with frustration, Zarrad paused outside the club, trying to let the warm breeze sort his disorganized thoughts. He didn't know which way was up any more, where Nona was concerned. He didn't know if, or how, she'd enspelled him. Though he was willing to admit that attempting to enspell her with a necklace was a very bad idea.

The only thing he was certain of was that he loved her.

Passionately. Desperately. Foolishly.

He had to get her back, make her talk to him. She had to see that he was the one for her. He would make things right for her.

Steeling himself and fearing what might happen next, Zarrad slipped inside.

Peppy pop music soothed his frazzled nerves, making him feel that he could succeed in his quest. His eyes took a moment to adjust to the pleasantly low mood lighting, after the glaring, harsh afternoon sun.

The crowd was thin, sipping and talking in a desultory way, rather than dancing and guzzling with the usual evening gusto. But that was to be expected this time of day.

Zarrad glanced around the room quickly. He didn't see Forrest—but he didn't expect to, since Forrest should still have been out scouting hotels—however, Nona and Mona were sitting at a cozy table near the bar.

Surrounded, of course, by three hideous admirers with delusions of Casanovahood.

Ignoring his irritation and the other men, Zarrad looked at Nona and Mona. He wanted to guess what sort of mood they were in, and gauge his ability to get them to talk to him.

Mona had her back to him, so Zarrad couldn't see her face, but gauging from the way her shoulders hunched, he guessed she wasn't happy.

Seeing her in Nona's clinging red dress, with the low-cut back and no wings, was odd. She didn't look bad in it—she was Nona's size and had Nona's build and coloring—but Zarrad had grown used to seeing gossamer, opalescent wings sprouting from the backs of Nona's dresses. Wings seemed appropriate somehow, and the lack detracted from Mona. She was undoubtedly a nice woman, but she wasn't his Nona.

Nona, ah Nona. She looked glorious: happy and flighty and flirty. Her wings fluttered, gently stirring the lace of her violet dress. Her eyes twinkled as she smiled, her full lips curving gently around whatever private amusement danced in her quicksilver mind. She was without a doubt the most beautiful woman in the world.

Zarrad dreaded the thought of ending her happiness, but hoped, hoped desperately, that this time it would all work out right.

Though she was facing his direction, she didn't look at him, or notice him, until he reached the table. He elbowed one of the surrounding idiots out of the way.

"Nona, can we talk?" Zarrad didn't dare smile, and he tried to sound pleading, without sounding groveling.

"Darling!" Mona shouted.

Turning to really look at her for the first time, Zarrad realized that above the low neckline of Nona's red dress something gold and silver glittered. She had the necklace on.

Mona abandoned her drink and her chair to fling her arms around his neck.

Chapter 12

"My darling. My sweet, precious love," Mona breathed into Jared's ear. The scent of him intoxicated her more than the frowzy, watered-down drink Nona had bought her.

How could she have ever left him?

Such strong arms, pushing her away. Such warm lips, trembling beneath hers, murmuring such sweet nothings as, "Oh, no! Wait! Ah—" Such silky soft hair, so wonderfully suited to running fingers through and twining, and such a good site to get a firm hold, so that he could never, never get away again.

Had she truly never noticed the way his chest heaved in and out as he breathed, in the most masculine and exciting sort of way? My, how his flat stomach quivered underneath her questing hand. And oh how he squeaked as she explored the truly desirable delights of him.

"You bastard!" Nona screamed. "And my own sister!"

"I can explain," Jared bleated as he pushed Mona's face away from his and tried to push the rest of Mona away too.

Mona's love remained unfazed by this seeming rejection. She knew now that Jared was the only one for her, and her devotion would be forever. She nibbled gently on his firm shoulder and down his muscular arm. She'd wrap herself around him forever, and never let him go.

She had previously noticed how very cute and sweet his behind was, but why had she never noticed the way his crisp, expensive suit pants clung so deliciously? There was something marvelously different about him today, but

Mona couldn't quite decide what it was, and truly didn't care.

"Oh. Can you?" Nona demanded of Jared.

Jared grabbed Mona's hands, giving her the opportunity to kiss the tip of each of his boundlessly dear fingers and savor their exquisite perfection.

"N—Not really," Jared said.

Looking into the frightened eyes of her beloved, Mona smiled. "Forgive me, dearest. I love you with all my being. Please, take me back. I'll never leave you again."

She soothingly nuzzled his elegant neck, breathing in the musky scent of his aftershave deeply. Such a wonderful, wonderful man, and he was all hers.

"Oh!" Nona screeched. She grabbed Mona's hair and flung her onto the table, spilling drinks, chairs, and men in all directions.

"You!" Mona shouted, jumping up from the table and tackling Nona. "You can't have him. He's mine!"

They fell into a tangle of legs and arms on the floor. Mona scratched at her sister as Nona rolled to sit on her.

Of course, Nona would be jealous. Nona had always thought that every man in the world should worship her and only her. Mona gloried in how angry Nona would be that one man, the one perfect man, Jared Silvan, would love Mona.

Nona screeched. Mona squirmed, pushing Nona away, trying to get up. They rolled again, through a puddle on the floor, and then both women sprang up.

"Ew!" Mona brushed at the spreading wet stain on the side of her hip; then she remembered that this was Nona's dress. Why should she care if it were stained? She looked to see Nona staring in horror at a similar wet spot on her own violet lace dress. Mona grinned. "Ha!" she taunted. "Serves you right for trying to take him from me."

"Oh! You!" Nona clawed at Mona, as Mona dodged. One hand connected with Mona's left shoulder, and ripping the seam.

Mona tackled Nona again, and they fell, writhing and slithering, across the wet floor.

Jared sighed at the looks on the hotel employees' faces as he walked through the door into the cool, quiet, pristine lobby. He hadn't done anything wrong or even improper. He was appropriately attired for a tourist in this weather. His fairy wings weren't openly displayed, but even that wasn't so unusual. A lot of fairies covered their wings. Not all clothes were made for wings. His were usually strapped down, but not today. Which was new for him and perhaps why he felt like everyone was staring at him so. He didn't want to feel like something the cat dragged in and though insanity might run through his family—his mother being a prime example—he knew he was sane.

It was just the world that was insane. And getting worse by the minute.

As he approached the main desk, the clerk, a human woman, plastered a false smile on her face. "How may I help you, Sir?"

Pulling the wad of cash from his pants pocket, Jared said, "I'd like to put this in the hotel safe, please."

She goggled at the money. Her mouth opened and closed for a moment. "How much is it, Sir?"

"I don't know." Jared unrolled the wad and spread it on the counter.

"All right," the clerk said slowly, as she stared down at the cash arrayed across the wooden counter. "Let me get my supervisor."

"Sure." Jared's voice sounded chipper and certain, in contrast to his stunned and confused feelings. Maybe he was just too numb to care any more.

He started piling the money by denominations, hundreds on the left, fifties on the right. He had two lovely, little, crisp, green money mountains built by the time the clerk's supervisor arrived.

This woman actually appeared to be younger than the clerk, and a fairy, and in the exact same uniform with the exact same decorations. Jared wondered how anyone was supposed to know that she was the supervisor. Or if she really was a supervisor. Not, Jared supposed, that it really mattered to him. Though the fact that she was a fairy might mean she'd been called, in case magic were required to deal with him. They obviously didn't know that he didn't know magic.

He couldn't help giggling at the idea that they didn't know that he didn't know magic. It seemed so apropos.

The clerk stood at the right hand of her alleged supervisor.

"How may I help you, Sir?" the supervisor asked.

Pointing at his two tiny mountains of clean, new cash, Jared said, "I'd like to put these into the hotel safe, please."

"And how much are they?" the supervisor asked.

"I don't know."

The supervisor pursed her lips and glanced at the clerk. "Perhaps we should count it."

"Good idea." Jared picked up the top bill from the crisp green pile of hundreds. "One hundred." He put it a little off to the side, starting a new pile, before picking up the next. "Two hundred."

The clerk much more efficiently counted out the fifties, and stacked and bundled them neatly with a rubber band.

The supervisor calmly picked up the two hundreds Jared had already counted, and patiently added each bill to her stack as he attempted to set them on the counter.

"Five thousand dollars. Does that sound correct, Mr. Silvan?" the supervisor asked.

"I suppose. I didn't think to count it when he gave it to me," Jared told her sunnily.

"Very good, Sir."

After they had disappeared to put the money in the hotel safe, Jared wandered over to the elevators.

What was it about that tough fairy lawyer that had seemed so familiar? There was something about his appearance that seemed memorable, but Jared would have sworn he'd never laid eyes on the man before. A distant relative of Mona's perhaps?

Riding the elevator up to his floor, Jared finally had to admit to himself that he had no way of finding Mona in this city. No way of finding Nona's address. He'd have to think of some other way to find Mona and set this weekend right. Otherwise, he didn't want to contemplate the rest of his life.

The maid had been by to make up the bed and straighten the room. Other than that, the room appeared as it had earlier, without any changes, so Mona probably hadn't been there. Her clothes were still gone, along with her suitcase, and her. The maid had re-opened the curtains, so Jared closed them, to shut out the rest of Miami.

He flopped onto the bed in his darkened room to look up at the textured ceiling. He had to think. Somehow. If only he could get this molasses-like mess out of his mind.

First things first. What did he need to do?

Check his pager for messages.

Finding he still didn't care if there were any messages,

Jared decided not to check his pager. If his business couldn't last one weekend without his presence, something was radically wrong. Boris could handle whatever came up.

Next. Amelia had asked him to find some unknown man in Miami.

Perhaps the hulking fairy with wads of cash?

No. Couldn't be him. Mother had said Jared would know him when he saw him, and Jared hadn't recognized the fairy at all. Well, at least Jared hadn't really recognized him, though he'd seemed familiar. Jared had expected, what with the way his mother had put it, that this whoever-it-was would immediately cause him to reach for the letter. Which the fairy hadn't made him do.

Good grief. He couldn't even find someone he did know in this town. How in the world was he supposed to find someone he didn't know?

It didn't matter. Jared had no intention of spending any of his precious, remaining weekend, looking for some unknown man, to run another fool errand for his crazy mother. End of subject.

Next thing to do?

Find Mona, tell her how sorry he was, tell her how much he loved her.

Jared sighed. He had no idea how to do that. He stared at the textured ceiling a moment, trying to think of a way around that.

He had no intention of giving up on Mona and their relationship. He'd worked far too hard for it.

One thing was certain, he couldn't find her, staring at the ceiling in his hotel room. Jared stood up. He had to get out of here. He had to think. Where would Mona go in Miami?

An art museum?

The theater? A movie?

The beach?

Oh, the beach. Mona had talked about going there. She'd wanted Jared to finally bare his wings in public. A possibility; perhaps she might have gone there.

Realizing he had many places yet to check, Jared stood up and squared his shoulders. He'd find Mona yet.

The hotel employees had taken to ducking, hiding, and heading away from him, but Jared didn't care. Let them think he was crazy. So what?

He was going to find Mona. No matter what.

In the hot sunshine, Jared momentarily considered heading for a cool museum, but knowing that Mona hadn't been to the beach in a long time, he figured that would be a more likely place to find her. Also, it would be the last place she'd expect him to be, or to check.

Jared stopped a passerby to ask for directions to the beach. The directions he received were complicated and the distance seemed more than he cared to walk. So he hailed a cab.

As he got in the cab, he noticed a large, shiny black car idling at the curb down the street. It didn't look like the tough fairy's, but it was similar. Not that he'd really know the difference.

Jared shrugged it off. There were undoubtedly many large, shiny black cars in Miami. Why would anyone follow him?

Zarrad stared in horrified fascination as Mona and Nona rolled through the icy puddle on the floor. He wanted to stop them, but if he pulled the necklace from Mona now, they would both surely know that it had been enspelled.

As would everyone else gathering around.

Mona clawed at Nona, ripping strips of lace to hang like banners from the violet dress. Nona retaliated by pulling Mona's hair while trying to get up from the floor. Halfway up, Nona slipped, her feet heading in opposite directions.

A soft, recurring, staccato, snapping sound accompanied the tearing of the side seams of Nona's dress. She flung herself on Mona, and the two screeched and pinched and slapped and tugged and clawed and tore.

The afternoon crowd was amused, and the troll bouncer gave no indication of wanting to end the show.

Scooping up some ice, Mona shoved it down the back of Nona's dress. Nona screamed and writhed, while trying to scratch her sister's face. Unfortunately, Mona chose that moment to try to slither away, and Nona's sharp fingernails stabbed into the red skirt of Mona's dress, ripping out a triangular section of the back. Mona turned and grabbed Nona's arms.

They slid on the floor, their legs flailing and kicking and wrapping around each other as their dresses mopped up the icy puddles on the floor.

"Stop it!" Zarrad shouted, but neither of the combatants listened to him. He had to find a way to save Nona from her sister. And himself from Mona, while he was at it.

He jumped out of the way as Mona slithered past him on the still-slick floor. She'd been pushed by Nona, who pounced after.

Someone had moved chairs and tables out of the way, and the crowd stood in a circle, calling directions, cheering, and hooting.

Nona clawed Mona's shoulder, leaving a row of deep red scratches. Mona kicked Nona. One violet shoe launched itself at the troll bouncer, who caught it and held it up as a trophy while the crowd cheered.

Zarrad looked around for some sort of help. Forrest, in rumpled T-shirt and faded blue jeans, not his usual crisp day wear, appeared at Zarrad's side. The whole world had gone mad, but Zarrad didn't have time to question or wonder about it.

"We've got to stop this," Forrest said.

"Yes. But how?" Zarrad asked. It was a real banner week for Forrest, behaving intelligently and efficiently. Amazing.

Mona slid out from under Nona, rolled to sit on her sister, and slapped Nona across the face.

Nona shrieked and clawed at Mona's neck, clutching the necklace.

"You grab one," Forrest said, "I'll grab the other. And we'll pull them to separate corners."

"Okay." Zarrad reached for Nona on the floor, just as Nona moved, rolling Mona to the floor.

Forrest easily plucked Nona from Mona and pulled her to the side. Zarrad had no choice but to pull Mona from the floor. He wished he'd been more specific as to who would grab which woman, when he'd agreed to Forrest's plan.

Though you'd think by now Forrest would know better.

The crowd booed and hissed and laughed.

"What is going on here?" a familiar voice boomed.

Zarrad turned in time to see his father pushing through the slowly quieting crowd.

Ageon looked at Zarrad and growled.

Jared stepped out of the cab. Between him and the beach was a parking lot and a building housing several shops. He could hear the roar of the waves and feel the sting of the salt spray. The smell of deep-fat fryers, hotdogs, and cotton candy floated on the sea breeze from the restaurants in the building.

Perhaps Mona had stopped to get something to eat? Probably not, if she'd been to one of the all-you-can-eat buffets Jared hadn't been able to check. He might have considered checking there, but his much-abused stomach threatened rebellion.

The parking lot's sign towered over him, providing him with a little shade, detailing the various charges for parking in the lot, and announcing that this section of beach was for the general public.

The beach farther on might have been for the public, but the parking lot was surrounded by a high, chain-link fence, as were the manicured grounds of the cheap hotel next door. Just down the street from where he stood, a small swath of weeds and sand served as a walkway between the two of them, to allow the public access to the beach.

A large, shiny black car pulled up to the curb just as Jared reached the walkway to the beach, and a young male fairy jumped out to block Jared's way. He had on Bermuda shorts and a loud print shirt, like a tourist, but the heavy navy jacket was completely unnecessary in the day's heat.

"Let's go for a ride," the fairy suggested, motioning with one hand in his jacket pocket.

"I don't think so." Jared tried to step around him, but the fairy again moved to block him.

"Oh, I do think so," the strange fairy said. Something concealed in the jacket pocket shoved painfully into Jared's stomach. "You wouldn't want me to do something we'd all regret. Would you?"

Jared grabbed the fairy's jacket-covered hand and whatever it held, lifting them above the startled fairy's head. The jacket nearly turned inside out around the young fairy's head, exposing his ugly shirt and giving Jared an opportunity to take some of his frustrations out on the exposed

135

torso with his right fist. He punched the fairy's stomach, and a shot rang out above his head.

He stared in horror at the barrel of the gun sticking out of the ragged hole in the jacket pocket, as a swarm of men tackled him and dragged him into the car.

Struggling and kicking seemed to be Jared's only options, but knowing these men would shoot him made it seem a futile option. He quickly found himself on his stomach on the floor in the rear of the car with his hands bound and several pairs of shoes digging into his back and legs.

Chapter 13

Nona struggled against Forrest's arms, trying to reach her traitorous sister. All she wanted was to claw Mona's face and pull all her hair out. The vicious, deceitful, human bitch.

Mona's necklace—the one Zarrad had given Mona—hung slack and broken in Nona's hand. She almost flung it at her sister, but something in the look on Mona's face stopped her. Mona should have looked ready to scratch her eyes out, but Mona looked surprised and confused.

"What is going on here?" Ageon demanded as he pushed through the crowd toward them.

For the first time, Nona noticed the crowd that had gathered around the empty space that had been cleared for the fight. Most of the people were grinning and laughing; a few booed at Zarrad. Tolly, the bouncer, held one of her shoes in his enormous troll hand.

Zarrad flinched, nearly cowering in front of his father, yet he still maintained his hold on Mona. Ageon growled at his son.

A tingling in her fingers drew Nona's attention back to the necklace dangling loosely in her hand. It appeared to be a simple, plain, braided chain, in mixed gold and silver. So why would it tingle? A sudden thought struck Nona.

It was enspelled.

Mona hadn't fallen on Zarrad because of extreme devotion or inexpressible love, but because the necklace compelled her to. Nona felt a snarl rising in her throat. Only a fairy would have noticed it. If they were looking for it, forewarned, or just suspicious. A human like Mona would have no way of knowing. Nona felt guilty for not checking it when Mona had first brought it out. But then, who would suspect Zarrad, a human, of enspelling a necklace. Zarrad! How could he?

That cad! That unspeakable villain! The nerve! The gall! The unmitigated vileness! Her poor sister.

Zarrad was blithering at his father, making no sense at all. Ageon merely glared at his son, as if trying to wither him down to nothing. Which he had a lot of practice doing. Zarrad bleated pitifully, as if that would help him.

Realizing she had in her hands a method of humiliating Zarrad, his stupid lackey Forrest, and Ageon, Nona grasped the necklace tight.

Twisting around, Nona managed to face Forrest, nearly hugging him. As long as she wasn't trying to break free of his grasp he paid no attention to her; he was too busy frowning at Zarrad and Ageon as if confused. A typical look for him.

The loop for the catch on the necklace had torn off, but Nona slipped the necklace around Forrest's neck and hooked the catch onto one of the braid loops, so that it would stay.

An immediate change in the expression on Forrest's face confirmed to Nona that the necklace was indeed enspelled. He released her, stepped around her, and flung himself at Zarrad.

"My love, my dearest," Forrest cried. He looked very strange clinging to Zarrad, what with Forrest in rumpled old clothes and Zarrad in a neat, crisp suit. Nona couldn't help noticing the lump under Forrest's wrinkled T-shirt. His wings looked more realistic than Zarrad's ever had.

However, that wasn't important now.

Nona leapt forward, snatching her sister from Zarrad's shocked and unresisting hands. She pulled Mona to her, whispering, "I'm sorry. That wasn't your fault. I'll explain later."

Mona shook her head, as if to shake off the last of her confusion and madness. "I . . . I . . . I'm sorry too. I think."

Quickly Nona realized that trying to put the shoulder of the red dress back together was futile. She did manage a bit of a mend spell, to keep the dresses from any further damage, but left the cloth sodden. No use wasting willpower on what would cure itself eventually. The tattered hem and lace of her own dress stuck damply to her legs. Even in the cool air-conditioned interior of the club, Nona didn't feel chilled. Hot fury at what Zarrad had done warmed her.

Boris clung desperately to Jared's strong, muscular arm. Why had he never noticed the gentle curve of Jared's nose before? The way his nostrils flared in surprise? The particularly cute way a blush crept over his face?

"Get off of me, you idiot!" Jared shoved, hard.

Such rejection didn't bother Boris. A few carefully-chosen magic words, and Boris' grip couldn't be loosened by anything but magic. Boris had never thought the day would come that he'd be glad that Jared had never learned magic. Boris could teach him now, he realized. Once Jared realized how much love and understanding there was between them. Once Jared knew they should never be separated.

Such soft, silky hair Jared had, just crying out to be stroked.

As Boris reached for his hair, Jared tried to shake him

off. Pouting, Boris oozed closer to Jared. "Let's go someplace where we can be alone."

Jared managed to push Boris away by using the arm that Boris clung to, keeping Boris at arm's length.

While nipping at Jared's fingertips, Boris waggled his eyebrows at Jared. "How have I never noticed that you have such a delicately curved behind?"

"Oh God, help me!" Zarrad heard his own voice crack in fear. The damn necklace seemed to have given Forrest the strength of ten. Zarrad couldn't shake him off.

"It's your own fault, you two-timing cheat!" Nona shouted as she huddled with her sister at the far end of the clear area. The crowd had yet to disperse. "It's your stupid necklace."

Zarrad stared at her with what he hoped was a look of uncomprehending horror. The horror at least was real. He had no intention of owning up to the necklace at this point. "What necklace?"

"Oh, please!" Nona let go of her sister to plant her fists on her hips. "The necklace you gave to Mona. The one that is enspelled to make whoever wears it lose their mind over you."

"You have such deliciously formed fingers," Forrest proclaimed and promptly began to lick Zarrad's thumb.

"Ahhgk," Zarrad shouted in disgust. But he couldn't get his hand away from Forrest. He turned back to Nona. "What are you babbling about? I never gave Mona a necklace. I swear it. I never met her until this morning at your apartment."

"Ha!" Nona shouted back. "You have the nerve to say that, after what you tried last night!"

"What are you talking about?" Zarrad demanded.

Mona, obviously brighter than her sister, turned to the highly entertained crowd around them and proclaimed, "That man married me, and then went out with my sister."

A soft and disapproving "oooh" sound rose and faded through the obviously greatly amused crowd.

"He did what?" Ageon roared, as Zarrad, stunned, whispered, "What?"

"He's mine now," Forrest sing-songed. "Forever, my little fairy boy."

"Yes. Poor thing." Nona put her arm protectively around her sister's shoulder, carefully avoiding the nasty scratches she had put there. "We found out about it last night when he tried to romance both of us at the same time." Mona leaned on Nona's shoulder, and put her arm around her sister's waist.

The club's bouncer troll started snickering. Someone from the crowd said, "I should come here more often."

"I have no idea what you two are babbling about," Zarrad said truthfully.

Ageon glared at him.

"Come away with me, my love." Forrest tried to get closer.

Zarrad held him off by shuffling to one side or the other, keeping Forrest at arm's length. He'd never liked having a boss-minion relationship with Forrest, but found he much preferred it to having Forrest madly, dangerously in love with him.

"Such a gorgeous chin." Forrest batted his eyelashes at Zarrad.

Ageon stopped their dance by placing a hand on each of their shoulders, while assisting Zarrad in holding Forrest at a distance.

"Are you married to that woman?" Ageon demanded, nodding his head at Mona.

"No," Zarrad said forcefully.

Mona gasped. "You liar!" She buried her face in her sister's shoulder, while clutching the torn shreds of her dress to her shoulder.

"Did you give her an enspelled necklace?" Ageon asked, quietly.

"No," Zarrad shouted. "I did not."

Mona sniffed, and looked up. Her voice was choked and rough as she said, "Technically, that blithering idiot gave it to me, not Jared." She smeared tears from her face. "Last night."

Nona made some soothing noises and hugged Mona tighter. "Not your fault. Poor thing."

When his father stared at him, Zarrad said, again truthfully, "I have no idea what Forrest did last night. *He* doesn't even know what he did last night. But I've never touched that necklace."

Frowning, Ageon turned his attention to Forrest, who was currently sniffing Zarrad's wrist, while whispering, "What a strong, well-formed arm."

Someone in the crowd giggled.

"What did you do last night?" Ageon shook Forrest to get his attention.

"Nothing. I sat at home." Forrest gazed doe-eyed at Zarrad and sighed. "Without him."

Zarrad shuddered.

A cunning look came into Ageon's eyes. "And what about Auveron?"

"Auveron?" For once, Forrest pulled his gaze from Zarrad to look at Ageon. "Who is Auveron?"

"Who is Auveron?" Ageon whispered. He choked, and turned to Zarrad. "Have you found anything out, with the money I gave you?"

"What money?" Zarrad asked.

"The money I gave you, earlier this afternoon." Ageon's face was turning dangerously purple.

"You didn't give me any money today." Zarrad made a fist with his hand to keep Forrest from nibbling any more on his fingertips.

Ageon said a few words of magic and groaned at the result. "You're enspelled."

"I know that." Zarrad glared at Nona. "She . . . Nona put some sort of spell on me. My memories are all messed up."

"No," Ageon whispered. "When I checked earlier today, I saw no ensorcelment. Though, with Auveron, the spell might not have to be on you to affect you." He looked at Forrest. "I can't tell anything about him around that blasted necklace." He looked back to Zarrad. "Are you certain about that necklace?"

"I never gave anyone that necklace." Zarrad shook his head, hoping to look thoroughly trustworthy. "I've never touched it."

"It was from him!" Mona shouted.

"Perhaps. Perhaps," Ageon murmured before lurching toward Forrest. He frowned at Forrest's back.

Forrest danced away, still holding Zarrad's hand and spinning Zarrad in a circle as Ageon tried to snatch the necklace. They spun into the surrounding crowd, which scattered and reformed around them.

"Enough of this," Ageon shouted. He grabbed Nona and Mona, dragging them by their arms while attempting to herd the struggling Zarrad and Forrest out of the club. "Into my car."

Both of the women squealed and struggled. Forrest didn't seem to care where they went, as long as he stayed attached to Zarrad.

The crowd parted in front of them, and closed in behind, as the club's patrons tried to keep track of what was happening.

Mona grabbed Ageon's hair and pulled. "Let go of me!"

Ageon growled, tucked his head down, and pushed forward.

Nona slapped at Ageon's arm. Nothing the women did seemed to slow Zarrad's father. Zarrad easily led Forrest out the door. Perhaps at home they could sort this out easier.

Outside another black behemoth of a car waited. Stig sat behind the wheel, patiently waiting for instructions. Hjell opened the back door, allowing Ageon to shove everyone into the back of the car. Zarrad easily pulled Forrest into the car. Ageon had a little more trouble with Nona and Mona.

Ageon whispered something to Hjell, as he pushed Nona and Mona inside. Zarrad didn't quite hear what his father said, but it didn't sound like they were going home.

Hjell slid into the car, catching Mona and Nona as they tried to escape. He sat between them, one large heavy troll hand on each, relieving Ageon of the need to restrain them.

"Where are we going?" Zarrad asked, feeling a stirring of alarm.

"Where to, Boss?" Stig asked.

"Mercy Hospital." Ageon didn't spare Zarrad the least glance.

"What? Wait. No." Zarrad reached for the door but was hampered by Forrest, still clinging to him and whispering sweet nothings.

Ageon's hand clamped down hard on Zarrad's shoulder. "You're going to Mercy. And you'll stay there until you're better."

"I am not crazy!"

Sighing, Ageon patted Zarrad's shoulder. "You might be enspelled to be crazy. Auveron. Not your fault, but you can bet I'll trace the source of this, and settle the score."

"Listen, punk, we just want to talk to you," a voice sitting above Jared said. "We can work things out without anyone getting hurt."

Jared glared at the rough carpeting beneath his nose, not believing a word they said. He tried to wonder what exactly was going on, but the thought had to compete with his anger and pain for his attention. Someone had their oversized feet planted right on his injured wing.

"All we want is—"

Sirens blared outside the car, sounding as if coming from several directions at once. As the driver hit the brakes, Jared slammed into the seat in front of him.

Someone quickly unbound his hands, and he was pulled off the floor. His arms ached, but nowhere near as badly as his back and wings. He tried to stretch a bit, but couldn't in the tight confines of the car.

Someone grabbed the back of his neck and the young fairy's face appeared nose to nose with his. "Play nice for the cops, punk. We're all friends, right?"

Jared snarled at him.

From outside the car someone shouted, "Everybody out."

An older man pulled Jared from the car and stood beside him, with an arm around his shoulders.

"Careful of the wings," Jared said, as he tried to slide out from under the encircling arm.

"Oh yeah," the man grinned and nodded knowingly. "The wings." He tightened his grip on Jared's far shoulder.

Four police cars surrounded them, sirens wailing, lights

145

flashing. Traffic on the street stood still, unable to proceed around the police cars. Several cops swarmed the area, most appearing ready to pull their weapons.

"What's up, officer?" the older man asked the closest officer.

"You were observed dragging this young man into the car." The officer, a female human, pointed to Jared. "And it sure sounded like someone fired a gun." She looked at the young fairy. "We're going to let you go downtown and explain that." She rewarded the older man with a grimace of a smile. "Turn around, up against the car, you know the drill."

Patting Jared's shoulder, the older man said, "We're just friends, goofing off. Having a fun day at the beach. There's no problem here." He smiled at Jared. "Right."

Jared shoved him away. "I don't know these people. I never met them before in my life."

The female officer's brows rose, and her expression became gleeful. The men that had snatched him glared and growled.

"Come along." She grabbed the older man by his arm and spun him around. "Don't be such a baby, Stake. You know how this works."

Another officer turned Jared around and began frisking him. Jared tried to turn around, but the officer pushed him back.

"But I didn't do anything!" Jared complained.

"We need you for questioning." The officer briskly attached handcuffs to Jared and led him to one of the police cars.

The back of the police car smelled of sweat and dirt. Although it beat riding on the floor of a nice car. At least none of the others were put in the back with Jared, though being cuffed and carted off was bad enough.

Chapter 14

Boris clung to Jared as they exited the car. He stumbled a bit over the curb but never released his grip on his marvelous Jared's perfect arm. Jared led him into a cool, antiseptic-smelling building, Boris didn't pay much attention. He didn't really care where they went, as long as they were together. He put his arm around Jared and bumped into the lump of Jared's wings. There was something odd about them, but Boris didn't care. Jared was perfect. Boris snuggled up to him and murmured, "You have such long eyelashes. Did you know that?"

"Him, yes," Jared shouted as he tried to shake Boris off. "He needs help. But, I'm not crazy. I don't belong here!"

The tough older fairy, Ageon, approached a desk nearby. Boris was relieved to have Jared all to himself. He was becoming jealous of Ageon's attachment to Jared.

At least those two women knew enough to keep their distance.

"Just you and me, partner," Boris whispered into Jared's ear, letting Jared's shampoo-smelling hair tickle his nose. "You and me and your cute little ears. They're so delicate and curved." Something at the back of his mind tried to get his attention, but he couldn't be bothered with details now. Not when he could admire the way Jared's manly neck muscles twitched, and Jared's pearly teeth ground. "That is the cutest little vein there, pulsing on your neck."

A troll grabbed Boris around the waist. "Come on, you. Let's go see the doctor, okay?"

Boris clutched tighter to Jared's arm. "No. No, he's mine! You can't have him."

"I don't want him," the troll said loudly into Boris' ear. "I don't want you either. You just need to go talk to the doctor." The troll tugged on Boris, trying to separate the two, but succeeding only in dragging both Boris and Jared toward a hallway.

"Help me," Boris pleaded with Jared.

Jared pushed Boris' shoulder, trying to push him away. Luckily, the spell Boris had spoken earlier was still in effect, and Boris stayed attached to Jared.

"Grab his legs," the troll instructed someone, continuing with several others. "You get a hold of him. You do the magic. And pull!"

Someone picked up Boris' legs and pulled. Another troll grabbed Jared's waist and pulled in the opposite direction. Boris only barely held onto Jared's arm, both of them being stretched apart. Someone standing close by started chanting.

The shoulder seam of Jared's sleeve gave way, and the sleeve ripped off, sliding down Jared's arm. Boris flailed desperately, trying to maintain some hold on Jared. Boris managed to grab Jared's bare elbow and could only admire the way Jared's skin smoothed so perfectly flawlessly over his biceps.

The grunting trolls continued tugging. Jared appeared red-faced, and he twisted and squirmed.

Boris' hands skidded down Jared's arm, leaving angry red streaks. Jared howled, and Boris felt instant remorse at hurting his beloved, but he couldn't bear to be parted from Jared. No matter what the cost.

"Stop!" Boris shouted. "Leave us alone! I love him!"

His grip had slipped to Jared's wrist, and Boris put the

full force of his will into holding on.

The chanting grew louder, and Boris realized someone was trying to break his hold spell. Another troll joined in, one enormous hand grabbing Jared's arm and one grabbing Boris', attempting to pull them apart.

Not even the spell Boris had cast could stand against four determined trolls and the annulment spell being chanted. He screamed incoherently as he felt Jared's hand slip from his grasp.

Two trolls dragged him away, kicking, struggling, and screaming to no avail.

Jared, the one person he loved above all others, disappeared from his sight. All Boris had left was Jared's sleeve.

Watching four trolls separate Forrest and Zarrad was painful for Ageon, though all in all, he was glad he didn't have to participate. Either as one of the separators or the separated. Zarrad was hauled away, rubbing the red streaks on his arm and complaining that he didn't belong there, he wasn't crazy.

Two men in white coats—Ageon wasn't certain if they were doctors, nurses, or just attendants—led Nona and Mona away, down separate hallways, to give their versions of what had happened in the last several days. They looked much the worse for wear, with tousled hair; damp, torn dresses; and a variety of scratches and bruises.

Almost made Ageon wish he were younger, and one of them was Amelia.

A white-coated fairy woman approached him. "Mr. Silvan? I'm Dr. Zequiel. I've been assigned to your son's case. Might I speak with you for a few moments?"

She led him into a small, neat office. A cluttered desk sat up against one wall, and several comfy chairs were spread around the room. Diplomas dotted the walls, along with seascapes. Dr. Zequiel picked up a notebook from the desk, then sat in a chair away from the desk, motioning for Ageon to take the one next to her.

They went through the preliminaries easily enough, with Dr. Zequiel gathering Zarrad's and Forrest's names, addresses, birth dates, other significant dates, occupations, species, medical histories, and what of their psychological histories Ageon knew. Then she took an account of Ageon's son's last several days, and what Ageon knew of Forrest's activities.

He didn't mention his rival Auveron, or anything about his own activities, but he did hint that he thought there might be an ensorcelment involved. Possibly as a prank, the young men were at that age.

"They've both been acting very strangely," Ageon concluded. "I know they aren't remembering things that they've done and everyone they know. But I don't really know why."

"I see." Dr. Zequiel frowned at her notes. "Is Zarrad's mother dead then?"

"Yes." Ageon grimaced, wishing he didn't have to go into this. Lying to Zarrad was hard enough. Though, in this case, he knew with a certainty there was no connection between then and now.

"I see." Dr. Zequiel made more notes. "So, Zarrad was separated from his twin shortly after birth?"

"Yes. I performed the separation myself."

"Ah." More notes. "Does his twin have any symptoms that we should know about?"

"His twin . . . died in the separation."

"I'm sorry." She scribbled another note. "It must have been very hard for you."

"It was a long time ago. I'm over it." Lying just became easier all the time. Next, Ageon would be telling her that he didn't still love Amelia.

"I see. Well." She closed her notebook. "We have the two of them checked in for observation for the next couple of days. Let me talk with them, and I can give you a report. Let's see . . . today is Saturday . . ." Dr. Zequiel checked her calendar. "Monday?"

"Monday would be fine."

"You can set up an appointment at the front desk." She nodded and smiled at him. "Good-bye, Mr. Silvan."

Hjell waited by the front desk. "Everything okay, Boss?"

"I don't know any more."

The hulking fairy-troll shrugged. "Sorry, Boss. Are we waiting for the girls?"

"The girls?"

"Nona and Mona." Hjell grinned. "Zarrad's girlfriend and wife."

"No." Ageon ran his hands through his hair in frustration. "They've caused enough trouble. Let them find their own way home."

Jared stared around the small interrogation room. At least he assumed it was an interrogation room. It consisted of cinder-block walls with no windows, one mirror that Jared assumed was more than just a simple mirror, one beat-up table, and three badly-used chairs.

He'd waited, sitting in one of the chairs, for a long, long time now. Thinking things over.

Since when did police fingerprint the victim of a crime?

No traces remained on his fingertips, just his memory. They'd used some sort of electronic pad. He'd had to put first his right, then his left hand, flat on it.

They'd done this right after they'd asked him his name. He'd never considered Jared to be that unusual a name, but he'd had to spell it for them. Silvan they'd got right the first time.

And what was so surprising about running an internet/mail order catalog business? Or a business named SilverProof? Or being a fairy? Or living in Wisconsin?

Or taking a weekend vacation with the wife in Miami?

The police acted as if they'd never had a real tourist in Miami before.

Something was very strange here.

Unfortunately, Jared didn't know what it was.

Jared had no more time to think about it. A large changeling, half human-half troll, entered. The policeman wore rumpled jeans and rumpled polo shirt, and nothing to indicate who he was, or what his position was.

Smiling at Jared, the changeling sat down in one of the empty chairs. "So, *Jared* Silvan. Tell me about this kidnapping."

"I'd taken a cab to the beach, to look for my wife."

"Your wife?"

"My wife, Mona Silvan. We had an argument, and she'd left. I was looking for her. We'd come here for the weekend, to get away from home."

"Because you live in Wisconsin." The cop didn't sound like he believed it.

"Yes. No." Jared clutched his hands in fists in frustration but hid them in his lap. "I mean we didn't come here because we live in Wisconsin. We've been having some marital problems, and we came here to have some time alone." He shook his head. "It doesn't matter. I was going to the beach to find Mona, when this car pulled up beside me. Then this dumb kid is threatening me. I don't know who he is. I've never seen him before in my life. When I tried to get rid of him, I heard this gunshot. Next thing I know, I'm surrounded by this gang, my hands are tied behind my back, and I'm dumped on the floor of the car. And I have no idea why."

"Right." The cop nodded his head skeptically, looking smug and suspicious. "You sure you want to go with that story?"

"It's the truth!"

"Let's take it from the top, with a little more detail this time." The cop sighed. "You're from—"

A knock on the door interrupted him. A stunned-looking uniformed cop entered, carrying a sheet of paper. He glanced at Jared before turning to the rumpled cop.

"Lieutenant, you're not going to believe this." The uniformed cop handed the paper over.

The rumpled officer read the paper for a moment. The smug, suspicious look on his face was replaced with surprised incredulity. He looked up at Jared, back to the paper for another quick read, then back up at Jared.

"You're Jared Silvan. From Wisconsin."

"Yes."

"Your wife is Mona."

"Yes."

"You vandalized your high school. In Wisconsin."

"That was a long time ago." Jared gaped in horror. They couldn't hold that against him now! Could they? "That was almost ten years ago. I was a kid. I haven't done anything since—"

The rumpled lieutenant held up a hand to stop Jared. "It's all right, Sir. It's all right." He looked from the paper in his hand, to Jared, then to the uniformed cop. He started breathing funny, in short huffs that started softly but gained volume quickly.

It took a moment for Jared to realize the rumpled lieutenant was laughing. The uniformed cop appeared stupefied. Jared tried to move his chair quietly away from both of them.

Taking a deep breath, the rumpled lieutenant stood up; his strange laughter stopped. "Excuse us." He motioned to the other cop to leave.

Before the door shut behind them, Jared thought he heard the rumpled lieutenant start huffing again as he said, "We've got them now. They grabbed the wrong guy."

Zarrad paced his small cell, furiously. How dare they commit him? He was perfectly sane.

Except for the spell Nona had put on him.

He would have felt sorry for trying to enspell her with the necklace, if it weren't for the fact that any spell this complex had to have been prepared in advance. She had to have been planning this for some time.

It hadn't taken him long to memorize the little room. Four white cinder-block walls, one small cot-like bed with a thin, white mattress and even thinner white blankets, one small white-plastic chair, and plain white-and-gray tile floor. No window. Light came from a single bulb that hid behind a transparent white dome surrounded by a steel cage.

Twitching the thin, white shirt and pants they'd forced him to wear didn't make them any more comfortable. They didn't fit, appearing to be made for someone much, much fatter than Zarrad. The edges of the hook-and-loop fastenings scratched his skin. The lack of proper underwear he could deal with, but he felt naked without his fake wings.

The suppressed laughter on the attendants' faces when they'd found his wings seared his memory.

There was nothing wrong with being human. He only wore the damn wings because his father insisted. Which you'd think his father would remember, before tossing him summarily in this place. But no, Ageon had forgotten the perfect fairy son had died, and all that was left was the defective human son.

Just as he reached the back of the room on his umpteenth round, the door opened. A white-coated doctor, a fairy woman, entered. Any hope Zarrad had of shoving her aside and escaping was dashed at the sight of a large troll standing silently in the corridor outside the room.

The troll glared at Zarrad, looking smug and sadistic. As if daring Zarrad to try something.

"Hello Zarrad." The doctor extended her hand as the door closed behind her. "I'm Dr. Zequiel. Perhaps we could talk."

"I'm not crazy!"

"Of course not," she said soothingly. "We just want to help you here. Things have been a little confusing lately." She sat in the small chair and opened her notebook.

"Look." Zarrad leaned against the back wall, folding his arms across his chest. The wall felt odd and cold against his back, without his fake wings, but he'd feel even more strange if she saw his back without them. "My girlfriend put some sort of spell on me. That's all. All I have to do is talk to her, and I can clear this whole thing up."

"Ah. Yes," Dr. Zequiel murmured, looking at her notes. "That would be Nona. Could you tell me about Mona, your wife?"

"Mona is not my wife!" Zarrad shouted. "I'm in love with Nona. I never met Mona before in my life."

155

"I see." Dr. Zequiel made a note in her notebook. "Could you tell me about your friend? Are you very good friends?"

Zarrad felt a blush spread across his face, and he ground his teeth. "We're friends, yes. But just friends. It was all that stupid necklace." He took a deep breath to calm himself. Getting upset wouldn't convince anyone he was sane. "At least that's what Nona thought."

"Yes. Your father thought there might be some sort of prank going on there. What do you think?"

Silently thanking his father, Zarrad nodded. "It wouldn't surprise me at all."

Dr. Zequiel nodded. "And who do you think might be pulling this prank?"

"I don't know. Maybe Nona."

She scribbled in her notebook. "Now, how about we talk about you? I've seen your wings. Do you wish you were a fairy?"

No, my father wishes I was a fairy. Zarrad couldn't bring himself to tell her that. He doubted that telling her he wished he were dead, or preferably never born, would help things, either.

Finally it was over. Mona found Nona waiting in the lobby by the front desk. Several men stood around, surreptitiously staring at her torn dress. It looked to Mona as if Nona might have enlarged a few strategic tears, just for the attention.

"Mona!" Nona ran to her and threw her arms around her. "Are you all right? You look like you've really been through it." Nona leaned back and tsked. "Of course you've been through it. The weekend from hell, poor thing." She herded Mona toward the door. "Let me get you home. You can rest a bit, and we'll go out this evening. Everything will be fine. You'll see."

The older man who'd whisked everyone to the hospital had disappeared. It was just as well. While Mona wanted to thank him for his assistance—helpful bystanders were so hard to come by—she hadn't much cared for his heavy-handed manner or his appalling superiority complex.

However, Mona didn't wish to go home with Nona. For one, Nona would want to go out tonight. Mona just wanted to lie down and cry. Alone. Secondly, Mona couldn't get their fight out of her mind. The necklace may have started it, and egged them on, but at the core, that fight had been coming for a long time.

And Mona didn't think they were finished with it yet.

Outside, the late afternoon sun wavered in the heat. Feeling vaguely wilted, both from the heat and her roiling emotions, Mona shrugged her sister's arm off her shoulder.

"Not tonight." Mona patted her sister's shoulder. "I'm tired." She glanced back at the hospital behind them. "Since he's safely locked up, perhaps I should go back to the hotel and use the room we rented." Smiling at her sister, Mona hoped Nona couldn't tell how upset she was. "Perhaps we could get together tomorrow for lunch?"

For a moment it looked as if her sister would argue. Nona opened her mouth, then shut it, her lips thinning and eyes narrowing in a calculating way. "Perhaps you're right." Then Nona's usual sunny cheer returned. "But we can share a cab."

Boris sat crossed-legged on his cot. Things were still fairly confused in his mind, but he'd offered the only chair in the plain, sparse room to the nice doctor fairy. He had that much presence of mind left. They'd exchanged pleas-

157

antries, like names and such, and the doctor appeared to be ready to go straight to whatever it was that caused Boris to be here.

"When can I see Jared?" Boris asked, hoping his previous cooperation would help.

"May I have your necklace?" Dr. Zequiel asked.

"What necklace?" Boris asked. "I don't have a necklace." It seemed an odd question. Boris knew he didn't look the type to drape himself in jewelry, like some fairies.

Dr. Zequiel pointed to his neck. "You do, right there."

Checking, Boris did find a necklace at his throat. "Well, what do you know?" He tried, but couldn't work the fastener. "I didn't bring any necklaces with me. I wonder where it came from? And how it got on me?"

"May I help?" Dr. Zequiel asked.

"Certainly." Boris turned around so that she could see to unfasten it, before he remembered his manners. "Please. Thank you." The Ploofs had tried long and hard to instill some sort of courtesy in their adopted sons. He wished they could know that some of it had taken.

The chain slithered off his neck, and he turned around. She held it in her hands, turning it over and examining it.

It looked like a braided chain of silver and gold. Boris whispered a few words, and the thing glowed greenly. He whistled.

"That thing's enspelled."

The memory of his recent obsession with Jared collided with the rest of their relationship in Boris' mind. Ouch. He cringed and hunched over, head in his hands.

"Oh my God! What did I do? Oh, I didn't." Boris groaned and closed his eyes, trying to stop himself from remembering any more. How horrible! How humiliating!

"Not your fault," Dr. Zequiel said soothingly. "But, with

this gone, I can check to see if there are any more spells on you."

Boris just sat hunched on his cot. He ground his teeth and sighed. Memories of various pranks played on him in his youth by school-age enemies added to his writhing embarrassment. This was worse. This was far, far worse. Someone was going to pay for this.

And Jared. What must Jared think?

He could almost hear Jared's good-natured laughter accompanying a few well-chosen, yet sharp, comments. Jared wouldn't hold this against him, though Jared would probably use it as fodder for ribbing harassment.

Still, someone would pay for this.

Folding his arms and straightening up, Boris tried to manage an irritated, but not deranged, demeanor. He grimaced at the doctor.

"Well, that's taken care of." Dr. Zequiel put the necklace in her pocket. "I can see another spell on you, though I can't tell what it is. I think we may have found the problem here. It appears to be a geas of some kind."

"That spell's not the problem. I think the necklace was the problem." Shaking his head sadly, Boris explained that there had always been some sort of geas spell on him and his twin brother. No one was certain what it was, but it was thought to be a remnant of the separation spell.

"Actually, it's been rather helpful in my life. For some reason it seems to give us extra immunity from other spells. Whatever it is, other spells can't shake it or mess with it. Some deep-seated something. One spellmaster said he thought it had something to do with our ability to make friends."

"Ah." Dr. Zequiel looked enlightened. "We're making progress. I'm certain of it. The problem is with you and your friend. Either another spell has tweaked this spell, or this spell is causing all the havoc."

"It's never been a problem before." Boris shrugged.

"What is your brother's name?"

"Forrest."

"Ah. I see." She made a notation in her notebook. "And do you and Forrest often trade places?"

Boris leaned forward on his cot. "We used to, as kids, but I haven't seen Forrest for six years now."

"I see." She scribbled happily in her notebook. "Forrest is human, and you are fairy, right?" She didn't look up from her notes to see Boris nod, but continued on. "Where does your brother live?"

"I believe he is here, in Miami."

"Ah-ha. Perhaps we should contact him."

Now there was a very good idea. Boris smiled. Yeah, Forrest would help. And it would be nice to see him again.

Ageon stepped through the front door. Home, finally; he could relax, put his feet up, listen to some classical music. And forget about his troubles for a while.

Merce held the door for him. "Yo, Boss, Erent is waiting in your library. He has news on Auveron."

So much for a few minutes to relax. Ageon sighed and headed for his library. His library was a small room next to his office, where people could wait for him and still be mildly entertained. The room contained a small bookshelf with coffee table books and various media disks, along with a TV and stereo.

The room almost appeared empty; Erent had a talent for disappearing while in plain sight, blending in with the crowd, even when there wasn't a crowd. It made him such a wonderful spy. He currently hid in a chair with a book. He was a compact human male, with wonderfully average features and a bland, mild temperament, covering a shrewd and quick mind. Ageon had learned not to underestimate him and not to doubt him. Humans weren't supposed to be able to perform magic, but Erent sometimes made Ageon wonder.

"My office?" Ageon motioned toward the door to his office.

Erent shook his head. "No need. I don't have that much information. But something is going on. Little Jimmy is in town. All I know is he partied pretty hard last night, and the police picked him up when he and his boys tried to snatch someone. They'll make bail soon. If they're smart, they're heading home."

Little Jimmy Auveron. Ageon shook his head in disgust. Every time he started feeling sorry for himself over his troubles with Zarrad, all he had to do was think of Little Jimmy.

Auveron's reputation kept him respected and feared far and wide, but Little Jimmy was the undisputed screw-up champion. If there was ever anybody that consistently chose the wrong place, time, and action for anything, it was Little Jimmy.

"Well, now we know what's wrong with Zarrad," Ageon muttered.

"At least Zarrad will be safe in the hospital. Little Jimmy can't get to him there." Erent nodded to Ageon and headed for the door. "That's all I've got for you. If I find out anything else, I'll let you know."

"Find Little Jimmy." Ageon sighed and pinched the bridge of his nose to stop the headache. "Don't pick him up. Don't talk to him. I just want to know where he's at, what he's doing."

"I'll find him and call you." Erent left the library.

Ageon sat for a moment in the chair Erent had vacated. If only Zarrad were a fairy and could do magic, none of this would have happened. If only he had both his sons here. If only Amelia hadn't taken the fairy boy and disappeared. If only . . .

Jared sighed and leaned back against the least-repaired section of the cab's seat. He'd wanted to tell the cabby to step on it, but with the way his day had been going, it would only get him in trouble. He'd get to the hotel fast enough.

The police had taken his statement and let him go. They'd seemed awfully happy about something. Jared decided that all in all he didn't want to know what. He was just glad to be away from them.

The cab had no air-conditioning, and the day's heat made him feel sticky. Between the lingering scent of greasy diners, the salty spray of the ocean, the confined frustration of the police station, and the heat of the cab, Jared's stunned stupefaction was giving way to a desperate need for a shower.

Perhaps the steam would clear his head, and some new idea for finding Mona would present itself. That was, after all, what he'd intended to do when he'd set out.

In the quiet cool of his hotel room, he sat on the hard bed. Now, how did one go about getting a shower?

Oh yes. First he had to take his clothes off.

He fumbled with the buttons of his shirt. If he just took this one step at a time, surely he'd get it figured out in the end.

Shirt. Off it came. Jared dangled it down the side of the bed before dropping it. He unwrapped his bandaged wings and dropped the bandage on top of the shirt. Little, browning red spots told him that his wings weren't doing as well as he'd hoped by this point.

Pants came next. Only when he got stuck did Jared remember that he had to take his shoes off first, before he could get his pants off.

Sighing, Jared reached for the waistband of his pants, currently drooping around his ankles. He promptly fell off the bed and onto the floor.

A few moments of struggle and he was back on the bed again. His pants and one shoe had joined his shirt on the floor. He glared dolefully at the shoe still on his foot.

One step at a time. He could think this through. And then he'd find Mona.

Off came the shoes, and socks, and underwear. Now he was ready. He stumbled into the bathroom.

Jared stood under the steamy stream of water, letting it comb his hair into slippery rivulets running over his face. He'd made it this far without coming up with any plan.

He needed a plan. He had to find Mona and rescue her from Nona. And tell her that he loved her.

The clean, wet heat refreshed his body, but only made his mind sleepy. While the idea of spending the rest of his life in the shower, until his skin shriveled permanently into wrinkles, had an appeal all its own, he doubted he could find Mona just by standing in the shower.

Shutting the water off, he flung the shower curtain open. The mirror had fogged over completely, and little beads of dew covered every surface in the bathroom. So why did it suddenly feel so cold?

The sound of the lock to the hotel room opening and someone entering the room outside the bathroom made Jared hold his breath.

Footsteps walked past the closed bathroom door, and

Jared heard someone flop onto the bed.

"Alone at last. Thank God!" Mona said.

Thank God she was back! Jared grinned to himself.

Apparently standing around in the shower *was* the secret to finding Mona in Miami.

Chapter 15

Mona sighed and rolled over onto her back to stare at the textured ceiling. Now that she was alone in her quiet, darkened hotel room and could have a good cry, she didn't feel like it. Strange.

It had been a strange weekend. Way too much going on. Maybe she just needed some time to take it all in.

The bathroom door opened. Mona sat up on the bed.

Jared, stark naked and dripping wet, walked out of the bathroom. He grinned like the demented loon he was.

"Mona! Mona, you're back!" He glanced at her disheveled appearance. "Are you all right? Did Nona do that?"

For a stunned and fearful moment Mona couldn't breathe. Jared spread his arms and studied her tentatively, as if either preparing to hug her, or just demonstrate that he had nothing in his hands.

"Mona?"

"Jared." Her voice sounded much calmer than she felt. She took a deep breath. If she acted unafraid, as if everything was normal, maybe he wouldn't do anything rash. Like hurt her.

He smiled again. "Thank you for coming back. I love you. I love you so much I don't know how to say it."

His hair dripped little streams onto his glistening, wet chest. The streams of water ran down his body, emphasizing every muscle, highlighting every feature, and coating him with an almost magical veneer. Mona couldn't help but admire the delightfully fascinating spectacle all the way down to his feet.

"Mona?"

Handsome, but crazy, Mona reminded herself.

A small, squishy puddle formed in the carpet at his feet. When he stepped forward, he started another puddle. In the cool of the room, he should have had goosebumps all over his arms and legs, but he didn't. He looked flushed and warm. Droplets of water trickled from his fragile wings, as they fluttered behind him like a dog shaking itself dry.

"You're getting the floor wet," Mona said, hoping his innate need for order and cleanliness would get him back into the bathroom, so she could run away.

"I don't care!" Jared flung himself to his knees. "Nothing matters except for you. You are the most important person in my life. I looked for you all day and couldn't find you. I thought I'd go insane. I couldn't stand to lose you again." His hands stretched out to her. "Please, I love you. It's always been only you."

The whipped puppy look had always worked on her before and, she had to admit, Jared, wearing nothing but that look and water, was incredibly appealing. With his hair clinging dark and damp against his face, and the rest of him so vulnerably exposed and slippery wet, how could she resist?

Except . . .

"I swear I never dated your sister, Nona. Never." Jared sighed, his chest and abdomen rippling. "I know I haven't been the best husband in the world, and I'm very sorry. I want to make it up to you. I want us to be together again. I'll do anything you ask. Please forgive me."

"Jared." Mona furiously tried to think of something to say to get her out of this.

"I'll cut my hair and let my ears show. I'll buy new shirts that let my wings stick out." Jared looked so vulnerable. "I'll only see my mother once a week, and I won't take care of all her problems. Anything you ask. I'll do it. I swear."

"Jared."

"Forgive me?" Jared pleaded.

"Okay." Mona scooted to the other side of the bed and stood up. This put her farther away from Jared, but also farther away from the door, and escape. "I didn't expect you to be here."

A new hopefulness had appeared in Jared's face. "After I looked everywhere I could think . . . well, not quite everywhere. I kept running into these strange people and even weirder problems. But that's not important. The important thing is I couldn't find you. I couldn't find where Nona lived. So I came back here. To try to think of some other way to find you. And now you're here." He sighed and smiled at her. "I love you."

He was still crazy. Handsome. Tempting. But, crazy. Mona sighed. She'd just wanted to be alone. Completely alone, not alone with an escaped, enspelled lunatic. Even if he was handsome, wet, and naked.

"Well," she said, "here we are."

Jared walked on his knees two steps toward her. "You do forgive me?"

"Yes." Mona hoped she sounded convincing.

"You do realize your sister needs a lot of help?"

"Oh, yes." Mona nodded vigorously.

"Ah . . ." Jared hesitated, waving his hand to indicate her, "what happened to you? Are you all right?"

Very, very crazy. Mona tried to smile. "Nona and I had a fight, but I'm all right."

"Are you sure?" Jared appeared terribly concerned. He

breathed deeply, rippling his glistening chest and abdomen again, causing small streams of water to join into temporarily raging rivers. "I'm sure your sister is very nice, but I think she's crazy."

"Nona is just upset." Mona tried not to think about how handsome and sweet and tempting he looked, kneeling naked and wet before her. He was still crazy and very dangerous.

"I love you so much." He crept closer, still on his knees.

"I love you, too," she said automatically.

He smiled and reached for her hands. "What would you like to do this evening?" His eyebrows waggled and he leered at her.

Suddenly—finally!—a thought occurred to her. "We never got out last night. How about a steak dinner? To celebrate." Mona smiled at him.

"Anything you say." Jared rose quickly to his feet, taking her in his arms. "My love."

She held her breath a moment, but all he did was hug her to him. She wrapped her arms around him, trying to get her fear under control and not think about how her dress was getting damp. Again. Oh well, it wasn't really her dress, and it wasn't in very good shape anyway.

Her hand touched his wing, and he flinched, releasing her.

"Ow." Jared stretched his arm and wing.

"What's the matter?" She turned him around.

A ragged wound slashed across his left wing. It appeared to be recent and untreated.

"What happened?"

"Nona," he muttered. "Last night. She dug her heel into me to keep me from following you."

Mona couldn't imagine her flighty sister hurting anyone.

Nona just didn't have it in her to willfully inflict pain on someone else.

Though Jared's wing might have been injured in an escape from the hospital. Mona could easily see one of the hulking troll attendant-guards injuring a fleeing maniac in an attempt to stop him.

"You need to get that treated."

Jared turned to face her, his face flushed. "It's nothing. It'll be okay. I'll be fine."

Simpering and smiling, Mona ran her finger up his wet arm. "But I worry about you."

"I'd rather you worried about other parts of me." Jared grinned back at her. He swooped down to kiss her.

Laughing around his kiss, Mona pushed him gently away. "You'll get me all wet."

"I don't mind."

"I do. We need to go get a steak dinner." She tickled his flat stomach with her finger. "To fortify ourselves for later."

He whispered in her ear, his breath hot on her neck, "Whatever you say."

She gently spanked him. "Go dry yourself in the bathroom. Shave and whatever. And get dressed. You can't go to a restaurant like that."

"Whatever you say. I'll even leave the wings unbound if you want."

"Wonderful!" Mona shooed Jared toward the bathroom. "Now, you go get dressed."

Jared bowed himself back into the bathroom and closed the door.

Mona fell on the phone, her hands shaking so much she could hardly dial Nona's number. She prayed while the phone rang.

Forrest had put off going to the hotel the Boss and Nona considered "theirs" until last. Originally he rather doubted he'd find Nona and Mona there, but now, being unable to find them anywhere else, he wondered if he should have started there.

He'd been checking everywhere in person, fearing hotel clerks might try to lie to him over the phone. He shifted his feet on the floor of the cab, itching to get out. He had long since tired of cab rides.

"Just let me off here on the corner," he told the cabby. "I can walk from here." It was just over a block away, but Forrest didn't care.

A cool breeze blew, softening the late afternoon heat. The sidewalks were filling up again, as tourists started getting out to find someplace to have dinner.

The smell of grilled seafood and baked potatoes drifted out of an open restaurant door. Forrest considered stopping in to get something to eat, and decided to come back after he'd checked the hotel.

"I have a message for Silvan," a voice behind him said.

Forrest turned to find a young male fairy in Bermuda shorts, a loud print shirt, and heavy navy jacket with a large tear in one pocket. Flanking the young man were three assorted, tough-looking characters dressed similarly: a human, a fairy, and a changeling human/fairy.

"Well, if it isn't Little Jimmy Auveron." Forrest loomed over Little Jimmy, smiling, and slowly pulled his hands out of his pants pockets. "Playing the tourist here in Miami."

Little Jimmy shoved a finger into Forrest's chest. "I got a message for your boss and his punk son."

"Uh-huh." Forrest added up the three toughs backing Little Jimmy and decided not to make an issue of the finger.

Instead he glared down Little Jimmy. "Who from?"

"From me."

Oh goody. Little Jimmy off on one of his jaunts. Just what everyone needed this weekend, as if things weren't bad enough. Forrest sneered. "Why don't you go home and see if Daddy has anything to say?"

"Shut up!" Little Jimmy shouted, turning red in the face. He jabbed Forrest again with his finger. "You tell your boss that if he doesn't want any trouble, he'll leave me and my business alone while I'm here. And you tell that punk that he'll pay for what happened today."

"Fine. I'll tell them." Forrest rolled his eyes. "In the meantime, if you don't want trouble, don't go making any trouble. Go play on the beach, or better yet, go home. Your Mommy is calling you."

The three men backing Little Jimmy shifted and glared at Forrest. Little Jimmy grabbed Forrest's shirt and pulled Forrest nose-to-nose with him.

"I could turn you into a warty toad any time I wanted to. In fact, I think I'll do it now." Little Jimmy took a deep breath, preparing himself for the spell.

Forrest easily broke Little Jimmy's grip and tossed him to his back-up. "What? Here on a public street? You're crazy." Looking at the three toughs, Forrest said, "Do yourselves a favor. Take him home."

Turning around, Forrest sauntered off toward the hotel, fully expecting to be jumped. When nothing happened, he glanced back. Little Jimmy was surrounded, and they were all arguing. Forrest wanted to run far away, but kept himself to his normal walking rhythm.

He'd have to pass on Little Jimmy's messages and warn Ageon and Zarrad.

Although, hadn't Zarrad mentioned something about

Auveron earlier? Something about problems with Little Jimmy being in town? Maybe the boss already knew about it. Forrest figured he'd go ahead and tell them.

If they did know, they'd think he was being stupid, like always. But there was always the chance they didn't know.

"Hello?" Nona voice sounded safe and wonderful over the phone. Mona wished she were there with Nona, not in her hotel room with a madman.

"Nona, it's me. Help!" Mona whispered, with one hand half-cupped around her mouth to try to stop any sound from going anywhere but the phone. She turned to face away from the bathroom, but kept glancing back to see if Jared was still in there or if he'd come out. "He's here. Jared is here in our hotel room."

"How'd he get out of the hospital?" Nona asked.

"I don't know." Mona glanced back again. Jared hadn't come out yet. "He must have been waiting for me to return. He just walked out of the bathroom when I got here, naked and dripping wet. About scared me to death."

"Ooooh. Naked and dripping wet, huh?"

"Nona! I'm alone here with an escaped lunatic. Help me."

"Yes, but he's a naked wet lunatic. Sounds fun."

"*Nona!*"

"Calm down, calm down. I'll always help you out with a wet, naked man." Nona giggled. "You lure him to the hospital. I'll get a hold of Ageon and have him waiting with some muscle outside the hospital."

Mona almost asked who Ageon was, then remembered the older man who'd bullied everyone to the hospital. She assumed he was a friend of Nona's. "All right. Are you sure he'll be there?"

"Of course. If it's about Zarrad, Ageon will even listen to me."

Oh, so he was a friend of Jared's. Mona sighed. "I think I can do that. I've got him convinced to take me out to dinner. I'll just have to give the cabby private instructions."

"See you there, Sis. Bye."

She missed on her first try at hanging up the phone, then used both shaking hands to get the handset in place.

Jared walked out of the bathroom. He'd shaved, and put on some cologne, but wore nothing more than that. He grinned at her. "I seem to be running out of clean clothes. Perhaps we should just order room service."

Spotting his clothes on the floor beside the bed—rumpled and tossed aside without care, very unlike Jared— Mona pounced on them. "Just put these back on. It won't be for very long."

Shuddering, Jared said, "Not those. I'll wear tomorrow's." He stopped as he opened up the drawer to get his clothes out. "What about you? Did you want to change?"

How to answer that? Mona did want to put something else on, anything but Nona's torn and redampened red dress, but not now, not with Jared right there and absolutely insane. Then she remembered, her clothes were still at Nona's apartment. Mona smiled sorrowfully. "I can't. I forgot my things at Nona's."

He pulled his clothes from the drawer. "We'll stop somewhere and get you some new things."

At first Mona tried to help Jared put his clothes on, but that only seemed to distract him. He kept coming up with other things to do rather than get dressed. So, to hurry things along, she stood by the door, with her hand on the doorknob, waiting.

"You must be hungry," Jared commented as they walked

through the quiet and unfortunately deserted corridors to the elevators.

"I didn't really get lunch." Which was true, the nibbles and frowzy drinks didn't really count as lunch. "Nona wanted to go to these expensive clubs; I wanted a buffet. Nona won." Then, remembering that she was supposed to be luring him along, she added, "However, she did point out this really great place to me, in passing. Some kind of Mexican seafood. Could we try there, rather than the steak place?"

The elevator was empty, but Mona found herself crowded into a corner anyway. Where was everyone today?

"Anything you want," he whispered as he ran his hands through her hair and kissed the split ends.

"I'll get the cab." Mona dashed out of the elevator, intending to run to the lobby and get a valet to grab a cab and give the driver the address.

However, Boris waved to them from the counter. "Hey, Boss. I see you found her."

Oh no! Mona groaned to herself. She didn't need another escaped lunatic to deal with. Though she should have expected it. Jared wouldn't have left the hospital without his partner.

Come to think of it, had Boris been helping Jared fool her all this time? There was no way Jared could have hidden his double life from Boris. Just what she needed. Why did they both have to be looking for her! Shouldn't Nona have to deal with at least one of them?

At least Boris no longer had that blasted necklace around him. Though it had been useful the last time in getting help for him and Jared.

"What are you doing here?" Jared demanded. "You're supposed to be home, minding the store."

Sighing, Boris muttered, "Not again."

Mona stepped aside and motioned one of the bellhops over. "Get us a cab. Quickly. Tell the driver he must take us to Mercy Hospital. All right? I'll pretend to give him other directions, but he must get us as quickly to Mercy as he can. Understand?"

The satyr eyed her torn dress and the two men arguing just out of earshot. "Absolutely. If you say so, Ma'am. I can see it's important."

"I'm just passing the message along, is all I'm saying," Boris shouted.

"You're not making any sense," Jared shouted back. "Just go home. Leave me alone."

"Quickly." Mona tried not to grimace as she turned from the bellhop and hurried to Jared, slipping her arm around his. She smiled up at him. "Why don't we take him with us to dinner? You can finish your discussion there, and then we can part ways."

"What?" Jared bellowed.

"Huh?" Boris frowned in confusion. "You want me to tag along?"

"Sure," Mona said breezily. "The more the merrier." Some acid bitterness in her made her flutter her eyelashes at Jared and add, "Don't you think so?"

"N . . ." Jared converted whatever he'd been about to say into a sigh. "Whatever you say."

"Well, all right, Boss." Boris stuck his hands into his pockets and slouched behind them. "If you say so."

The bellhop approached them. "Your cab is waiting." He winked at Mona.

"Thank you." She herded the two men into the cab.

The cabby, an old, wrinkled gnome, looked back at them. "Where to?"

Mona gave him a made-up address.

He nodded and winked at her. "No problem. I'll have you there in a jiffy."

Oh, if only it were that easy, Mona thought, as she leaned back, uneasily squeezing herself between two escaped lunatics.

Chapter 16

Forrest sat stiffly in the cab, one hand on the door handle, trying to figure out what was going on now. Whatever weirdness was going down was getting much too weird for him.

Since when did Zarrad not know who Little Jimmy was? Or Auveron? Had Nona's spell affected his memory that much? Was this really a spell of Nona's or was the little problem with Auveron really a big problem?

And Zarrad and Nona did *not* take him with them when they went out. Never. Ever. Didn't happen. Would never happen. Forrest didn't want it to happen.

But . . .

Here he was, with Zarrad shooting him suspicious and rather irritated glances and Nona smiling falsely while her hands shook nervously. Had Zarrad talked with Nona about whatever spell it was that Nona had put on them?

Nona couldn't have removed it, since Zarrad obviously didn't know what he was supposed to know. If it wasn't Nona's, then perhaps it was affecting her too. Forrest feared what new turn the spell might take. Unfortunately, as a human there was little he could do about a magic spell.

Though why wasn't he immune like always? Life just wasn't fair. Why would his immunity let him down now?

Perhaps he could slip away when the cab stopped at whatever restaurant they were heading to. He could at least try.

There was no help for it now. He'd just have to deal with

whatever happened. He'd dealt with it all day now. It hadn't been too bad.

Only when the cab pulled up in front of Mercy Hospital and he spotted Ageon did Forrest realize that someone else had control over whatever was happening.

Which was fine with Forrest. He sure didn't want either Zarrad or Nona in control.

Jared spotted the tough fairy lawyer who'd given him money standing outside the building as the cab pulled to the curb and stopped. Beside the fairy was a half-troll, another fairy, and a human. They all looked large, and vaguely annoyed.

"What's this?" he asked, grabbing Mona's hand as she and Boris piled from the car. He didn't want to deal with Nona's lawyer, or whatever the tough fairy was. He'd had enough for one day.

Mona tugged gently. "Please. It's for the best. Come on out. We just want to help you."

Spotting a notice on a window, Jared realized they were at some sort of a hospital. He stepped out of the car, sighing. "I'm not hurt that bad. I don't need a hospital. My wing is fine."

"Get inside." The half-troll jerked his head toward the doors.

"Really, this isn't necessary." Jared tried to pull Mona to him. "We don't need lawyers or other complications. Let's just go out to eat, and we can talk and work this all out."

Mona squealed, pulling her hand out of Jared's, and ran behind the hulking fairy lawyer. Where, it turned out, Nona was hiding. The two women clung to each other, staring at him with large, frightened eyes. Nona was behind this. Jared tried not to grimace at her. What exactly did the crazy woman have against him?

"Ageon, help!" Nona squealed.

Boris, who'd been watching all this, scowled at Jared. "You been hurt?"

"My left wing. It's not that bad. Just a scratch, really." Jared waved his hand, as if to shoo away any concern.

Boris frowned and squinted at Jared. "What?"

"Let's see what the doctors say," the tough, aging fairy suggested.

"Let's not." Jared stepped up to the fairy, surprised to find that he was actually taller. So how did the man manage to make him feel smaller? "I know when I do and don't need a doctor. I appreciate your concern, but it's not your business. Now, I'll thank you to leave us alone." He looked past the fairy to Mona. "We can work this out. Please, let's just go have dinner."

The fairy's eyes widened in shock. He obviously hadn't expected Jared to argue. Suddenly his eyes narrowed in anger. He waved to the half-troll. "Get him inside."

The half-troll lunged at Jared, who stepped aside and brought his fist down on the man's back. His blow landed directly between two tiny fairy wings Jared hadn't known were there, effectively debilitating the man. The troll-fairy fell to the sidewalk, gasping.

Everyone stared at Jared, stunned, with their mouths hanging open, and for a moment nobody moved.

"When did you learn that?" Boris asked.

"What?" Jared stared at him. They'd taken martial arts classes together. He'd known Boris for years, but he couldn't figure out Boris, or Boris' actions tonight.

"Get him!" the tough fairy shouted as he himself lunged at Jared.

Jared dodged the older fairy, but the younger one tackled

him around the waist. The human piled on, trying to secure Jared to the ground.

"Get him, Axel! Pin him!" the tough, older fairy shouted as he backed out of the way, and the human on top of Jared grinned.

A well-aimed fist wiped the grin off the human Axel's face. Jared managed to free one leg and kicked the young fairy in the knee.

The older fairy stepped farther back, beside Mona and Nona, shouting encouragement to Jared's opponents.

Axel, blood seeping from his nose, threw himself on top of Jared, rolling them and the young fairy over the groaning half-troll. Jared bit Axel's arm, gagging at the taste of the man's dry, sandy sleeve. Axel let go of Jared long enough for Jared to wriggle out of the young fairy's grasp and stand up.

The young fairy and Axel jumped to their feet, crouching in preparation. The half-troll slowly staggered upward to gain his feet. Jared danced on his toes, trying to keep all three where he could see them.

He bumped into Boris.

"Help me!" Jared whispered.

"Ah, Boss, are you sure about this?" With Boris behind him, Jared couldn't see him, but Boris made no move to either stand beside Jared, or with his back to Jared.

"Of course I'm sure," Jared growled. Boris had never failed him before; Jared wondered what was going on now. "I don't like the odds." Why was everyone trying to kidnap him today? And where were the police, like last time?

The half-troll swung at Jared. A punch Jared easily ducked. Then both Axel and the young fairy lunged at him.

Jared dodged them, earning himself a blow to the stomach from the young fairy. Boris was still just standing there, staring stupidly. Jared only realized he'd lost track of the half-troll when he felt a mighty impact on the back of his head.

Everything went black as Jared fell to the sidewalk.

Staring at Zarrad, Ageon only realized Hjell was tottering and panting beside him when Hjell said, "I didn't know he had that much fight in him."

Ageon nodded. His son had surprised him, too. Maybe insanity had given Zarrad extra strength, but when had Zarrad suddenly acquired a talent for fighting? "Let's get him inside."

They didn't have to bother. Some of the hospital's attendants had apparently been waiting to see the outcome of the fight, and they immediately dragged Zarrad off.

"He always seemed so quiet," Axel said, dabbing at his still-bleeding nose.

"It's the quiet ones you have to look out for," one of the troll attendants said. He added to Forrest, "Come along."

"Me too?" Forrest's forehead creased. It wasn't quite a frown, but it was close. "Why?"

The hulking attendant swatted him on the back, and Forrest staggered. "Just for a little rest. Wouldn't you like a little rest?"

After a moment's pause, Forrest nodded. "Actually, after today, maybe it'd be a good idea."

"There we go." The attendant smiled at Forrest. "Come along."

"One minute, got to tell my boss something." Forrest stepped over to Ageon and whispered, "I ran into Little Jimmy. He's here, dressed like a tourist and acting like a clown. He didn't say why he was here, but he told me to tell you to leave him and his business alone. Oh, and he said

Zarrad's going to pay for something. He didn't make much sense."

"Never does." Ageon nodded toward the hospital. "Go on. Don't worry about it. I've got everything under control." Didn't he wish . . .

A grinning Forrest allowed the troll to usher him inside.

"Well, that's taken care of." Ageon glanced at Mona and Nona, still clinging to each other. "You both all right now?"

"I think we can manage," Mona said stiffly.

Ageon looked them over. They still wore the same torn dresses they'd had on earlier. He didn't know what they'd been up to, or why they hadn't changed, but a part of him wished he were younger and could find out. They reminded him in some ways of Amelia. His son certainly felt the same way about them as he felt, still, about Amelia. If there was one thing Ageon knew, it was how a man could lose himself over a woman.

Which he didn't want Zarrad to do. Zarrad should make his own mistakes, not Ageon's. Ageon took a deep breath of the cool evening air, and nodded curtly to the women. "Good night."

Stig held the door to the car open for him, but Ageon paused. Turning back to Hjell and Axel, he said, "I need you two to stay here and keep an eye on Zarrad. I don't want him escaping again."

"Sure, Boss," they said in unison.

Ageon sat back in the cushiony seats as the car pulled away from the hospital. He had the horrible feeling he'd be back here tonight. First he had to find out where Little Jimmy was, and what he was up to, and what this spell on Zarrad was, and how to set everything right.

Nona whispered to Mona as Stig closed the car door.

"Maybe we should see if Ageon could protect us." The sun was lowering in the distance, and she feared what might happen that evening, and feared even more what might happen that night.

"I can take care of myself," Mona said. "I don't need some domineering fairy pushing me around."

"So that's why you called me all frantic when you found Zarrad naked and wet in your hotel room," Nona said sarcastically. She pushed Mona away from her, planning on catching a ride even if Mona wanted to stand around. But it was too late, the car had pulled away. Nona watched it go with mingled fear and relief. The price of Ageon's protection was undoubtedly too steep.

"I didn't mean you." Mona ran her fingers through her hair. "Though I probably shouldn't go back to that hotel tonight. If he should escape again . . ."

"Oh. I hadn't thought of that." Nona bit her lip. "My apartment probably isn't safe either."

The unspoken, "Now what do we do?" hung between them.

Hjell, the half-troll, cleared his throat. Both women turned to him.

"I don't want to stick my nose in where it isn't wanted. But, perhaps you should stay together. Maybe get yourselves a room somewhere nearby." He shrugged, and stretched his enormous, sinewy arms and tiny, delicate wings. "If you let me know how to contact you, I'll let you know if he escapes. And you might want to . . . uh . . . find something else to wear."

The warm sea breeze blew Mona's hair into her face, so that Nona couldn't read it.

Mona pushed her hair back. "What do you think?"

Nona didn't dare look at Hjell. Ageon's right-hand man

would never, never go against any orders. So, either he had no orders on this subject—other than standing guard to make certain Zarrad didn't escape again—so he could do as he pleased, or he had orders Nona didn't know about.

Like maybe keeping an eye on her, or finding out where she was staying, or getting rid of two inconvenient women who were complicating his son's life.

Barely lifting her shoulders, Nona hoped Mona would be able to interpret her gesture as the supreme I-don't-know.

"It couldn't hurt." Mona scowled disgustedly. Nona watched as she looked Hjell up and down, measuring him, and apparently not happy with the end result. "So, where's the nearest hotel?"

They exchanged information with the half-troll, getting his phone number and promising to call him when they'd found a place to stay.

Zarrad startled awake, cold and stiff and bleary. He tried to focus on the indistinct gloom around him. It took him a moment to remember where he was and why. The loony ward at Mercy Hospital. Because everyone thought he was crazy.

Though, considering his position lurking under the cot, perhaps they were right.

He pulled himself back into the darkness, as close to the wall as he could get. The cot above him was rather rudimentary, but securely bolted to the wall. The floor underneath was as clean as the rest of his room, making his hiding place as comfortable as possible.

Though Zarrad didn't much consider the antiseptic-smelling, cold, hard floor and frigid, rough block wall in the dark, confined underbelly of his crude prison cot particularly comfortable. For that he'd need real clothes, at least.

Not these thin hospital garments.

The sound that had startled him from his uneven sleep was the sound of the lock being opened.

Finally they'd come for him. Zarrad felt rather stiff and frozen after waiting hours under the bed for the staff to come in and not find him.

If all went well, the idiot oafs would look in, see him gone, and run for help, leaving the door open. Or at least unlocked, both magically and unmagically. Whereupon he would saunter out to freedom.

Hopefully.

A small eternity passed between the lock opening and the sound of the door handle being moved. If this was the best Mercy Hospital could field against him, Zarrad figured he'd just walk out without a problem. It shouldn't take this long just to get a door open.

Finally, the door banged against the opposite wall, and stayed open.

Two sets of heavy-booted troll feet stomped in.

"I swear. Gordy said he had fake wings," one troll rumbled in a low, soft bass. "Not real ones. He said they were made out of gauze and plastic with an aluminum frame."

"Gordy was throwing pixie dust in your face," another rumbled back. "Why do you listen to him?"

They heaved something onto the cot, nearly pinning Zarrad to the floor.

"So, how come his file doesn't mention the injury on his wing? I'm telling you, something screwy is going on here."

"Look around! Where are we at? Something screwy is always going on here."

Two sets of heavy-booted troll feet stomped back to the door.

"Yeah. And we're the ones that always have to pay for

it." The door handle clattered in a rough grip. "I'm telling you—"

The rest was lost as the door clanged shut.

Followed by the unmistakable sound of the lock being safely secured, both magically and unmagically.

Chapter 17

Zarrad lay still, stunned.

They hadn't even noticed he was missing. They acted like they expected to find this room empty. What kind of place was this? What kind of records did they keep? What kind of idiots worked here?

His long, lithe, muscular body had easily slid under the empty bed, but with this weight, it sagged severely. Zarrad had to squirm, wiggle, and inch his way out. It would have been harder, he realized, if he'd had his fake wings on. Or if he'd been the fairy son his father always wanted, with real wings. Being human occasionally had its advantages.

Whoever they'd thrown on the bed weighed a ton. Or the springs were as deficient as everything else here.

If the idiots that ran this place thought he, Zarrad Silvan, would share a room with someone, they were crazier than he was.

For pity's sake, there was only one bed in the room. And it was his. He certainly wouldn't share it with anyone.

Well, if she was really cute . . . No. He loved Nona. He wouldn't let them tempt him like that.

Whatever, or whoever, was on the bed made no sound. They didn't even stir when Zarrad pushed up from the bottom to get himself a little extra wiggle space. Not that it helped much.

He finally pulled himself out and sat up, panting.

Someone lay on the bed in white hospital clothes similar to his, but this person had fairy wings sticking out of slits in the back. One wing had a reddish wound peeping through the slit in the shirt. Since whoever it was faced the wall, Zarrad couldn't tell much more about him, except that he looked tall and muscularly male from the back.

He stood up, preparing to defend his room and his pitiful, sagging prison cot from this interloper. Reaching over, Zarrad grabbed the other man's shoulder and rolled him onto his back.

Zarrad looked down at himself, while the room spun and little dots gathered at the edges of his vision.

Then the floor hit his head and he lost consciousness.

Mona looked around the little hotel room she and Nona had rented. Did hotels really have that little imagination, or did everyone really just want exactly the same thing in every hotel room?

The room had two double beds with ghastly print spreads, one nightstand between them with a plain, black digital clock-radio, one fake dark-wood wardrobe to hide the television, with a few drawers for clothes, a table masquerading as a desk with a phone sitting on it, two hard chairs disguised with cushions, and one small table with a lamp.

Nona had appropriated the bed nearest the window for her own and was currently flipping television channels with the remote. Which left the bed nearest the bathroom for Mona.

They hadn't stopped to pick up any of their things, fearing they'd find Jared waiting for them in Nona's apartment. So Mona was left with little to do, except worry.

"Is there anything you want to watch?" Nona asked. "I can't find anything. We could order room service and watch a movie."

"I don't think I could concentrate enough to watch a movie." Mona slumped onto her bed. "Besides, we need to call that half-troll, what's-his-name."

"Hjell."

"Whatever. And we need to do something about clothes, at least for tomorrow. I suppose we could wear these for tonight."

Brushing her clothes as if suddenly realizing she wasn't up to her usual perfectness, Nona hummed. She looked up brightly. "I know. We could go shopping! We'll buy some nice stuff." Grinning wickedly, she added in a murmur, "Best of all, we can put it on his card."

Mona sat up. "The poor man has gone nuts. He's not responsible for himself any more, and you want to add to his bills!"

"Better than adding to mine." Nona grinned unrepentantly.

"We're big girls. I think we should pay for our own stuff," Mona scolded.

Sighing, Nona picked up the remote again. "There has to be something on."

Flopping back onto her bed, Mona privately didn't agree. There was never anything on.

After a moment, she got up and went to sit by the phone. Nona watched her curiously, while absently flipping channels.

"What're you doing?" Nona asked.

"Calling Hjell."

"I don't know if we should tell him where we're at." Nona put the remote down and crawled over her bed, leaving the ugly spread wrinkled and in shambles. "He's Ageon's right hand. And if Ageon decides we're the problem, we'll be eliminated. Somehow."

189

Mona paused with the phone in her hand. "I thought Ageon was your friend."

"Heavens no!" Nona looked horrified. "You should know that, since . . . Oh, wait, I forgot. Zarrad kept you hidden away in Wisconsin. You don't know anyone here. Ageon hates me. He only tolerates me because of Zarrad."

"Oh." Mona wondered when exactly Nona had acquired the lisp, or odd accent, or whatever-it-was on Jared's name. Perhaps it was another Nona quirk, or worse, some pet-name thing between Nona and Jared. Mona decided not to pursue that line of thought. She realized she still had the phone in her hand. She'd been about to call the half-troll. "Still, we need Hjell to let us know if Jared escapes the hospital again."

Nona frowned at Mona, then sighed. She leaned forward and gently took the phone from Mona, setting it back in its rest. "We can call later. After we go shopping and get some dinner. That's a good excuse to delay calling."

"I thought we agreed not to go shopping."

"It's either that or X-rated movies on the TV." Nona bounced up off the bed to leer down at Mona. "And that's not something I want to do with my sister."

"Fine. A quick—and I do mean quick—bout of shopping, and then dinner. Sensible and economical clothes, and someplace with an all-you-can-eat buffet for dinner. Then we call Hjell."

"Of course."

Forrest followed the attendant quietly. He'd considered fighting to get away, but it hadn't helped Zarrad any. And besides, he'd be safe enough here from any more confusion.

He hoped.

The attendant opened a door and held it for Forrest. "In you go."

190

The door shut behind him without the attendant even looking to see that Forrest had gotten all the way in. Typical. No one ever paid him any mind. Don't worry about Forrest, he'll be okay, no matter what.

The lumpy covers on the bed undulated. Something large inside them made a noise somewhere between a grunt and a groan. Whatever, or whoever, had covered their head completely.

Very gingerly, Forrest picked up a corner of the blanket with two fingers and peeked inside.

Flinging the covers back, he cried, "Boris!"

"Huh?" Boris rubbed his eyes, and sat up. He blinked up a moment, then recognition lit his face. "Forrest!"

Their arms went around each other for a second before they started back-slapping, hair-ruffling, and shoulder-punching. Then their reunion degenerated into their normal wrestling tussle for dominance.

Jared blinked. Above him, he found a plain white ceiling. Beside him, plain white block walls. Beneath him, a sagging, lumpy mattress with white sheets and covers. He had to be in the hospital. He'd definitely lost the fight. Too bad he didn't know magic. That would have helped. He gingerly felt his head for lumps. He found a tender spot but no lump.

Why in the world were they so worried about his wing? Was it really worth forcing him into the hospital? And if they were so dead set on doctoring his wing, why hadn't they done anything about it while he was out? His back and wing still hurt.

Since he was in a room, Jared assumed he'd already been checked in, but, looking around, he didn't see any call button. How was he supposed to get hold of a nurse or an attendant or a doctor to find out how he was doing? Or when they would let him go?

A groan from the floor attracted his attention. He rolled onto his side to peer at the floor.

A human male in white hospital clothes lay curled on the floor, facing away from him. The man appeared to be scrubbing his face with his hands, as if trying to rearrange his features.

When Jared's last memories caught up with the fact that a human male lay on the floor, Jared bounced up from the bed, to land in a fighter's crouch. What had the human's name been?

Ah, yes. Axel.

The man turned at the sound of Jared's leap and sat up.

It wasn't Axel.

Jared stared into his own face and sat back down on the bed. Human. This other Jared was human. His shocked mind couldn't get beyond that one simple fact.

"Maybe they're right. Maybe I have gone crazy. This is definitely not the sort of thing that happens to sane people," the other Jared said, slowly and quietly. He rocked back and forth, barely tipping his body each way.

This couldn't be real. Jared knew he had to be dreaming. Reaching with one finger, starting and stopping, as if afraid the other Jared would pop like a balloon at his touch, Jared gently nudged the other's shoulder. Human, and exactly like him.

"You feel real enough," Jared whispered hoarsely. He examined his finger, wondering if it were real. Exactly like him. Same face, hair, build, everything. Except, the other Jared was human.

"Just out of curiosity," the other Jared waved his hand, "how do you explain this?"

"I think I'm dreaming," Jared said.

"That's a good one." The other nodded vigorously. "I may use that myself."

Jared looked around at the small, white room. He couldn't think any more. He didn't dare think any more. Not about two people so similar they could be . . . "So, how do we get out of here?"

"The door is locked." The other Jared got up off the floor and started pacing. "I tried fooling the guards, but that didn't work. If I were a fairy, I could use magic and try opening the lock, but I'm not."

"I'm a fairy," Jared volunteered. The other turned on him swiftly, with an alarming expression. "But I don't know any magic."

The other Jared threw back his head and laughed maniacally. "I know magic, but can't use it. You can use it, but don't know it. Is that classic or what?"

The laugh echoed in the close confines of the room and did nothing to soothe Jared's shattered nerves. He covered his ears with his hands. When it looked like the other Jared had stopped laughing and returned to pacing, Jared took his hands away.

He watched the other Jared pace for a bit, afraid if he spoke he'd provoke another strange outburst. Finally, gathering his courage, Jared said, "If you tell me what to do, I'll try opening the lock."

"Yes." The other Jared hurried to the door. "Yes." He glared back at Jared. "First, you need to come over here."

Jared approached cautiously. He tried nudging the other Jared with his finger again, with the same results. He seemed real enough. Completely human, and exactly like him. How odd. Jared considered the entirety of the weekend. Either he'd gone crazy, or . . .

"Is there a problem?" the other Jared inquired patiently.

"If you're real," Jared whispered, "if this isn't a dream, I think I have a letter for you."

"Oh," the other said, surprised. "Where is it?"

Spreading his arms out to demonstrate his apparel, Jared said, "In my other suit."

"Of course. Whatever." The other Jared pointed at the door. "Now about the lock."

Nona towed Mona away from the clearance racks. It was bad enough having to buy something off the rack, without having to either buy it in a dump, or buy last season's dregs. Unfortunately, no place with any claim to class was open at this hour on a Saturday.

Mona, annoyingly, kept insisting on something cheap.

And everywhere they went, people stared at them. Of course, Nona knew she and her sister were worth a stare or two. With or without the torn dresses. However, Mona obviously found the whole thing embarrassing, and after a bit even Nona began to be exasperated.

"Dearheart," Nona repeated patiently for the umpteenth time, "you will save money in the long run if you buy something nice that you can wear again on another occasion, rather than buying any old thing cheap, just because you hadn't planned on buying anything."

"Just because it's cheap doesn't mean I won't wear it again." Mona struggled in Nona's grasp. "I have no intention of spending money just so I can say I spent it."

Sighing, Nona stopped in front of a display rack covered in sensible women's business suits for middle-class matrons with delusions of executive positions following maternity leave.

"Look, here we go. Just for you. You can buy yourself an

ugly pseudo-power suit that you can wear while you soar through the bureaucracy in your tiny, partitioned cubicle."

"Don't make fun of my job. At least I can pay my own bills." Mona shook Nona off and fingered one of the skirts. "That's more than I can say for you."

"I have a commission," Nona replied smugly, "I'll have you know. I've had it for over a year now."

"Over a year now?" Mona said incredulously. "You've been sitting on someone's money for over a year now without producing anything?"

"No." Nona folded her arms. "Actually, they've been sending me a monthly stipend."

"And what have you produced?"

Nona hesitated, knowing Mona would mock her even if she'd produced several paintings. "A few sketches."

Releasing the hem of the skirt, Mona stared at Nona in shock. "Someone sends you money every month for over a year, and all you've done is a few sketches! Who is this fool? And how can I get in on this?"

"I don't know." Nona shrugged, and tried to pretend to be interested in the business suits. "Everything all goes through this lawyer's office."

"You don't know who you're working for?" How Mona was able to talk with her jaw hanging open, Nona couldn't figure. "Do you even know what they want?"

"Well, not really. They want something that could work either as a small, little piece or possibly a mural. Every now and then, they talk about perhaps doing some statuary. I don't think they know what they want." Nona waved her hands helplessly.

"There's something wrong there," Mona declared. "No one just throws money at someone for nothing."

Tightening her mouth wouldn't help, Nona realized.

Mona might not understand the artistic temperament, but she did understand business. "Actually, I have a suspicion that it might be Ageon."

"Ageon?" Mona frowned. "Why Ageon? I thought you said he hated you."

"Yes, but you see, I can only work in the country, I can't seem to work here in the city. So, I have to get away to go work, and that gets me away from Zarrad."

"Why would Ageon do it that way?"

Nona goggled at her sister. "That's a dumb question."

"No, I mean, if Ageon really wanted to separate you two, surely he could do a better job than that."

"I hadn't thought of that."

"Tell me about these sketches," Mona demanded. "Do you talk to this lawyer much?"

"I just sketch whatever. Beach scenes usually. The waves and the sand. Sometimes people."

"And the lawyer? Do you see him often?"

"Occasionally. Not often." Nona shrugged. "We have lunch once a month, maybe a little oftener, and talk. Just chit-chat, really. He complains to me about his wife; I usually end up talking with him about . . ." Nona covered her mouth with her hand, a horrible thought taking over her mind.

Zarrad. She usually talked about Zarrad.

"What?" Mona shook Nona.

"Auveron. Ageon mentioned Auveron." Nona bit her lip. How could she have been so dense? "Auveron would pay a monthly stipend for information on Zarrad and Ageon."

Mona pulled out her cell phone. "We have to call Hjell."

A young fairy stepped up behind Mona, putting one hand on her shoulder while his other hand grabbed her cell phone. "I don't think so." He snatched the phone from her hand and tried to turn her around by her shoulder.

Unfortunately, the much-abused remaining shoulder of her red dress couldn't take the strain and ripped. Leaving the stunned fairy clutching the back of Mona's—really Nona's—dress. Leaving Mona to catch the front of the dress before it plunged too far.

"You little creep!" Nona lunged past Mona, grabbing the fairy by his heavy navy jacket and tossing him into the women's business suit display. Red, black, and purple suits flew off the shelves to litter the floor and nearby racks.

A human man stepped in to rescue the fairy, looming over Nona and growling. Mona punched him, all the while clutching the top of her dress to keep it from falling.

He staggered back, holding his nose and howling, knocking over a circular rack of skirts. Plastic clip-hangers skidded over the floor, dragging denim and khaki. The aluminum rack rolled ringingly across the scarred linoleum. The clattering echoed in the warehouse-like building.

"My phone!" Mona screamed. "Where's my phone?"

Nona pounced on the dazed fairy, checking his hand for the phone. It wasn't there. It wasn't in his jacket pockets, one of which had a terrible rip. She opened his jacket; his loud tourist print shirt had two pockets over his chest. It wasn't there. The only place left were the pockets of his hideous Bermuda shorts.

"Hey!" he shouted as she checked his pants pockets. He tried to shove her off him, succeeding only in completely ripping the right side seam of her dress.

"Oh!" Nona screamed. "Help!"

"I just want to know why you put Zarrad in the hospital," the fairy said as he tried to crawl away. "He didn't seem to want to go."

"We're going to put you in the hospital!" Mona kicked at the fairy. He dodged into a flat rack, sending flimsy, pastel, button-down summer shirts scattering.

The rack started to topple, then stopped, leaning against the next rack over. For a moment it paused, then the rack it leaned against slowly tilted. Nona watched in fascinated horror as a whole series of racks fell like dominoes.

The clothes might be cheap and ugly, but they didn't deserve to be treated like trash.

"My phone!" Mona shrieked. "He stole my phone and ripped our clothes! Help! Help!"

The human dodged past Nona but knocked Mona down as he tried to reach the fairy. Mona let go of her clothes to try to break her fall. The red dress tangled around her legs. The human had succeeded in getting the fairy up from the floor, and it was obvious they were going to make a run for it.

Nona grabbed their ankles as they passed her.

The three of them fell in a heap on scattered clothes, slipping and sliding on the fabric-covered linoleum.

Scrambling to get up, the human's foot connected with the skirt of Nona's tattered dress, ripping it completely off.

"Excuse me, Ma'am," he murmured.

In response, Nona punched his nose again.

He howled as his nose began bleeding.

Mona, dressed only in bra and panties, leapt into the fray, kicking and clawing at the fairy.

Skidding through the layers of clothes on the floor, the men crawled for a clear section of floor with Nona and Mona in hot pursuit. Two other men assisted the ones on the floor, and they escaped the women's wrath, running out of the store faster than Nona had ever seen anyone move.

Nona looked up into the wide-eyed, open-mouthed expressions of the clerks and customers around them. Mona tossed her something, and she clutched it to cover strategic portions of herself.

Similarly arrayed, Mona stood up. "We'll take these. Do you have fitting rooms nearby?"

A stern, frowning gnome woman pointed to the right. "The fitting rooms are there. We've called the police."

Of course. Nona smiled at her, and trotted behind her sister to the fitting rooms.

Chapter 18

The cold, hard floor pressed against Boris' chest and stomach. Forrest held his arms behind his back, and Forrest's knee pressed, gently, against the tender spot between Boris' wings.

"I surrender," Boris gasped.

Forrest held him a moment longer, as if to make certain Boris wasn't playing for sympathy. Then he let Boris go.

"Ha!" Forrest crowed.

Boris stretched his aching arms. "Where'd you learn that?"

"Working for Zarrad. His father, Ageon, had me take martial arts lessons so I could bodyguard, along with whatever else they wanted me to do."

"I've had martial arts training, too," Boris complained as he sat carefully on the bed. His back had taken a pounding. "Obviously not as good. So who's Zarrad?"

"I met him shortly after we'd separated, after running off from the Ploofs. He's a human, but his father wishes he were a fairy. Ageon's a fairy. He seems to think only a fairy can take over his business." Forrest sat next to Boris on the bed, also cautiously, but Boris knew Forrest was waiting for the fight to resume.

"What business is that?" Boris had no wish to resume their play-fight. Not without magic. A fairy needed every little advantage he could get.

"They're connected."

"Oh."

"So, what've you been doing for the last six years?"

"Well." Boris leaned back against the wall. It was hard against his wings, but the cool made his back feel better. "I ran into a fairy. His mother wants him to be human. We opened an Internet/catalog company. We're partners, but mostly it's his; he had more start-up cash. You'll never guess his name."

Forrest shrugged.

"Jared."

Boris could almost see the cogwheels in Forrest's head turning.

"Zarrad and Jared. Hmmm." Forrest also leaned back against the wall, finally relaxing. "Let me guess. Jared's twin supposedly died in separation, but his mother doesn't really talk about it."

"Yup."

"And, how did you end up here? In the hospital, not Miami. We'll get to that later."

"I don't want to talk about it." Boris examined his hands a moment. He knew his brother would learn all about his humiliation, but why rush things . . .

"I ended up here when Zarrad, most uncharacteristically, attacked his father and his father's men. It seems they thought he'd gone crazy. He certainly acted like it. He didn't even recognize his own father."

"Jared," Boris said.

"Jared," Forrest agreed. "And you?"

"Do you know anything about a necklace?"

"A gold-and-silver braided necklace that makes the wearer fall in love with Zarrad?" Forrest grinned.

"Yup."

"Yeah. I know a little. What about it?"

Boris examined his hands again. "I was wearing it, when they put me in here."

Forrest snickered. "I'd have paid to see that."

"Bet they think I was you." It cheered Boris to see Forrest stop snickering. "Not so funny now."

"Actually, I was thinking that we have a serious problem here." Forrest sat up, frowning.

"What would that be?"

"We're going to rot here, until they finally figure this out." Forrest's right fist hit his left hand. "And the way they're going about it, that could be a long time."

Boris gently punched his brother's arm. "Naw. Jared'll spring me. I'm sure of it."

"And just where do you think Jared is now?"

"Don't know. Probably the next cell over." Boris wilted a bit, slumping farther onto the lumpy mattress. Forrest might be right. They could be in for a long wait, if Jared couldn't convince anyone of his sanity. "Where's Zarrad?"

"Who knows?" Forrest said glumly, slumping a bit himself. "Could be a cell. Could be he's escaped. Probably as far away from here as he can get."

"Maybe Jared'll escape. He's pretty good about that sort of thing."

Forrest sighed and looked at the door.

Bored with sitting and seeing his chance, Boris pounced. "Gotcha!"

They rolled to the floor, struggling and flailing.

"Winner gets the bed," Boris shouted.

He opened his mouth again, preparing a spell. Forrest shoved a sock into it.

Zarrad had just about had enough of his other self, dream or not. Why couldn't he go faster? They had to get out of these hospital corridors fast. This idiot fairy just didn't seem to get it. "Forget the letter, let's get out of here."

"It's important," the fairy insisted. "Where do you think they'd keep our clothes?"

"Who cares?" Zarrad looked down the night-quiet corridor around the corner. There was a promising exit sign above a door at the end and no one in sight. He wanted out of here. "Looks like a back door this way."

"But, Amelia's letter—"

"Who is Amelia?" Zarrad grabbed the fairy's thin hospital shirt-front and shook him. "I've never heard of her. Why is she so important?"

"Mother," the fairy whispered.

"Mother?" Zarrad breathed. He let go, and the fairy straightened his hospital tunic. Zarrad shook his head. This couldn't be happening. He really would go crazy, if he didn't get a hold on himself. "No. No. No. I am not crazy. I will not *be* crazy. My mother is dead."

"So's my father." The fairy sounded as if he was on the wrong side of hysterical.

"Shut up." Zarrad ground his teeth. "Just shut up. Don't say another word."

"Hey!" a bass voice far behind them shouted. "What're you doing out? Hey!"

"Run!" Zarrad grabbed the fairy's arm and fled toward the exit.

The footsteps behind them sounded like a thundering herd of elephants getting a stampede underway. The exit door broke open to a loud, wailing alarm as Zarrad crashed into it. Zarrad stumbled out into the cool darkness with his doppelganger beside him.

Outside, Axel whirled around to face them, standing just inside the circle of light by the door, ready to block any escape. His eyes bugged out of his head, and his jaw dropped as he stared at them.

The fairy Zarrad dropped him with a single, well-placed kick to the head.

"Wow!" Zarrad stood looking at Axel, spread-eagle on the ground, out cold. "How'd you do that?"

Grabbing Zarrad's arm, the fairy shouted, "Run!"

The sound of the thundering elephant stampede gaining ground and momentum behind them urged them away from the revealing streetlights and toward the comforting recesses of the dark night.

The police were waiting when Mona stepped out of the fitting room. A rumpled, half-troll half-human changeling seemed to be in charge. She'd ended up with an apple-red power-suit skirt and pastel-orange, flimsy, spaghetti-strap summer shirt. Not exactly how she wanted to greet the police. Or anyone else.

The rumpled changeling glanced at her clothes and smiled. He also held up a cell phone. "Is this yours?"

"Yes. Thank you." Mona slipped the phone back into her purse.

Nona hesitantly exited the fitting room. She glared at Mona, exasperated. "Would you look at this?" Her hands smoothed over an embroidered, denim peasant blouse and tight, lime-green polyester Capri pants. "You couldn't have paid attention to what you threw me? This is hideous! I'll never live this down. It's a nightmare."

"Well, pick something else out," Mona drawled, trying to keep her temper in check.

"I will!" Nona stalked off. "And I'll get you something else too. We cannot be seen in public like this."

The policeman still had his smile plastered on his face. It looked permanent. "I'm Lieutenant Wight, Miami Police Department. Can you tell me what happened?"

Mona explained that she and her sister had been shopping for clothes when a fairy and a human attacked them, took her cell phone, and ripped their clothes off. She told him there were other men with the two that attacked them, but they didn't get involved with the fight, just the escape. The lieutenant took notes as she talked. When she was done, he asked for a description of the men. She had to repeat her descriptions three times, and each time he seemed more amused.

Nona returned before he could ask any more questions. "Here, this is for you." She handed Mona a muted, pale-blue print dress. "This is for me." Nona held a short, black miniskirt and tight, elastic blouse up to herself. After Mona admired her outfit, Nona began trying to herd Mona back into the changing rooms. "Come on. Let's get changed. Before anyone else sees us like this."

"I need to finish talking to Lieutenant Wight. And I want blue jeans. Sturdy, heavy duty, denim, with lots of pockets, blue jeans. And a durable shirt."

Sighing with exasperation, Nona snatched the dress from Mona's unresisting hand and stalked off.

Lieutenant Wight shrugged. "If you'll just answer one question, we'll hold off on the others until you're changed." After Mona nodded, he asked, "I just have to know, would one of you two happen to be Mona Silvan, from Wisconsin?"

"I'm Mona Silvan."

To Mona's surprise, the Lieutenant grinned like an idiot. "Thought so."

Nona hustled over, flinging blue jeans and a knit blouse at Mona, before pushing her over to the fitting rooms. "Come on."

"I'll be waiting here when you're done," Lieutenant

205

Wight called to them, as he waved his notebook.

Mona pulled the curtain across the door to one cubicle. As she pulled off her mismatched clothes, she said, "We need to call Hjell."

"Wait until after the police are gone," Nona whispered from the next booth. "He doesn't get along well with the police."

Ageon stormed through the corridors of his house, Hjell having loosed the current crisis. Though Ageon couldn't really blame him, he was just the messenger; the problem had been going on a long time.

Auveron. Everywhere he turned today, there was Auveron. Did the man never sleep?

Wishing he could drop with exhaustion, Ageon arrived at the top of the stairs to the foyer.

Below him, one of his guards, Merce, sat in a hard, wooden chair by the reinforced, bulletproof front window, keeping an eye on the front of the house.

"Merce!" Ageon called, glad to see that at least this once Merce wasn't sleeping at his post. Though, as uncomfortable as the hard chair was to Merce's wings, it was amazing that the man could sleep there at all. Ageon wondered if someone had warned Merce about Hjell's call, and that was why Merce was ready and waiting.

"Yo, Boss." Merce turned and looked away from the window, up at Ageon.

"Stig will be arriving soon, with Nona and Mona. Let them in and send them up to my office."

"Sure, Boss." Merce appeared confused. "Who's Mona?"

"Nona's sister. Zarrad's wife."

"Zarrad's married to Nona's sister?" Merce shouted, as

he started to stand up in surprise.

"Shut up. Sit down." Ageon ran his hands through his hair. He didn't need this from his subordinates. It was bad enough Zarrad had gone off the deep end, without everyone making a scandal out of it. Though, in truth, Ageon saw no way to hush this up and avoid a scandal. Merce's reaction was merely the tip of an iceberg Ageon desperately wanted to avoid. "Just watch for them and send them up."

"Sure, no problem, Boss." Merce sat back down and turned to watch out the window.

Ageon headed for his office, wishing he could rest. He'd endured enough scandal when Amelia had run off, right after their son was born. He pushed thoughts of Amelia from his mind. He had to concentrate on the current problem, not old ones.

He couldn't help thinking about that old scandal. It brought back all those old feelings. It made this situation seem so familiar. So, why was he so certain that something was slipping through his fingers? Again.

Jared leaned against the shadowy, splintered wooden fence, trying to ease the stitch in his side without piercing himself with slivers or stabbing his wounded wing. The other Jared, the human Jared, walked in slow circles on the sidewalk nearby. They'd lost their pursuit a while back, but they still kept to the dark areas of the street, away from the streetlights, trying not to call attention to themselves.

Remembering that Boris was still at the hospital, Jared groaned. "We have to go back."

"What?" the other Jared asked, incredulous. "We barely got away."

"Boris is back there," Jared gasped out. "We've got to help him."

"If that idiot can't get out himself, he can stay locked up." The other Jared stopped circling. "After all the trouble he's put me through today."

"It's not his fault." Jared pushed himself carefully away from the fence, avoiding any splinters. "This whole day has to be Amelia's fault. All this confusion, it's typical of her. Besides, I still need to get that letter for you."

The other Jared shook his head, but Jared couldn't read his expression in the dark. "Then we're splitting up, because I'm not going back there."

"Can we?"

"Can we what?"

"Can we split up?"

Several splinters stabbed into Jared's back and wings, as the other Jared slammed him into the fence.

"I am not crazy. You do not exist." The other Jared straightened himself up. "I'm going to Nona's apartment, and I'm going to talk with her, and get her to release me from this stupid spell." He pointed at Jared. "You can do what you want. I don't care."

"You know where Nona's apartment is?" Jared asked as he pulled out the splinters he could reach.

"Of course." The other Jared rattled off an address.

While trying to memorize it, Jared wondered about his ability to recall correctly through this craziness. Or perhaps it was a dream; his head had been hit pretty hard. In which case, the address was a figment of his imagination anyway. Like the other Jared. The human Jared. But . . . "I spent all day looking for Nona's apartment. Couldn't find it."

The other Jared stalked off purposefully down the sidewalk. "I'm leaving. You don't exist. I'm not crazy." He passed under a streetlight, then faded into the darkness beyond, until Jared could only hear his footsteps, and then they faded away, leaving Jared alone, listening to the far-off sounds of night traffic, electrical transformers, and the occasional dog barking.

Jared waited a moment to see if he would dissolve into nothingness, or fade into invisibility, or disappear off the face of the earth.

It didn't happen.

"Maybe *you* don't exist," Jared muttered to the darkness where the other Jared had disappeared.

He started back the way he'd come. He wouldn't abandon Boris. They were friends. Even if Boris hadn't backed him up in the fight. Which was as strange as the rest of the day. Maybe Boris was crazy.

There had to be a good reason. And some sound and sane explanation for everything that had happened.

Right?

Mona hadn't been thrilled about getting into the car Ageon had sent for them. She was even less thrilled about going into his house. If the hints she'd been getting from Nona could be believed, she worried that they were stepping out of the frying pan and into the fire.

But Hjell had insisted that they tell Ageon what they knew. He'd even come to the store, to personally convince them. After he'd made certain the police weren't there any longer.

Hjell hadn't tried any rough stuff. Instead, he'd been polite, concerned, and kind. He'd spoken very quietly and very gently, and he'd practically begged them to talk to Ageon. To help him and Ageon. When that hadn't worked, he'd begged them to help Jared.

That was an appeal Mona found hard to resist. Jared didn't deserve to be abandoned when he had clearly lost his senses. He might be a two-timing rat, but he'd cared for her once. Probably still did.

So, Hjell had eased them into Ageon's car and into the care of Stig, the driver. Then Hjell had returned to the hospital. Mona almost wished he'd come with them.

Exiting the car, Nona's hand shook as she grasped Mona's arm. Mona tossed her head back, and straightened her back. She'd be damned if she let some high-priced hoodlum scare her.

Stig ushered them up to the front door, where a heavy fairy smiled at them. "Nona, Mona, meet Merce."

Merce shook hands with both of them. "Nice to meet you." He stared at Mona longer than she cared for, before turning to Stig. "The Boss said to take them up to his office."

"Follow me, ladies." Stig led the way up the stairs.

Ageon's mansion was huge, hushed, and expensively decorated. Lush, deep carpet made a path down the center of a light oak floor. Tasteful art, by artists both living and dead, graced the walls of the hallways Stig led them through.

None of it by Nona, Mona noticed, wondering if Nona noticed, or cared. It sure irritated Mona. Didn't anyone know or see what a wonderful artist her sister was? Ageon should have been paying Nona a stipend for art that Mona considered every bit as good as the stuff hanging on the walls.

Ageon's office was guarded by a heavy, dark, wood door. Stig pounded on the door, and a muffled sound came from within. Stig opened the door, waving them in, and announcing, "Nona Bryce and Mona Silvan."

The office was sparse. A conference table with ten identical black chairs, unadorned cream walls, and lush carpet.

No phone, no desk, no computer, no bookcases or books. Mona guessed it was a supplementary office, for when he conferenced or just didn't want to let someone into the inner sanctum.

Moving his chair closer to the head of the table, Ageon waved to the left side of the table. "Have a seat."

After they'd both sat, he stared first at one, then the other for a moment, before settling on Mona. "What happened at the store?"

Between the two of them, Mona and Nona managed to get the story out. Ageon listened to the whole thing before asking questions.

"Describe the fairy again," he said.

Mona did so, adding, "The lieutenant had me repeat the fairy's description three times. Do you know the fairy?"

Ageon grimaced. "It sounds like Little Jimmy Auveron."

"*Little* Jimmy?" Mona said.

"He's a junior. Named after his father." Ageon leaned back in his chair, causing it to squeak. "And he's on the short side. And not the brightest. And apparently all over Miami today. And possibly the cause of Zarrad's little problem."

"Auveron," Nona whispered. "Little Jimmy asked about Zarrad."

"Can you remember exactly what he said?" Ageon prompted.

"He wanted to know why we'd put Zarrad in the hospital." Nona cowered in her chair.

Covering his face with his hands, Ageon leaned forward to rest his elbows on the table. He sighed.

"Why are you concerned about this Little Jimmy Auveron?" Mona asked.

"His father wants to take over my business." Ageon sat

up, drumming his fingers against the polished tabletop. He focused his attention on Nona. "Tell me about your commission."

"Well, see," Nona sputtered. "It's through this lawyer."

"This lawyer have a name?" Ageon growled.

Nona winced and whispered, "Tergal Delpresti."

Ageon also winced. He slumped down in his chair.

"Do you know him?" Mona asked.

Grimacing at her, Ageon said, "He's been known to do legal work for Little Jimmy." He closed his eyes a moment before looking at Nona again. "Let me guess. You've just had, or just scheduled, a meeting with Delpresti."

Nona nodded.

Slumping farther down into his chair, Ageon said, "All right. Tell me about your commission."

Chapter 19

Zarrad stormed off down the sidewalk, chanting to himself, "I am not crazy. I am not crazy!" There was no fairy Zarrad. Just him. Just the human. Being human was good enough. Deciding he'd had enough of skulking around in the shadows, he walked through the glare of a streetlight and into the darkness beyond.

Four figures appeared in front of him in the darkness.

"Maybe you are. Maybe you're not."

Little Jimmy. It had to be. Zarrad sighed. Forrest had been right, Auveron was here. That explained a lot about today.

"Now, we're going to settle up over what happened with the police today." Little Jimmy stepped forward. He didn't appear quite as Zarrad remembered him. He was still a scrappy little fairy irritant. The clothes were unusual, but Zarrad had seen him in stranger things. As Little Jimmy took another step forward, Zarrad realized it was the eyes. There was something wild and furious in Little Jimmy's eyes.

Under other circumstances, Zarrad would have dismissed Little Jimmy as a lunatic, what with his babbling on about the police and the madness in those eyes. But it had been a very long day, and Zarrad was no longer certain just where sanity was.

"What are you talking about?" Zarrad took a step back. "What about the police?"

"You had us arrested!" Little Jimmy screamed. "Don't

you dare stand there and act all innocent, like you weren't arrested today."

"I wasn't." Zarrad took another step back. "You're nuts!"

"You were there with us!" Little Jimmy aimed his fist at Zarrad and shook it. "Don't tell me that idiot didn't give you my message."

"This is the first time I've seen you today!" Zarrad dodged Little Jimmy's shaky fist. "I heard you were in town, but no one gave me any messages. Have you lost your mind?"

"You're not going to get to me this time," Little Jimmy said, nostrils flaring, eyes flaming mad. "I know you know me. I know you got my message. And you're not messing with my mind any more."

"Right. Sure." Zarrad backed away again. He had enough troubles without Little Jimmy adding to them. "Why don't you go home?"

Little Jimmy screamed incoherently and began flailing at Zarrad.

Zarrad took off running, back the way he'd come, wishing he'd learned more about defending himself without any weapons. It had never seemed necessary before. Now, with Little Jimmy hot on his heels and no weapon at hand, it seemed a vital gap in his education.

After passing into the semi-dark beyond the streetlight, he dodged into an alley to get deeper into the darkness of night. Little Jimmy ran past the opening of the alley, obviously not realizing Zarrad had turned aside.

Little Jimmy's men followed behind Little Jimmy, slower and not as certain.

Breathing with his mouth open to keep from making any noise, Zarrad began stealthily following them.

★ ★ ★ ★ ★

A knock at the door interrupted Nona as she told Ageon about her commission. Not that there'd been all that much to tell. And there was really no reason for Mona and Ageon to keep exchanging patronizing glances about what she'd said.

So she didn't know much about business. Nona could barely contain herself from flinging the fact that she'd managed to support herself—and very well, thank you, better than Mona'd done—without knowing everything they knew. Yes, the money had come from Zarrad, and probably originated with Ageon, but it was hers now. She wasn't quite as stupid as all that.

Stig's entrance was a relief.

"Call for you, Boss." Stig held out a cell phone. "It's Hjell."

"Speak," Ageon said as he put the phone to his ear. "Uh-huh." He closed his eyes. "Uh-huh." He switched ears and sighed. "Is he all right?" The answer to that took a while. Ageon pinched the bridge of his nose. "Is he coherent at all?" A short pause while Ageon studied Nona. "Meet me here. I have an idea."

His scrutiny unnerved Nona. She didn't want to know but asked anyway, "Is everything all right?"

"Zarrad escaped. He got completely away." Ageon tossed the phone to Stig. "Knocked Axel out. They think Axel has a concussion. He's not making much sense. He says Zarrad attacked him from both sides at once."

"Oh, no." Mona grabbed Nona's hand.

"The hospital has no idea where he's at. He disappeared, and they say he had someone with him. Probably that idiot, Ploof, with the necklace." He rolled his eyes.

Nona clutched Mona. "Oh, no." They looked at each

215

other, frightened. What to do now?

"Would you be willing to help me catch him again?" Ageon asked.

"How?" Mona asked cautiously. Nona's unease increased. Whatever Ageon had in mind, it couldn't be good.

Ageon placed his hands flat on the table. "The first time he escaped, he headed for you." He nodded at Mona. "I think this time he'll head for your apartment." He stared straight into Nona's eyes. "If you're willing to be the bait, I think we can trap him."

A shiver ran through Nona, and her wings fluttered. Could she do this? Could she face Zarrad? A crazed Zarrad?

Memories of her and Zarrad in happier times drifted through her mind. A laughing Zarrad on the beach. Zarrad with flowers and candy and jewelry, trying desperately to impress her. He'd always praised her art and her talent. He'd always listened to her rant and rave and complain. The way he smiled, and the little crinkles that appeared around his eyes when he did.

She nodded, not trusting herself to speak. Zarrad would have done the same for her, if he'd had to. Right?

"Are you sure?" Mona whispered, leaning close.

"He needs help." Nona half-smiled. "And he can be very sweet."

Mona nodded, half-smiling herself.

"What do we do now?" Nona asked, straightening and trying to convince herself that she was brave and strong.

Forrest lay on the lumpy uncomfortable bed, on top of the tousled covers, staring at the plain white ceiling of his little room. Or perhaps it was Boris' room. It was difficult to tell any more. The bed was definitely his. "I spy with my little eye—"

"Oh give it up, we've spied everything in this room," Boris grumbled from the floor.

"I still think that crack along the ceiling looks like a worm."

"It's not moving."

"Well, no. It's just badly-applied plaster." Forrest rolled onto his side to peer down at his brother on the floor. Boris lay on his back, with his eyes closed and his arms up, pillowing his head. The picture of perfect misery on the cold, hard floor. "You said you thought Jared would spring us. Do you think we should just spring ourselves?"

Boris rolled onto his stomach, and put his arms over his head. His voice was muffled by the floor and his arms. "No. The hospital staff would just put us back in here. Go to sleep."

"I'm not tired."

"I am."

Forrest flung himself back on the bed to stare at the ceiling. Though he'd won the bed, he'd considered letting Boris have it to sleep, but since Boris usually won their fights, it seemed a shame to surrender his few, rare spoils.

"You ever consider taking another partner in your business?" Forrest asked.

"No. Now let me sleep." Boris shifted on the floor. "I'd pay money to get you to let me sleep."

"Really?" Forrest grinned to himself. Here was an opportunity to sell his well-won spoils at a very good price. "I'll tell you what. I'll let you have the bed and let you sleep, if you take me on as a partner in your business." He rolled to his side to peer down at Boris again.

Boris propped himself up on one arm. "I can't do that without Jared's say-so. However, if you let me have the bed and let me sleep, I'll do what I can to convince him."

"Good enough." Forrest swung his legs off the side of the bed and stood up. "And if he won't let me become a partner, then you'll just owe me."

"Okay." Boris crawled into the bed.

In seconds, his snores echoed off the walls.

Forrest sat in the plain, white plastic chair, grinning. He slouched down, letting his head fall forward, as he'd seen Merce do so many times.

Soon two sets of snores struggled for dominance in the little room.

Jared heard screaming and yelling off in the distant darkness, from the direction the other Jared had taken. For a moment he feared that the other Jared had dissolved in some horrible, tortured way into nothingness. He stood under a streetlight, grateful for the comfort of the light in this dark, strange city. Then he heard several sets of running footsteps headed his way. Had someone tried to hurt his other self? Was the other Jared in trouble? Jared tensed, preparing to fight.

The young fairy in the heavy navy jacket ran into view, the bossy, annoying, punk fairy that had tried to kidnap him today. The punk fairy stopped when he saw Jared waiting for him.

Pointing at Jared, he said, "You're going to pay!"

"For what?" Jared demanded. "You're the one who tried to kidnap me."

"So, now you admit you know me." The young fairy circled in, trying to find a good vantage point to throw a punch.

"I have no idea who you are." Jared kept his eye on the fairy, while waiting for whoever belonged to the other footsteps to appear. "You're just some nutcase that tries to kidnap people."

The fairy screamed incoherently and jumped forward, flailing at Jared.

Jared dodged him and brought his own fist down hard on the sensitive spot between the fairy's wings. The fairy fell to the sidewalk as his associates appeared. Jared backed away, holding his hands up. "He attacked me first."

"We know," one man said, looking at Jared like Jared was an idiot.

"I don't want any trouble here," Jared said. "I just want to be left alone." And to spring Boris from the hospital, and to find Mona, and to tell her that he loved her, and set this crazy weekend straight. But these people didn't need to know all that.

The young fairy on the ground rolled over to sit, panting. "So, just answer me a few questions. That's all I ask."

"Okay," Jared said hesitantly. Answering questions didn't sound so bad. Of course it depended on the questions. "What?"

"Why did they force you to go to the hospital?"

"How did you know about that?" Jared asked suspiciously.

"I followed Ploof." The young fairy stood. "Why the hospital?"

"I injured my wing. They thought it needed medical attention. It didn't." Jared had no intention of adding any details; they were none of this fool's business.

"Oh come on!" The young fairy threw up his hands in disgust. "Everyone knows you're human. You're not fooling anyone."

"I am a fairy. I have wings. One was injured." Jared wanted to wipe the incredulous look off the fairy's face with a swift right, but didn't dare throw the first punch with the odds stacked against him.

"Prove to this idiot that he's human." The fairy waved to his associates. "Show him his fake wings. Rip the shirt off his back."

"Like you did with his girlfriend?" one of the men said.

"Shut up!" the fairy said.

"What?" Jared shouted.

Before he could pursue this new wrinkle on his troubles, Jared found himself surrounded. It was a short struggle. The fabric of his hospital tunic was no match for the other men. They easily ripped it off him just by grabbing and pulling. He punched the nearest man.

Someone tackled him. Jared hit the sidewalk, scraping his hands and elbows on a section of loose cement, sending pebbles and dust scattering. Someone sitting on his back grabbed the tops of his wings and pulled painfully. Jared screamed.

"They're attached." Whoever was sitting on him let go of the wings but remained sitting heavily. Hands shoved his head and shoulders down, pushing his face into the dusty sidewalk. Grit coated the side of his face and was ground into his mouth. "He's a fairy!" Jared squirmed and tried to roll over as they spread his wings out. "There's a wound on this one."

Jared quit trying to roll and grabbed some of the cement gravel and dust from the loose patch with both hands. He threw one handful into the face of the man on his back. The man howled. Jared knocked him off and got up, throwing his other handful into the face of his nearest attacker. The third he punched in the stomach, leaving him facing only the young fairy.

"You're lying!" the fairy shouted at him.

"Really?" Jared grabbed the fairy's heavy navy jacket and

pulled it over his head. "Is this a lie?" He punched the fairy in the stomach and ran to hide behind a nearby car.

"Where'd he go?" one of the men rubbing his face demanded.

"I'm right here."

Jared watched himself step out of the darkness on the far side of the fight from where he hid. He pinched himself, to make certain he was still where he was at. Sure enough he was. And unfortunately, he wasn't dreaming. His human doppelganger was back.

The other Jared swaggered over to the young fairy. He still had a hospital shirt on. "Any more questions?"

The young fairy pulled his jacket off and threw it on the ground. "I challenge you to a spell-duel."

"You can't do that. I'm human." The other Jared shrugged. "It's illegal. It's immoral. And it's a really tacky, uncouth thing to do."

"We all saw your wings!" one of the other men shouted. "You're a fairy."

"No, I'm not." The other Jared pulled his shirt off and turned around in a circle, spotlighted by the streetlight, so that they could all see his bare, wingless, back. "I'm human. I can't spell-duel. Just not possible. I can't do magic."

"We saw!" the young fairy shrieked.

His associates were rapidly moving away from the scene. The other Jared growled at the young fairy, then howled like a wolf at the moonless sky. When the echoes of his howl died away, he grinned dementedly at the young fairy, who swiftly ran screaming down the street.

Jared cautiously stood up from his hiding place behind the car. He approached the other Jared, who was still grinning dementedly. Cautiously, carefully, Jared poked the other on the shoulder. He was real.

221

"That was fun." The other pulled his shirt over his head. "And I can't think of anyone more deserving than him."

"Who was that?" Jared asked.

"Little Jimmy Auveron. The bane of my existence." The other Jared stopped grinning like a lunatic, settling for a merely self-satisfied expression. "So, are you still going to rescue Ploof?"

"Yes." Jared shrugged. "You still going to find Nona?"

"Yes." The other frowned a moment. "Do you think he really ripped the shirt off Nona?"

"Don't know." Jared looked himself in the eye. He'd never been able to do that before, but now it seemed exactly right. "It wouldn't be a good idea with Mona. She'd knock him into next week."

"I can't see Nona putting up with that." The other shook his head.

"Ask when you see her."

"I'll do that."

They nodded to each other and parted ways.

Mona leaned against the wall in the dim recesses of the hallway leading to Nona's bedroom. She wished there was some better way to do this. She didn't much like the idea of her sister being bait for an insane Jared.

Hjell stood in front of her, his large bulk nearly blocking her view. Stig hid in the dark kitchen. Ageon sat behind the flimsy wicker couch. He'd been crouching for a long time in an uncomfortable squat, but his legs had finally given out.

Nona sat in the wicker couch, quiet and nervous, pretending to read a book. No one said anything.

As Nona shifted her legs, to tuck them under her, the wicker creaked and twanged. "I don't think he's coming."

"Patience," Ageon whispered. "Is the door unlocked?"

"Yes." Nona had answered that question the same way the last five times Ageon had asked.

Just as Hjell took a step forward, they heard the click of the door handle turning. Everyone froze.

"Nona!" Jared said. "Oh Nona. You look wonderful!" Jared still had on his wrinkled hospital clothes, which flapped loosely around him. His hair stood up on his head in almost every direction, and he looked tired and much, much older, more exhausted than crazy.

He closed the door behind him. Hjell wrapped a hand around Mona to keep her from running forward. She wanted so badly to protect her sister.

"Zarrad, how have you been?" Nona asked.

Mona hoped Jared missed the nervous quaver in her sister's voice.

"What a question!" Jared flung himself on the couch beside Nona. "You would not believe." He scrubbed his face with his hands. "Forget me, though. Are you all right? I ran into Little Jimmy. He said he'd ripped your shirt off. Did he hurt you?"

"Not my shirt, my dress. And one of his men did it. He got Mona's dress."

Jared turned away from Nona and punched the arm of the couch. "I'm going to skin that little bastard."

Hjell's hand dropped and he surged forward, with Mona on his heels. Stig popped out of the kitchen, and Ageon slowly unfolded from the floor.

They must have made too much noise, either that or Jared was prepared for them, because he turned back and grabbed Nona before she could jump off the couch.

"Take this spell off me! Please." Jared had his arms around Nona's waist, and her attempted flight had pulled him from the couch onto his knees on the floor. "I love you!"

Mona grabbed her sister's arms and pulled. Stig and Hjell grabbed various bits of Jared and pulled.

"Stop! No!" Jared shouted. "Help me! Please take this spell off me!" He clawed at Nona, slowly losing his grip, and tearing her new skirt.

"Be careful with him," Ageon shouted. "Don't hurt him."

"Don't hurt him?" Mona pulled Nona away from the tussle on the living room floor. "What about her?"

Nona had tears streaming down her face. Mona hugged her sister, allowing Nona to sob onto Mona's shoulder.

"She'll be fine." Ageon waved his hand dismissively.

"Don't you dare hurt her!" Jared shouted from somewhere in the mass of struggling bodies. "Let me go!"

Finally, Hjell and Stig had Jared trussed but unfortunately not gagged.

Ageon sighed. "Calm down. Calm down." He patted Jared's shoulder. "Everything is going to be all right." He turned back to Mona and Nona. "If you want to come with us, she'd better get changed."

Nona nodded. Mona helped her back to the bedroom and into another dress.

"We do seem to be going through clothes today," Mona joked.

"Yes." Nona smiled, wiping tears from her face. "We seem to do that every time we're together."

Back in the living room, Jared lay on the wicker couch, attempting to wriggle out of his bonds, held down by Hjell. The wicker creaked and groaned, warping this way and that beneath him.

"Let's go." Ageon held the door, first for Hjell and Stig

carrying Jared, then for Mona and Nona.

"I don't know about this," Nona whispered frantically to Ageon. "He'll just escape again."

"Not this time." Ageon took a deep breath. He whispered quickly, before they caught up with the others, "I'm going to have them tranquilize him, so he'll sleep the rest of the night."

Nona sighed. She leaned on Mona as they waited for the elevator.

Mona wondered if that would be enough. Everything about this situation screamed Amelia. Leaving Mona to ponder exactly how Amelia had engineered all this. This would have taken time and money. It seemed a bit much for Amelia to have handled, but yet it felt exactly like being in one of Amelia's situations.

Jared crept quietly down the hospital's deserted basement hall, reading the labels on the doors. How handy of hospitals to label all the rooms. It made finding things so much easier. Too bad being indoors without a shirt was just as cold as outside without a shirt. Or maybe it was just his imagination. He'd never gone shirtless before, to his knowledge.

Finally he found the room he was looking for, the laundry.

It didn't take long to locate a clean hospital shirt and clean white coat. He pulled on a pair of blue paper slippers in the hope they would add to his costume. He wanted to be mistaken for someone that worked at the hospital, a nurse or doctor or attendant. He wouldn't pass a close inspection, but at a distance no one would notice him.

He tiptoed out. Now to locate Boris.

Chapter 20

Finding an empty office with a computer made Jared feel all the more lucky. He closed the door behind him, turned the lights on, and made himself at home. The cluttered office spoke of a busy occupant, with a disordered desk covered in notes, papers, and junk. The walls were lined with filing cabinets and bookcases. None of that mattered to Jared; he powered up the computer and took it for a spin, made all the more easy by the fact that the computer's owner had taped his ID and password to the top of the monitor.

However, even after accessing the hospital's admittance routines, Jared couldn't find Boris. The hospital's software was too straightforward for Jared to suspect he hadn't broken in properly. No Boris Ploof was listed as a patient. No Boris Ploof was listed as having been treated in the last week.

Hoping they'd spelled his name wrong, Jared tried several variations on Boris, then on Ploof.

There was a Forrest Ploof registered.

Boris. Forrest. There was something familiar there. Jared tried to remember if Boris ever mentioned having a brother. Wouldn't it be funny if it turned out he had a brother? Forrest even had the same birthday as Boris. Twins, perhaps? Or had they originally been born a single half-breed, like himself?

But then, how would his twin have ended up here?

Weird, very weird. However, the whole day had been very weird. Maybe they'd just misunderstood Boris when he'd said his name. There were any of a number of explanations. Each stranger than the last. Jared decided he didn't care what the reason was.

Jared jotted down the room number given for Forrest Ploof on the unused top sheet of a small pad of paper and pocketed it. He closed what he'd been doing on the computer, powered it down, turned off the lights, and peeked out of the office.

No one was in sight. His luck was still holding. He wondered how long it would.

Walking confidently, as if he had business—which he actually did, sort of, just not the kind hospitals generally approved of—Jared headed through the quiet nighttime hospital for the elevators and the third-floor mental ward.

He stepped out of the elevator when the doors opened onto the third floor with as much confidence as when he'd entered. He realized his mistake as the doors closed behind him.

A troll waited behind a heavy reception desk in the starkly clean lobby by the elevators. The only way to get to the third floor rooms was past him. He recognized Jared, in a very negative way.

"Hey! You!" The troll scrambled from behind the desk.

Grabbing one of the two visitor chairs, Jared threw it at the troll. The troll knocked it out of the air, continuing his forward progress without pause. Jared tried a straightforward punch, but the troll grabbed his arm and tossed him.

He flew through the air, landing on the desk, rolling off onto the chair behind it, and tumbling to the floor.

While pulling himself up, he accidentally opened a desk drawer. It gave him added leverage to get up, and a bit more. Inside Jared saw what looked like a boxy stun-gun. He grabbed it and thrust it at the troll rounding the desk.

He connected with the troll's arm and the trigger at the same time.

Electricity arced. Sparks danced in front of Jared's eyes, and a strange, burning, ozone smell filled his nostrils. The troll jerked like a puppet on strings, eyes rolling back into his head, his mouth chomping on nothing, before collapsing on the floor.

A frantic search revealed no keys on the desk, or in any drawers. Jared shoved the troll and found a large key ring filled with keys attached to his belt.

Leaving the troll drooling on the floor, Jared raced down the corridor, slowing only to read the numbers on the doors. He found Boris' room and began flipping through the keys. The click and tinkle of the keys echoed in the bare corridor as he searched, but no one came to see what was going on. The keys had some code on them that Jared assumed would let anyone in the know pick the right one. Jared wished he'd been in the know.

He began systematically trying the keys.

The lock opened on the seventh one.

"Boris?" Jared said as he opened the door.

One man slept slumped in a white plastic chair. He looked like Boris. An identical one drew covers over his head and mumbled for whoever-it-was to go away. Definitely twins. Boris had a brother.

It had been a very weird day. Jared wasn't about to question anything he found any more.

"Hurry. Wake up! We have to get out of here." Jared leaned back to check the corridor, but the troll hadn't roused and no one had noticed yet.

The man in the chair stretched and yawned, twisting and turning to straighten his back. He blinked up at Jared and grinned. "Jared Silvan, I presume?"

Since the one on the chair had no wings, Jared concluded the one on the bed was Boris. He hesitantly held out his hand. "Forrest Ploof?"

"Ah. Yes. Pleased to meet you." Forrest stood and shook Jared's hand, before smacking his brother's shoulder. "Wake up. Now."

Boris sat up and glanced from Jared to Forrest. "You couldn't let me sleep."

"Things are just getting interesting." Forrest grabbed Boris by the arm and hauled him to his feet. "I think Jared knows."

Wondering what he was supposed to know, Jared said, "Not a clue. Trust me, not a clue. Life has been very weird today." He grabbed Forrest's arm. "But we have to hurry, if we're going to get out of here." As they raced down the hall, Jared looked back to ask, "Did you ever tell me you had a brother?"

"I don't remember. I might have," Boris said from the rear of their little parade. As they passed the still unconscious troll, he added, "Glad you got him. He was obnoxious."

They made it into the elevator without anyone the wiser.

"Do either of you know where they keep patients' clothes here?" Jared asked.

"First floor. In admittance. There's a room with a whole bunch of lockers." Forrest grinned smugly. "Some of us actually cooperated."

"Good for you," Boris grumbled.

The elevator doors opened. Jared motioned for Forrest to go first. "Could you lead us?"

"Follow me."

It seemed odd, seeing two Borises walking along, arguing quietly with each other. Yet, it felt right. They were obviously very comfortable with each other. Jared wondered if he'd ever see the other Jared again. If the other Jared was real. If he should mention all this to Boris and Forrest. He'd probably just sound crazy again. Perhaps later, after they'd escaped.

They found the locker room, abandoned, dark, and quiet. Boris jimmied the lock with magic, and they let themselves in. Small lockers of the sort usually found in malls and other public gathering places to hold packages or coats were stacked six deep around the walls, and there was a wall of free-standing lockers in the center of the room; two long benches were the only furniture in the room. Each small locker had a name taped to it. They searched until they found their names. Boris had to jimmy the locks again.

Jared gladly traded his hospital togs and borrowed white coat for his own clothes.

Amelia's letter was still in his pants pocket.

He could give it to the other Jared. Assuming the other Jared was real, and he could find him. How hard could it be? He'd found the man in just over a day, out of all the millions in Miami. Surely he could do it again.

Boris had fallen asleep on a hard, wooden bench. It took both of them to wake him.

"Come on." Forrest took one arm, as Jared took the other, and they lifted Boris to his feet.

"I swear," Boris muttered as they got under way, "I'm going to sleep for a whole day, if I can ever get away from the two of you."

Most of the corridors they'd walked were empty or nearly empty, but Jared knew they'd start meeting up with more people as they got closer to the entrance.

Jared checked around the corner of the next corridor before they entered it. He looked at Boris. "You're going to have to walk on your own, or we're going to draw too much attention. Let's get out of here. Then we'll find someplace to sleep."

And Mona. He still had to rescue Mona. And tell her he loved her. And set this weekend—no, his life—right.

First things first. Get out of here and find Mona. He helped Forrest herd Boris toward the hospital's front door.

Ageon finally allowed Hjell to gag Jared. Mona wasn't sure if this was a good thing or not. It was undoubtedly the right thing. They'd all tired of the constant nagging, pleading, and begging. An uneasy quiet descended on the cowed group in the car. Mona wondered if Jared would ever be well.

She watched the lights and glamour of Miami's nightlife speed by outside her window. She'd come here with so much hope. All shattered now. She had trouble accepting that her life would never be the same again. It was all too much too fast.

The quiet interior of the car seemed stifling and closed, boxing her into a future she had no control over and didn't want. When Mona glanced at Jared, she caught him looking at her. He had his whipped puppy look on, but it didn't affect her like it usually did. She was too scared.

The car sped through the night, through streets she didn't know, to a place she didn't know, with people she didn't know. Except for Nona, but considering that Nona had been seeing Jared without Mona's knowledge, maybe she didn't know Nona either.

No comfort there.

They slowly exited the dark car, after Stig pulled up to the well-lit curb in front of Mercy Hospital, except for Jared who remained seated, bound and gagged, in the car. Mona stood by Nona while the men gathered around the car's open door.

Hjell glanced in the car, probably worried about the trussed and gagged Zarrad. "We can't take him in all tied up like that."

"No," Ageon agreed wearily. "But can you two get him in, if we release him?"

Stig glanced in at Jared, then at Hjell. "We can try."

"Should I get some of the hospital's attendants?" Ageon asked.

Hjell shook his head. "No. They're only allowed to help once we get him inside or if he's unconscious. Some sort of insurance rules." He looked at Stig. "Let's do it."

Taking opposite sides of the car, Ageon's men began to untie Jared. Mona knew the moment they removed the gag, because Jared immediately began screaming at them.

"Let me go! I am not crazy! Just listen to me, please!"

The car bounced and shook with their struggles. Finally Stig emerged, red faced with exertion.

Jared exited the car feet first, Stig had his arms wrapped firmly around Jared's unbound ankles and legs. Jared wiggled and squirmed as he came into view. Hjell had Jared's arms in some sort of a lock-hold and was trying to make sure Jared's head didn't hit anything as they eased him out of the car.

"Let me go!" Jared bared his teeth at Ageon. "You can't do this to me! Would you just once please listen to me? I'm not crazy." He struggled and squirmed futilely. "It doesn't matter. I'll just get away again. And again and again, if necessary. As many times as it takes to get you to listen. You can't keep me locked up. I'm not crazy! It's just a spell. Nona, please!"

Mona shivered, not because of the cool night breeze.

The only thing that kept her there was the certain knowledge that she really had nowhere to run. She wondered if Jared had often felt the same way when confronted with his mother's chaos. Amelia had to be behind all this. Somehow.

She sighed and put her arm around her shivering sister. "Poor Jared. All this confusion has to be Amelia's fault."

Ageon whirled around to stare at her. Jared stopped struggling and stared at her. They both said, "You know Amelia?"

Chapter 21

Everyone came to a full stop. Hjell and Stig stood with their mouths open and Jared slowly slipping from their grasp.

"Of course I know Jared's mother." Mona stared back at all of them. "How could I not know her? She's everywhere in his life. A force of nature, like a tornado or an earthquake. You can't get rid of her."

Ageon whirled to stare at Jared. "You know Amelia?"

"No. But the other Zarrad told me she'd sent a letter for me. He said she was his mother." Jared shook off his captors and pulled himself up, as if daring anyone to contradict him.

"The other Zarrad?" Ageon screamed.

At that moment, three men ran out of the hospital's front door. Mona recognized Jared, and was startled to see two Borises.

The new Jared dropped into a fighter's crouch, looking from Ageon to Hjell to Stig, who were beginning to resemble statues in variations of shock and surprise.

"See," the Jared from the car said. "The other Zarrad."

"Jared?" Mona asked, looking from first one to the other.

"Zarrad?" Nona echoed Mona's actions.

Mona turned a surprised look on her sister. "I thought you were lisping."

"*I* thought *you* were lisping."

"Finally," one of the Borises crowed, "everyone is all together."

The Jared from the hospital, realizing that no one was going to attack him, slowly came out of his crouch and relaxed. He carefully reached for a pocket on his thigh. "I'm just going to get the letter out and give it to him." He pointed at the Jared from the car. "Just a letter. That's all."

Ageon just stood, open-mouthed, stunned.

Jared stepped up to his mirror image and handed over a sealed envelope. "I didn't think I'd ever find you again. I wasn't sure you really existed."

"Of course he existed; he's your brother, Zarrad. Twin, or the other half-changeling. He's the human one," one of the Borises said. The other sat on a concrete bench, looking completely exhausted. He said, "Can I get some sleep now?"

"Zarrad?" Jared looked at his mirror image in awe. The tiny fairy wings beneath his shirt fluttered briefly.

"Yeah. And you are?" Zarrad demanded.

"Jared," Ageon breathed.

"Let me guess, the fairy one. The perfect fairy son you always wanted." Zarrad opened the letter, skimming over it quickly.

"Excuse me," Mona said. "Could someone explain what is going on here, for those of us that are completely confused?"

"Mona," Jared breathed. He started toward her, but stopped warily. "Are you all right?"

"Nona is mine," Zarrad said, while still examining the letter.

"Fine with me." Jared glanced over his shoulder at his twin. "I just want to spend some time with my wife. The woman I love with all my heart." He ran his fingers through his hair. "And straighten things out." He looked at her with pleading eyes. "If I still can."

"Jared." Mona threw herself at her husband, wrapping her arms around him, caressing his wings to make certain they and he were real. "I'm sorry. I didn't know. I thought—"

His answering kiss was everything she could have wanted.

Ageon cleared his throat, breaking things up. "Who has the money I gave one of you this afternoon?"

Grinning down at Mona, Jared said, "I put it in the hotel safe. I didn't know what else to do with it."

Zarrad refolded the letter. "You idiot." He glared at Jared. "Everything is explained here in the letter. You could have avoided all this trouble, if you'd bothered to open the letter and read it."

"Open someone else's letter and read it?" Jared stared at his brother, looking shocked, but Mona was pleased to note he didn't take his arms from around her. "That would be wrong."

"And what happened here was right?" Zarrad countered.

Squeezing Jared, Mona said, "No. It was just Amelia all over."

"Amelia." Ageon snatched the letter from Zarrad, holding it reverently, nearly caressing it as he opened it.

"You lied to me." Zarrad glared at Ageon. "All these years." He seemed near tears. "And now that you've got your perfect fairy son, I suppose you won't be wanting me around any more. The ugly, human screw-up."

"Who is he?" Jared asked Zarrad, pointing at Ageon with one hand while keeping the other around Mona's waist. "Why do you bother with him?"

Zarrad's eyes nearly popped out of his head in surprise. "He's my father." He frowned a moment. "Your father too, I suppose."

"Yes," Ageon said, without looking up from the letter.

"So, you and Mom are divorced?" Jared sounded uncertain.

"No." Ageon looked up quickly and intently at Jared. "She just ran off, in the night, with you. I couldn't find her."

"Too bad," Zarrad snarled. "I guess she was supposed to run off with me."

Ageon rounded on his son. "I didn't want her running off with anyone. I wanted to work things out. She wouldn't listen. I loved her then. I still love her. More than I ever thought possible. You, at least, are the one thing she left me. You're my son. Everything I have is yours."

Zarrad didn't appear the least bit appeased. Ageon reached for him, but Zarrad backed away.

"Sounds like Amelia," Mona said. Jared shushed her gently.

Nona, standing with her fists on her hips, looking very angry, said, "And who was responsible for that awful necklace?"

Silence descended on the little group, as everyone looked from one to another to find the guilty party. A cool night breeze blew through, scattering litter across the sidewalk. The distant wail of a siren drew closer, then shut off as a police car pulled up to park behind Ageon's car. The red and blue lights remained on and flashing. An unmarked car stopped behind the police car.

A familiar lieutenant stepped out of the front seat. "So, everyone is here. Good. Perhaps one of you can explain this." Lieutenant Wight walked over to the other police car and opened the door.

Two unformed cops pulled Little Jimmy from the back seat of the police car. His hands were cuffed behind his back, and he was babbling on, as the cops dragged him toward the front doors of the hospital.

"It's a new kind of changeling. He can be either a fairy or a human or a wolf or anything that he wants." Little Jimmy spied Zarrad and began struggling in earnest against his captors. "There he is! It's black magic, I tell you. His family is delving in new, sinister magics. They've changed his very being! He just looks human. He's not! You have to listen to me! They're going to take over the world!"

Finally the cops wrestled Little Jimmy inside. Lieutenant Wight turned to Ageon. "Do you have an explanation for this?"

A smug look appeared on Ageon's face. "Not me. Perhaps my sons can explain it."

"Sons?"

Ageon held one hand out to Zarrad and the other to Jared. "I've finally found my lost son."

"Gentlemen?" Lieutenant Wight prompted.

"He tried to kidnap me, then he was going to beat me up," Jared said. Mona hugged him tight for comfort. He smiled down at her.

Zarrad nodded. "He did, I saw him. He tried to beat me up at the same time. And he bragged he and his men had stripped our girls. We couldn't put up with that."

"So, what did you do?"

Jared and Zarrad exchanged glances. Zarrad shrugged and turned to Lieutenant Wight. "We just played a bit of a switch on him, which convinced him that we were one person that could be either fairy or human."

"And how did you change into a wolf?" The lieutenant glared at Jared. "Did you use magic?"

"That was him." Jared pointed at Zarrad.

"I howled at the streetlight." Zarrad grinned. "That was all it took. He ran off."

The cops just stared disbelievingly at Zarrad, so he threw his head back and howled for all he was worth. It sent a shiver down everyone's spine. He grinned when he finished. "It was just so much fun to give him a taste of the confusion I've had all day. I'm sorry. I couldn't resist."

Lieutenant Wight sighed and looked at the assembled group. "Will any of you be pressing charges for anything that's happened this weekend?"

"I don't think so," Ageon said.

Mona sputtered in protest. Personally, she thought Little Jimmy should be locked up forever. Jared smoothed her hair. "Now, now. Being cooped up in the loony bin is punishment enough. Besides, there's all the paperwork and coming back for the trial . . ."

Sighing, Mona looked at Nona. Nona nodded. "Let the poor idiot go."

"Oh, all right." Mona snuggled into Jared, who said, "That's it. Forget him, he's not worth it."

"I thought it might be like that." Lieutenant Wight saluted them and headed into the hospital.

"The necklace?" Nona demanded. "Who was responsible for the necklace?"

"Little Jimmy?" Ageon offered.

"No. I arranged for the necklace," Zarrad said in a small voice. He turned whipped puppy eyes on Nona. "You deserve the truth. I won't lie to you any more. I knew you were going to try to break up with me, and I just couldn't stand to lose you. I love you so much. I shouldn't have tried to enspell you. It was wrong, and I'm sorry. Really, truly sorry."

Sighing, Nona turned to face the darkness, away from Zarrad and the hospital.

"Please forgive me." Zarrad walked to her, putting his hands on her shoulders.

Mona patted Jared's arm, before letting him go. She walked over to her sister. "I think he means well. And if he's anything like Jared, he'd be worth salvaging."

She glanced up to see Zarrad smiling hopefully down at her. He whispered to Nona, "I'll make it up to you, somehow."

"How?" Nona asked.

"However you want." Zarrad squeezed her shoulders. "Anything you want. I couldn't bear to lose you."

Nona sniffed.

"He did say he was sorry. When is the last time he did that?" Mona asked.

"Never," Nona said.

"I am sorry," Zarrad whispered to her. "Things have changed. I've changed. Really, I promise. I love you."

"Besides," Mona said, "if you don't give him a chance, you'll never get to meet the woman that can throw this much confusion and chaos into so many lives. Including yours, from such a distance." She motioned to the other seven people standing around the hospital sidewalk with them.

Only then did she notice the crowd of people, hanging at the edges of the pool of light by the hospital doors, or just inside the doors, watching and listening. Several troll attendants waited patiently, with restraint jackets hanging limply in their enormous fists.

"Amelia," Ageon said the name as if it could either be a blessing or a curse. He turned Jared to face him. "Where is she?"

"She's in the hospital back at home." Jared shrugged off Ageon. "Recovering from minor surgery to remove a potential tumor."

"A tumor?" Ageon bellowed. "Cancer?"

"Probably benign." Jared backed away from a suddenly dangerous-looking Ageon. "Almost certainly so, since neither the physician nor Amelia ever contacted me." He shrugged. "She always has to make a big production of everything. It should have been outpatient surgery, but she insisted on a hospital stay. Everything has to be a production with her. She's a real drama queen."

"Of course she should be in the hospital! What are you thinking? Coming here for the weekend and abandoning her! What sort of son are you? Poor, frail thing." Ageon started herding everyone to the car. "All alone, with no one to help her." He opened the back door before Stig could get it, and began waving people in. "We have to get to her, right away. Get in. Get in." Ageon grabbed Jared's arm, pushing him in the door. "Where is home, by the way?"

"Wisconsin."

Ageon rolled his eyes. "Typical of the woman." He grabbed Mona next, and shoved her into the car.

She stumbled out of the way as Nona was pushed in on top of her. Cuddled up with Jared—actually, sitting in his lap since they were running out of seats—in the dark of the car, Mona whispered, "I don't know if we should be doing this. Your father is a dangerous and scary man."

Jared kissed her gently on the cheek. "We need to pick our battles, love," he murmured. "I've learned that in all my years with Mother. He wins this one." One finger stroked her arm. "He loses on anything that really matters. Like us."

Nona and Zarrad sat next to them, with Nona on Zarrad's lap, pretending to ignore him. Boris and Forrest took seats opposite each other, both muttering something about not allowing anyone to sit on their laps. Ageon stuffed Hjell in, then squeezed in himself.

"To the Carpet Terminal," Ageon said to Stig.

"No," Mona said firmly, but careful not to shout in Jared's ear. "We need to go back to the hotel and get our stuff."

"And your money," Jared added.

"And I need to stop by my apartment," Nona said. "I'm not going anywhere without some of my things. And Mona's things are still there."

Ageon stirred in his seat, forcing a bobbling wave of movement through the people in the car. "I'll get all of you new things when we get there."

Nona gasped. "I wouldn't dream of it. I have my own things. And I want my own things."

"I'm not getting on any flying carpets without the stuff I brought here," Mona declared.

Growling, Ageon glared at Jared and Zarrad in turn.

"I agree with Mona," Jared said stoically.

"And I agree with Nona," Zarrad declared more forcefully. "Nona's apartment first, Stig."

"You two are the most hen-ridden, milquetoasty wimps I've ever met," Ageon said.

"Have you looked in the mirror?"

It sounded suspiciously like Hjell, but Ageon glared at the apparently sleeping Boris beside him.

Nona glared at Zarrad. "I can't believe you thought you could get away with that."

"I love you. I'm sorry." Zarrad caressed her back below her wings. "I won't ever be that stupid again, and I'll try to make it up to you."

"Oh yes. You'll definitely be paying for it," Nona said.

"Good." Zarrad smiled at her. "If you're making me pay, that means you'll be with me. So, I guess we're staying together?"

Nona glared at him and sniffed. "We'll see."

"Will you come to Wisconsin with us?" Zarrad pulled her closer. "Will you marry me?"

Now that the words were out, now that he'd actually finally said them, Nona felt her eyes tear up. He really did love her and, as Mona had said, he was salvageable. She couldn't imagine life without him. But that didn't mean she'd make it easy for him. "I'll think about it."

Zarrad kissed her.

Stig stopped the car in front of Nona's apartment building. Nona got out, pulling Mona with her. "Come on. I have some of the most divine little dresses I want you to have. They'll look so cute on you."

Mona grabbed Jared, whispering, "Help me."

"There's nothing I can do," Jared whispered back as he was dragged from the car. "She's your sister."

Zarrad bailed from the car after them, trailed by Ageon.

They paraded up to Nona's apartment. Luckily the Ploofs, Hjell, and Stig all elected to remain in the car, so it wasn't as bad as it could have been.

Chapter 22

Jared quietly tiptoed into his mother's hospital room. Everything was as he'd last seen it. The walls were a pale rose, two chairs with rose and blue cushions sat in a corner as if conversing, and Amelia lay in an ugly hospital bed with its attendant IV. The acid, antiseptic smell remained, along with the beeping machines, and hospital clutter.

Life all around her had changed. Nothing would ever be the same again for anyone else. She remained yet untouched by all that. But not, Jared reminded himself, for long.

Amelia was pouring some water from a plastic pitcher into a small cup. She looked up as he walked into the room. "Jared!" She only slopped a little water from the pitcher as she set it down hard. "Jared! It's just been awful. You have no idea what I've been through."

"Yes. I know." Jared couldn't help grinning as he approached the bed. "Same here."

"Whatever do you mean?" She held him in a tight hug and kissed his cheek. As she did so, she noticed his new shirt, with the slits in the back allowing his wings to protrude. "Jared? You've changed. What happened?"

"I just got back from Miami."

"Oh." Amelia shrank back against her pillows. "Did you look for the man, like I asked?"

"No. I'm sorry. I didn't bother." Jared sat in one of the chairs. Its cushions were deceptive; they were harder than any metal chair he'd ever sat in. "I didn't think I could find him, no matter what I did. So I took Mona with me for a romantic weekend. It was, without a doubt, a weekend we'll never forget. Everything has changed."

"Jared Silvan!" Amelia sat up and shook her finger at her son. "How dare you! I ask you to do one little thing for me, and you can't even do that. You selfishly go off with that woman and just completely forget about me, here alone, going under the knife, dying, in the hospital." She fell back against her pillow, as if in a swoon.

"I had a very interesting weekend," Jared burbled happily. He couldn't stop grinning, and expected she'd catch on any minute to the fact that the hall outside her room was filled with eager eavesdroppers. "Priceless in every sense of the word."

"I'll just bet!" Amelia complained to the ceiling. "You probably sat around on the beach, soaking up the sun and nuzzling with that woman." She shivered. "Never giving me a single thought."

"Actually, I thought about you an awful lot. I made some new friends." Jared stood up and walked to the partly-open door. "Would you like to meet them?"

He flung the door open.

Ageon was the first in. He and Amelia stared at each other for a moment. Amelia burst into tears. Ageon rushed to the bed, put his arms around her, and began comforting her.

"Hush, now." Ageon kissed her forehead. "Everything is all right." He leaned back from her. "You're even more beautiful than I remember."

Amelia clung to him, still crying.

Boris and Forrest had taken the chairs in the corner, keeping, more or less, to themselves. Mona stood next to Jared. Zarrad hung back by the doorway. Nona tried to urge him farther in, without much success.

Jared grabbed Zarrad's arm and hauled him forward to the foot of their mother's bed. "I don't know if you'll remember this chap. He's changed a lot since you last saw him." Jared pushed Zarrad to the opposite side of Amelia's bed from Ageon.

"My baby! My sweet little boy!" she cried, abandoning Ageon to throw her arms around Zarrad and squeeze him until he couldn't breathe. "Oh, my precious baby." Amelia let him go enough to ruffle his hair and look into his eyes, but she still kept her arms around him. "Are you okay? Has he been treating you all right?" She poked at his ribs. "Goodness, doesn't anyone ever feed you?"

"I do what I can for my boy." Ageon reached across to ruffle Zarrad's hair. "But he's a stubborn cuss. Takes after his father, you know."

"He's probably a perfect angel, compared with Jared." Amelia kept Zarrad's hand in hers, but let him stand up. "Jared never listens to a word I say. He spends all his time worrying about things. Money mostly. Bills and taxes and foolishness. And that silly business of his. Nothing of importance. And that wom—"

She stopped as she noticed Nona sidle up to Zarrad and put her arm around his waist. Amelia quickly looked to where Jared and Mona were standing at the foot of her bed, with their arms around each other's waists.

"Oh, no!" Amelia breathed. "There's two of them!"

"Kids these days." Ageon leaned forward to kiss Amelia's cheek. "Can't tell them a thing."

"So true," Jared whispered to Mona, smiling. "So true."

"Well." Amelia sighed and looked at Zarrad. "My sweet Zarrad. So tell me everything. All about yourself. Don't leave a single detail out. I want to know absolutely everything that has happened since I last saw you."

Zarrad pulled Nona close, smiling at her. "This is Nona Bryce, the love of my life. She's agreed to marry me."

"No, no, no," Amelia said. "Just the important stuff."

"Nona is the most important person in my life," Zarrad replied, never taking his eyes off Nona, who smiled back and blushed slightly.

"Kids!" Amelia let go of Zarrad's hand to turn to Ageon. "He probably doesn't remember that far back. Tell me everything. What was his first word? When did he start walking? How did he do in school?"

Ageon patted her hand. "I looked everywhere for you. I couldn't find you. I thought I'd go insane, wondering what had happened to you. He was a good baby."

"You were supposed to find us," Amelia said petulantly. "I thought for sure you'd find us. I didn't think I could hide that well. I expected every day to see you at the front door, taking charge, bringing us home. I knew you'd want your fairy son back." Amelia leaned toward Ageon. "I'm sorry."

"I should have found you. I can't believe I didn't. What I really wanted was you." Ageon rested his forehead on hers. "But now we're back together and everything will be fine."

"Only if someone will please tell me about Zarrad," Amelia said.

"I still have the little booties we bought for him." Ageon smiled. "And a whole library full of pictures, and scrapbooks, and you wouldn't believe."

Forrest turned to Boris. "I think that's our cue to leave for a while."

"Definitely."

The Ploofs abandoned the chairs and made their exit. Jared appropriated one chair and kicked the other toward Zarrad. Then Jared sat in his chair with Mona on his lap, and Zarrad did the same with Nona.

"I'll tell you about Zarrad, if you'll tell me all about Jared," Ageon said to Amelia.

"That sounds fair."

Ageon settled onto the bed to sit beside Amelia. "I'll never forget the day I caught him sliding down the stairs on a cookie sheet."

"Papa!" Zarrad wailed. Nona giggled.

"Merce slept through it all," Ageon continued, ignoring all of his audience except Amelia.

Epilogue

"Atlas is gaining ground." Zarrad handed his jacket to his brother with a smirk. "You sure you don't want to consider a merger?"

"No." Jared put Zarrad's jacket with his own and handed both to Merce, standing patiently by the open door. He murmured a quick, "Thanks," before returning to his conversation with Zarrad. They'd argued in the car the whole way back from the store. "SilverProof is holding its own. Atlas must be gaining against someone else."

Zarrad's smirk hadn't changed a bit, though he had walked away from the cool breeze coming in the open door of the foyer. "Oh, I think we've been doing better than you know."

"That may be. But I'm happy with things the way they are." The more Jared learned of his father Ageon, the less Jared wanted Ageon to have anything to do with SilverProof. Jared suspected some of Zarrad's booming business wouldn't stand too close a scrutiny by law enforcement. Though he had no proof, and his suspicions could have been nothing more than sibling rivalry.

Luckily, they were interrupted as Amelia came skipping down the stairs from the second floor, followed by Ageon at a more sedate pace.

"Boys, boys! Did you remember to get the ribbons like I asked?" Amelia planted a quick kiss on each of her sons' cheeks.

Jared pulled two lengths of thin, silky ribbon from his

pants pocket, one pale violet and one brilliant white. Zarrad also pulled two lengths of thin, silky ribbon from his pocket, one sky blue and one perfectly pink.

"Perfect!" Amelia snatched the ribbons from their hands. "Oh, they're so cute!" She ran off, back up the stairs.

"You will remember which is which?" Jared shouted after her, but she didn't even glance back, heedless of him.

"We'd better go after her." Ageon smiled indulgently. "No telling what could happen." He frowned at Merce, standing mesmerized by the open door. "Shut the door and keep watch."

"Yes, Boss." Merce slammed the door, dumped the jackets into the closet, and eased himself into his chair by the window.

Ageon and his sons trudged through the mansion, up to the nursery. Hjell sat in a chair in the hall by the nursery door. He nodded to them, and pushed gently against the partly-opened door. "Shhhh."

The nursery had been redecorated with a rainbow-and-butterflies theme. Rainbow curtains arched over the windows, and little delicate rainbow-colored butterflies dotted the walls. The carpet, a study in the many uses of rainbows and butterflies and how the two could be mixed up completely, was firmly tacked to the wooden floor, to prevent any accidental slips. Nothing but the best for Amelia's grandchildren.

Two sturdy cribs—Mona had insisted—stood head-to-head against the far wall. Mona and Nona gently rocked back and forth in two rocking chairs, facing each other from opposite walls. Each woman held a sleeping baby tightly in her arms.

Amelia looked up from what she'd been doing in the crib

by Nona and motioned the men to be quiet. She tiptoed over and whispered, "We've got the ribbons on the boys. I'm just putting the ribbons on the girls."

She tiptoed back to the crib by Mona, dangling the white ribbon in her hand.

Jared exchanged a look with Zarrad. They tiptoed in behind her to check that the right ribbons were on the right infants.

Mona smiled and blew Jared a kiss. He knew she'd have checked, but he wanted to recheck. He couldn't be too careful around his mother.

Though now that his father was back in her life, Amelia didn't cause Jared anywhere near as many problems as before. Especially now that she lived in Florida, and he lived in Wisconsin. However, being back in Miami, in the same house with Amelia, made him cautious.

A pale violet ribbon had been tied around little Price's ankle; Mona made certain he saw it, by briefly lifting the blanket from their son's foot. Jared peeked in the crib. Amelia was just putting the finishing touches on the white bow around his daughter Bryce's ankle. He smiled at her cherubic face, completely undisturbed by all the adults around her.

Zarrad whispered in his ear, "Everything is set with Emily and Egan."

Tiptoeing out, Jared marveled again that they should each have a set of twins—a boy and a girl each—within days of each other. And that the infants should all appear so identical.

Amazing, but Jared smiled fondly at Mona from the hallway, knowing that many amazing things had happened in his life, one of them rocking in a chair with a tiny baby.

Mona and Nona carefully put the sleeping boys in with

their sisters. Mona turned the intercom on, and Nona cast a quick spell over her twins. They tiptoed out with Amelia. Amelia closed the door behind them, and pointed at Mona and Nona. "You two go sleep. I'll put these men to work, and we'll have that playroom ready in no time."

"They're not going to need a playroom anytime soon," Mona said wearily.

"Go rest, sweetheart." Jared kissed Mona's forehead. "You deserve it."

"You too," Zarrad echoed, kissing Nona.

Shooing everyone down the hall, Amelia began issuing orders.

Ageon glanced back at his sons. "We'll need to separate the children soon. We can't wait much longer."

Mona groaned. "I can't handle twins. How am I going to handle quads?"

"It's not so bad, being a changeling," Hjell said. His delicate fairy wings fluttered as he adjusted his great troll frame on the little chair.

Nona burst into sobs, joined by Mona.

"Hush, hush," Jared soothed. "Everything will be all right." He glared first at Hjell, then Ageon. He mouthed, "Later."

Zarrad put his arm around Nona. "You rest. I'll worry about everything else."

Men! Amelia stalked down the hall toward the nursery. Did they ever do anything but argue?

At this rate the playroom wouldn't be ready before the grandchildren had children.

She paused in front of the door to the nursery to calm herself. Hjell studied her suspiciously.

"Just checking on the babies. I don't have a monitor and

don't want to bother the girls," she whispered as she motioned for him to remain seated. Very, very quietly she eased the door open and tiptoed in, quietly closing the door behind her. That would keep that nosy half-troll Hjell out.

Amelia just wanted to see the babies, not disturb those women, so she tried not to make a sound that would be heard on the intercom. She didn't want to be interrupted during her brief time with her grandbabies.

Peeking into the cribs, Amelia found her little angels still sleeping. Egan had found his thumb, and was industriously sucking on it, while his sister Emily's mouth moved around a non-existent pacifier. Bryce and Price had cuddled up to each other, mixing arms and legs into a precious tangle.

Mixing. Amelia stared at the children, thinking furiously. All she had to do was take off the ribbons, and all that would be left would be four identical infants. If their parents were ever to sort it out, they'd have to stop arguing. It would serve them all right.

No. She sighed. There'd be two identical boys, and two identical girls, not completely mixed-up children. That wouldn't work.

On second thought, maybe it would.

Amelia reached into a crib.

She paused. Maybe she should wait until after the separations.

Decisions, decisions.

Boris peered over his hand of cards at Stig, calculating the odds. Beside him, Forrest rearranged his own hand. Axel waited patiently, having won more than anyone else at this game. Erent had folded, and was currently blending into the wallpaper behind him.

A small pile of money huddled in the center of the table.

A bare bulb provided the small room with its only light. A few bowls with nibbles sat half-full, and drinks were being moved efficiently from a refrigerator on one side of the room to a trash can on the other side of the room by way of the occupants. As far as Boris was concerned, the ambiance of this spare, little basement storage room was perfect.

As Boris opened his mouth, his phone rang. Folding his cards in one hand, he used his other to pull his phone out.

"Are you going to play or what?" Forrest complained.

He looked at the message on the phone silently for a moment, then read aloud to the others, "Amelia just went in with the kids. Alone."

"What's going on?" Stig demanded.

"I asked Hjell to let me know if Amelia tried to get the kids alone." Boris stood, tossing his cards on the table. "Come on. We've got to go rescue the kids. There's no telling what she'll do." He ran to the door. "Come on!"

"She's their grandmother, for pity's sake," Axel said. "It's not like she'll hurt them. What could she do?"

After a moment's silence to contemplate the damage Amelia could do to a house full of grown, wary, cynical adults, then another moment to imagine the chaos she could unloose on four innocent newborns, they all stood and ran after Boris.

About the Author

A passionate reader, Rebecca Lickiss began telling stories at an early age. She finally decided to write them down for publication, since it was better than cleaning house again. Her husband and children humor her; otherwise, they're making their own dinner. Her husband also writes, 'cause he doesn't want to clean house either. Worried that taking care of her five children and home, going to work, and writing novels wouldn't be enough to keep her busy, Rebecca has returned to school to get her master's degree.